Fading into Focus

Jade Paspalis

Contents

Prologue

I think there was a rope, or maybe it was pills, it is not clear to me. I can barely remember because the world was spinning and it feels like it happened a billion years ago. I remember the screams, all inside my head. Hurtful words that keep pushing me and pushing me. Far and farther.

In all my life I never did anything to anyone. I always minded my own business and people didn't notice me, unless it was to make me the most miserable creature on Earth.

I think there was a kitty crying, a new member in this small family. Just some desperate attempt Mum had tried to help me to cope. It kept meowing, adding to the chaos in my mind.

I remember I wanted it to stop. I remember I just wanted everyone to stop screaming at me, telling me what to do. I just wanted to be left alone.

I remember the salty flavour in my mouth. I think it was tears. I can't really remember. I was choking on my own agony.

As time passes by it gets harder and harder to remember that day. The pain, the hatred, the desperation, and the despair. I don't remember what I did, I just remember I wanted it all to stop. Nothing else mattered.

But that was long ago. I've moved on. Whatever I really did, it worked. People stopped pestering me, calling me names and pushing me to the floor. People even stopped looking at me when they found out.

I was finally in peace. I could finally hear my own thoughts instead of other's insults. No one bothered me, no one hurt me, no one saw me and I couldn't have it any other way.

I was free from them.

Chapter 1

"Oh, he'll be head over heels for me," Roxette beams, fanning her face and batting her long faker-than-meat-in-hamburgers eyelashes. "The moment he walks in and we make eye contact, he'll be lost."

"Keep dreaming, sweetie," replies Adeline, her supposed best friend. I snicker, but keep watching without making a sound. I'm very good at that. "He'll be mine. That bad boy will be my next favourite mistake."

I gag and have to look away. The boy hasn't even showed up yet and they are already fighting for the illusion they have of him. Whoever he is! I would die laughing if he turns out to be some super geek, covered in acne and overweight hobbit. I don't think I could control myself after seeing the faces of these girls falling to the ground, all their fantasies broken.

It would be delightful.

Rumour has it we'll have a new class mate. Something exciting in Strode College for once! Although every year many kids join the establishment, we don't get many transfer students in the mid of January. So of course it has caused uproar, especially among the female community when it was made public that our future classmate would be a male.

Oh, wouldn't it be funny if he's studying something like... uh... Beauty! And he's gay? I would pay to see the moment Roxette and Adeline realise they won't get a new boyfriend. But that will not happen. I mean he is also taking the Level 3 diploma in Arts and Design so we share all of our lessons. And he is joining our group as we are the smaller one. The other group has twenty students already.

The moment they found out a new transfer student was joining us, all sort of rumours began. I don't really know which one is more ridiculous. First I heard he was expelled from his previous college after assaulting a teacher and setting his car on fire. Then I heard his family is part of a mafia and they just moved here. I also heard that he killed someone so he is hiding here in Street, England. Then I heard a variation of that in which he saw someone being murdered so he is hiding to save his life. I also heard that he is probably this mysterious boy with a dark secret that everyone wants to unravel, of course.

It seems very curious to me that in all these silly rumours this poor boy is some sort of bad boy. No one has thought that maybe his parents were offered a good job here and moved to stay together. Or that maybe he lost his parents and now has come to live with some relative. No, they immediately think he is some sort of lost cause and that thrills them because all of them want to fix him.

Isn't that sad? The boy hasn't shown up and all what his classmates want is to change him, to shape him into what they consider the perfect guy.

What is it with people wanting to change the other person they choose to be with? Isn't it easier and less time consuming being with someone you actually like and whom you wouldn't change? We don't even know his name, for crying out loud.

"What if he's a nerd?" I ask but as usual they ignore me. I'm too lame for them but, hey, surely I get points for trying.

"Can you imagine our tragic story? Everyone opposing to us because he's not good for me but they don't know us, they don't know I love him and I make him a better person, that we need each other. They don't see that we have to be together, they just try to tear us apart," Roxi dramatises and I roll my eyes. This girl is going to end up writing soap operas scripts, I'm calling it. "We'll be a modern version of Romeo and Juliet, and everyone will swoon over our love story."

"Romeo and Juliet wasn't a love story, you dumb. It was a tragedy and a satire. As usual, Shakespeare was laughing at all of us, especially at teenagers who think they know about love but only got everyone killed."

I shake my head. I don't even understand how people find that play romantic, I think it's infuriating and most amusing at the same time. I laugh so hard that sometimes I think Shakespeare wrote a comedy instead of a tragedy.

Of course, even if I would want to have a serious conversation with Roxi she would not hear me. Or maybe she can't understand my words and will just roll her eyes, saying whatevs and continue rambling about love and whatnot.

"I can't wait to see him!" Adeline chirps, her voice so high that it hurts my ears and I cringe.

"Woman! Control those vocal cords of yours," I scold her but she's too preoccupied fantasising to pay me attention.

I tap my ears softly just to make sure I can still hear properly. Everything working normally.

"You know what's likely? He's some supernatural creature. What about a vampire?" I suggest and everyone laughs, although I think they are laughing at Adeline and not what I said but oh well, I continue. "No, vampire is old story, no one wants vampires anymore. Werewolf? Nah, too hairy. Fallen angel? I think those are popular nowadays. The whole fallen from the sky, supposed to be good but in reality they are just demons. That's what you want, right?" I ask placing my hand on Roxi's shoulder and she turns but before she can reply Regina, our Art History teacher, walks in. And she's walking alone.

I go to my desk, ignoring completely all the things written over there. No one sits by my side and I don't blame them. People really avoid me and I like it better like that. I prefer them ignoring me than bullying me.

I take a peek over my shoulder watching Roxi and Adeline, who watch Regina with furrowed brows. Oh right, they were expecting their bad boy soon-to-be boyfriend to arrive with her. He is supposed to join us today.

I laugh under my breath. I just enjoy their disappointment so much.

I am not mean, okay? And yeah, maybe I make fun of them a lot and insult them and mock their lack of intellect, but who can blame me? Considering what they did to me before, this is nothing.

I sit here, running my finger over all the messages written on my desk. The insults are still there, all the hurtful words people threw at me before, but the apologies are also here, hiding the damage they did before. They can't hide them from me, I know them too well.

We are a small group, only sixteen people including me so I'm not the only one sitting alone... except today there's someone else sitting alone. Today there's seventeen of us and my eyes focus on the new figure that everyone else seems to ignore, even Regina who has just started her lesson introducing us to The Fauves.

It's a guy, of that I'm sure. He is not looking up and he does not pull the hoodie down. It's a grey, workout hoodie that has clearly seen better days. His ripped dark jeans and combat boots are also worn out, and so is the black backup at his side on the floor. I don't know if he is paying attention, but he is scribbling something on his notebook.

There're two people between the mysterious new student and myself so I can't just stand up and go talk to him. I mean, I can but I shouldn't and I won't do it. Instead, I keep watching him but he barely moves. And I'm impressed that the whole class passes by and no one notices him.

I am used to people ignoring me and pretending I'm not there. I mean, I wanted this and fought for this, but I never saw someone else who could manage to be completely ignored like that. Not even Regina saw him until she was walking out the room and he stood up to leave as well, a small piece of paper in his hands.

"James?" Regina says and other classmates stop, noticing Regina is talking to someone... someone no one saw before. Well, no one besides me, that's it.

The guy, James, hangs his backpack from his right shoulder and stands straighter, and he is his good thirty centimetres taller than Regina. I'm a few centimetres taller than her, one point sixty-five metres to be exact, so he should still be like a head taller than me. He didn't look that tall when he was sitting.

I notice Roxi and Adeline approaching, finally noticing who can only be their bad boy soon-to-be boyfriend. Well, they are pretty lousy future girlfriends if they didn't notice the love of their lives was there before. They were talking about him and he was sitting there, probably listening.

Isn't that mortifying?

"Yeah," he replies.

If the two girls were expecting a deep voice that sends shiver down your spine, they are surely feeling disappointed now. He has your regular teenager boy's voice. Not high but not that deep. Normal. Maybe too low, a bit raspy like when you scream too much and then your throat is sore. Or like someone who does not speak much and is not used to say anything at all.

I have a hunch it's the latter option.

"I thought you were late and probably with the headmaster, that's why I didn't wait for you. I had to introduce you to the institution and your classmates. My deepest apologies!" she cries out and he just shrugs before scratching the back of his neck in an uncomfortable gesture. This makes the hoodie finally drop and I see dreadlocks falling past his shoulders, almost reaching the mid of his back, of a light brown and I just blink. I have never seen a guy with dreadlocks before. Not that I go out much or anything, but still.

I look at his hair, not knowing exactly what to think. It's just tangled hair, isn't it? Like knot after knot and you can't even untangle them, you have to cut them off. Does he wash his hair? I once heard that for the dreadlocks to have their consistency you had to keep them dirty.

Is that so?

"It's okay. I arrived earlier," he says and his voice sounds a bit less raspy, like he's getting used to speaking. It sounds manlier now.

"You should've waited," Regina insists but he shrugs again.

"The headmaster gave me the talk. 'S all good," he insists and I can tell by the way he buried his hands in the pockets of his hoodie that he just wants to leave and stop talking to this woman. He wants to disappear. I know it because that is how I used to feel.

Regina looks around, noticing that almost everyone is gone, except from Roxi and well, me, but it's not like she is going to ask loser Paige for help.

"Oh great, Roxette is still here. Roxette, please come," she calls and James looks at the door with such longing I can't help chuckling. I sit on my desk, watching the scene unfold. "Dear, this is your new classmate. You remember we talked about him? James, this is your classmate Roxette. Could you help him out to get settled? Show him around and you know, make friends."

"Of course. I'd love to," she replies and her eyes focus on James.

He turns around, allowing me for the first time to see more than his back and I nod in appreciation. He isn't a Greek god or a TopMan model, but he is handsome, I guess. His features are sharp and interesting. His jaw is very chiselled, and are those freckles all over his cheeks and nose? He also has arched eyebrows, I think blue eyes and a nose ring. And he looks the most uncomfortable in front of Roxette, a hot and not shy at all girl with too few clothes and the fakest red hair you could imagine. Last week her hair was black. Next it's going to be blue or something. It's not like she can stand one hair colour for too long. I think she's naturally brunette, like me, but I am not sure.

"I'll leave it to you, then. Welcome, James," Regina says once again and then leaves the room. I keep watching, resting my elbows on my knees and cupping my cheeks to adopt a more comfortable position.

"So you are the mysterious transfer student," Roxi muses and James looks everywhere, dying to leave. I consider for a second to cause a distraction, then I tell myself nah, not my problem.

"I'm all right, no need to help. Bye." He says and then turns around and leaves.

It's not exactly rude, but it is and Roxi stays with her mouth hanging open and I laugh out loud. I think I already like James, not because I like asocial people, but because he rejected Roxi in the most obvious way and I would've loved if someone else could've seen it.

Chapter 2

I follow James because I have nothing better to do and I'm curious. I certainly don't want to stay around Roxi, so following the new kid sounds like a pretty sensible and amusing plan. It's not like he's going to mind or anything. He won't even notice me unless I'm really obnoxious and I don't really want to get his attention, I just want to see him better.

He walks quickly, avoiding everyone and quite managing himself. I wonder if he came before. Art History isn't our first subject so I wonder where he was during Printmaking. Maybe he was taking a look around to learn where everything is so he wouldn't need anyone to show him the place. Well that is clever, if that is what he did.

I follow him outside the C block where we have Art History. Our campus consists of several blocks and it is very well equipped. We, Art students, spend most of our time in the E block; sometimes the C block and we go to the rectory for food and other things. We barely see other students like the Beauty students or the A Level ones.

I see him cursing when he realises it's raining. Big shock, huh? He pulls the hoodie up and hurries to the library right in front. I wonder if he really despises his hair getting wet so much that he pulled the hoodie on. It's from one block to the other, it isn't that large of a distance and rain hasn't killed anyone that I know of. I know everyone complains about it, but they are just being crybabies.

I follow him, not minding the rain at all and if I get wet, I'll get dry later. It's natural, after all. I won't catch a cold or anything of the like so I have no worries, even if I'm just wearing army boots, a dress and my denim jacket. My hair is curly and messy so rain doesn't do anything worse to it.

I think James is more sensitive about his looks than I gave him credit for.

He goes to the farthest corner in the library, where no one can bother him, I see. He sits down and pulls his backpack on the table and then rummages inside, looking for something. He takes out some pamphlets and other papers.

"Oh, I see. Catching up, uh?" I mumble but he completely ignores me. I take no offence, I'm used to it. "Mate, you'll get tired pretty soon. Wait until the teachers give you your briefs. You'll be crazy. It doesn't even matter if we have Mondays off, you'll spend it all working," I keep telling him even if he is not paying attention and keeps reading.

I sit across from him and put my elbow on the table to then cup my cheek with my hand, watching him.

"So, what's your deal? Are you some misunderstood artist? What are you gonna do with this course? Why did you pick it?" I ask him not expecting an answer to be honest, but because I don't like silence.

For so many years I used to have people screaming at me, telling me horrible things or just mocking me that I got used to the background noise. I could never hear my thoughts until they stopped and I was finally alone with my own voice.

I couldn't stand it.

That's when I started talking so much, even if no one pays me attention. I need to hear something besides my own thoughts or I feel like I'm disappearing. No one has shouted at me to shut up so I guess they don't mind.

"What are you?" I ask next. "Everyone has such crazy rumours about you, did you know? I bet you do. You probably heard Roxi and Adeline talking today," I ramble, making all different sorts of gestures with my hands. "I guess I also said things but I wasn't mocking you or anything, I was mocking those two. I just really dislike them. If you knew our history together then you would understand."

He is really impassive, isn't he? In all this time he hasn't even frowned. My voice is clearly annoying him. Other people ignore me but when I talk so much in front of them it tends to give them a headache and they leave to get some aspirin.

"You're good, uh? A pro at ignoring others. Congrats! I'm a pro at being ignored." I smile at him but he does not react.

Well, let's see for how long you can keep up.

"I'm Paige, by the way. Very nice to meet you, James. Welcome to Strode College and to the Level 3 Diploma in Arts and Design!" I state ceremoniously, stretching my arms to make it more dramatic. "I hope you enjoy your stay here and accomplish what you dream of. There are many talented people in this course and our teachers are pretty cool."

Nothing. Absolutely nothing.

I hold my face in both hands now, leaning a bit closer to him, narrowing my eyes hoping to decipher him.

"So, James… what brings you to Street? Are you really son of a mafia godfather or something?" Nothing. "Did you kill someone?" Nothing again. I heave a sigh. "Did you see someone being killed?" Zero response. "Ugh, you're so taciturn! Don't you have expression or something!" I rant, frustrated that he doesn't even blink when I scream at him.

Okay, not screaming, I'm just… raising my voice a wee bit.

"Like this you won't make friends, are you aware of that? And the rumours will continue. The kids will carry on coming up with crazy theories and then no one will believe you when you actually tell the truth: that you wanted a change on your life and less chaotic life." Silence.

Ugh, I hate silence! I feel this urge to fill it and that's why I never come to the library.

"I thought you would be more interesting," I complain, heaving a bored sigh and looking away. I focus my gaze on the window and the rain I can see pouring outside.

I like the rain, even if it is most inconvenient at times. It's has this comforting sound and it gives me peace. I can listen to it and feel it like a lullaby. It makes me want to snuggle in a blanket with a warm cup of tea and Luna next to me, purring.

Luna is my cat, a fluffy black cat that keeps me company. And yes I do have to admit that I named her after the cat in Sailor Moon. No shame. It's a pretty name after all and Luna was amazing and super clever. It's an honour to be named after her.

"Are you gonna stay here the rest of the day? We don't have other lessons so it's just catching up with work. Do you even have work to catch up with?" I speak although I'm not looking at him, I keep my eyes on the window.

I take a glimpse at him and I see him he's taking a sketch notebook and he's drawing. "Uhhh, arty things!" I get excited and start watching him drawing.

I tilt my head to the right, trying to see better what is taking shape in front of me. I think it's some sort of monster, I'm not sure. It looks very creepy with its jaw open and the fangs and saliva drooling. I pull back a bit, repulsed with the drawing even if it's well executed. I like how he uses ink and gives texture to it, making it come alive. Which is really, really creepy. But he's really, really good.

"That won't help you, my friend. If you make those drawings of monsters then people will keep saying you're some sort of werewolf of creature of the night. They'll think this is a self-portrait— wait! Is it? Is this how you really look during full moon?"

He finally sighs! It's not a verbal reply, but it's a reaction and I clap. He doesn't say anything else, though and it's not like I expect him to, but at least I know I got to him, even if it was just to annoy him.

I giggle at that.

"I hope you keep your clothes on when you change, though," I muse as I stand up. "But just to be safe, I won't go out during full moon." Again, nothing. He keeps drawing. "Well, it's my a real pleasure to get to know you. You're such a talkative person, did someone ever tell you that? I'll see you tomorrow, don't be late!"

And like that I leave him. He doesn't say goodbye or anything and I'm off. I don't have anything better to do and I'm bored already. I decide to leave.

It's still raining but like I said, I don't mind. I leave the campus and walk back home, taking my time and enjoying the view. People running or waiting for the rain to stop, all the colourful umbrellas, and the animals looking for shelter. No one seems to mind the girl walking in the rain, with a grin on her face. I keep my hands at my back, my fingers laced together and I almost march on the street, although it's more like a child's marching, picturesque and silly, not regal and serious.

I find a stray cat on my way and stay there, playing with it. I didn't like cats before, or any sort of animals. But with time I've realised what beautiful creatures they are, always nice and loving. Animals don't bully, or I think so. I know it's the survival of the fittest in nature, but that is not made with malice, so I think they are still better than people.

I think I spend hours with the cat because by the time it decides to leave to look for food, it is not raining anymore. I stand up and stretch before resuming my way. I don't live too far from College, normally a good fifteen or twenty minutes walk, which is quite reasonable and agreeable.

When I get home I'm not surprised to find Mum in the kitchen. Our house is your typical English house, not too big, not too small. Cosy and appropriate for a middle class small family. My room is in the first floor and Mum's, the kitchen, living room and bathroom are on the ground floor. I don't have siblings so I practically live alone in the first floor. My window faces the street so I can watch people passing by and other things. Not that much happens, though.

"Hello, Mum!" I call walking in and going to the kitchen. Luna is there and when she sees me she jumps down the table and comes to rub herself against my boots. "Hi, Luna. Did you miss me?" I say stroking her black fur and she purrs. "I missed you loads, baby."

Mum doesn't say anything. She's in working out clothes although I bet she's barely moved. She's reading the newspaper but her look is lost. It's been like that for so long, since Dad left her. I haven't seen him in so long I barely remember him.

"Did you do something interesting today?" I ask Mum but she doesn't reply. "We got a new classmate. Total bore. He didn't say a thing and he completely avoided everyone. The only cool thing he did was rejecting Roxi." I laugh at the memory. "He's cute, I guess. I'm not fond of his hair, though. I don't know how to feel about dreadlocks. What do you think? They gave me this dirty vibe." Mum doesn't say anything and I sigh. "I'm probably being judgmental, aren't I? Maybe I should ask him. Like, hey, do you happen to wash your hair at least once a week? Is that too offensive?" Mum only shrugs, but I think it's a reflex, she's not really answering me. "His eyes are wicked. Blue but kinda greyish, like storm clouds. You think he's like those people whose eye colours change according to the weather? That's cool, right? I wish mine changed. Pff, boring brown eyes."

I get tired of talking to mum and not receiving reply and it seems it is making her feel worse. Her eyes start to water and she seems about to cry. So I decide to leave her alone.

"Okay, I'll go to my room. Make more tea, Mum. Yours got cold," I tell her and lean in to kiss her cheek. She freezes but doesn't move. When I'm climbing the stairs I can hear her the first sob and I feel bad again.

She is always crying and I think it's always my fault. It makes me feel horrible that I can't do anything to make her feel better.

I decide to hide, Luna follows me upstairs and I hide in my room for the rest of the day and night until it's morning again and I have to go to college.

Chapter 3

"Well, isn't it lovely, Luna? It's raining again. What should I wear?" I ask out loud walking up to my wardrobe. Luna meows back at me before turning on herself and become a ball of fur on my bed, her tail wrapped around her. "Yes, I understand fashion is not of your concern, but you should help me out or I'll end up wearing the same as usual."

I put my hands on my hips and watch what I have. It's all wrinkled and looks so old fashioned. If I wear anything of what I have here, I'm sure someone will push me off the stairs for being a criminal. Some beauty student would run to the E block and say she or he was just doing it for the world, and I would agree.

I should ask Mum to go shopping because I urgently need new clothes, but she won't listen and considering our situation I don't think it's sensible to ask for such a petty thing. I can survive with my clothes.

"I guess the same, then," I mutter closing the doors and just sighing. "I'll see you later, Luna. Sleep well!" I bid her, giving her a kiss on the top of her head before running down stairs. "Bye, Mum. Have a good day," I shout crossing the door without receiving a reply; Not that I wait for one.

I take my time on my way, not minding the rain. I've never been an umbrella type of gal. I find them more troublesome than helpful and it's like all that they protect is your hair and shoulders -barely because the rest of your body gets soaked wet anyways so I don't see a point for them.

Even if I take longer than usual, I'm still the first to arrive to Ceramics and I distract myself watching everything around me. The room starts filling without me noticing it. I turn around and find an amusing scene that has me smiling.

"It seems I'm not the only one being ignored," I mumble folding my arms as I watch how Roxi and Adeline keep talking to James, in a contest to find out which one will get his attention first.

That's not the best part, though, far from it. Seeing the best friends competing for one guy isn't the really amusing part, it's that James is ignoring them just like he was ignoring me, not even reacting to the girls asking him question after question. It has to be worse than me nagging him yesterday, because now it's twice as annoying.

I chuckle because I can see how the girls are getting annoyed, as well. Frustrated that James is not reacting, he keeps checking his notebook. Is he pasting his briefs? I think so. Hm, so he was given the briefs already. Good luck, my friend, you have loads to catch up with.

"We can help you with that," Roxi says at some point, putting her finger on top of one of the briefs. "I bet you feel overwhelmed with all the workload, but it's okay. I'm really good and I have no problem sparing time to help you catch up."

I take my index to my mouth and make gagging sounds. It's not just her word choice what is lame, it's her tone that gives me the creeps.

James just flips the page and Roxi has to remove her finger. He does not reply, he keeps working and I see Roxi gasping whilst Adeline giggles. Roxi glares daggers at her best friend and I think we are five seconds to witness a cat fight. Then Lauren, our Ceramic teacher, arrives for the lesson and I go to my usual spot and so do Roxi and Adeline.

My spot this time is next to James but I decide not to nag him this time with questions. It's clear he won't reply and I think he's had enough with Roxi and Adeline. I feel sorry for him that he has the two hottest girls in our class fighting to get his attention. I don't even think they are seeing him properly, I think they just see their fantasies in him and ignore the real picture.

As everyone starts working on their current projects, I watch James. He works silently, not making eye contact with anyone, not even Lauren when she approaches him asking if he needs help with anything. He just shakes his head and mumbles, "I've got this." And that's it.

I wonder if he's shy and that's why he doesn't talk to any-one. No, I don't think that's it because the way he ignores the people that talk to him isn't the sort of someone that's shy, it's kind of rude. Did he have friends wherever he lived before or was he this asocial there, too? Luna is my only friend but I wish I could have someone, why does he reject everyone that tries to approach him? In my case, people don't want to befriend me, but I know everyone in this group is quite curious about him and wouldn't mind talking to him.

Oh! Maybe the rumours are true and he has some tragic backstory, like his best friend died in an accident that was his fault so he feels remorseful and he is scared to make new friends because he is dangerous so he is just trying to protect us all.

"I cracked the code!" I shout, slamming my fists against the desk, making everything on it jump with a loud thud and everyone leaps. Gasps and cries of surprise escape their lips and everyone looks in my direction. "Oops, sorry," I say, sticking my tongue out and getting smaller.

No one says anything and they get back to their works, but I see Roxi shivering and then whispering something to Adeline but she just shushes her.

I look at James and he doesn't seem affected by what I did, but I put my elbow on the table, facing him as I cup my left cheek. "I did, you know?" I tell him but of course he ignores me. He's so good at that. "I know why you ignore us all." Nothing, still nothing. "You got your friend killed, didn't you? But it wasn't your fault, James. You can't be afraid of making new friends. Maybe not Roxi and Adeline, but there are other very nice people in this group." He keeps working and I sigh. "Whatever. I'm not asking you to be my friend, I'm just saying that you don't need to be scared of making friends. Be thankful that people actually want to be your friends."

After that I look away and don't watch him anymore.

After Sculpture we have the rest of the morning free so everyone goes to catch up on work and get some snacks. I notice James dashing out first, wondering what's up with him, then I notice how Roxi and Adeline were on their way to him.

Ah, that makes sense.

"It seems not everyone likes you," I mumble walking past them with a smirk of my face.

It's still raining when I leave the C block so I just go to the library to wait until our next class: Photography, which is my favourite, with Rick who is also my favourite teacher. I don't know why I go to the library, I normally can go anywhere to wait for the following class, but well, the rec is just in front so it seems like a logical option. Only when I'm inside do I notice James is there, exactly where he was the day before.

"Oh, what the hell, I'm bored," I mumble and then walk up where he is. All the other tables are available but I sit across from him next to the radiator. He doesn't react to my proximity. "Don't worry, I won't annoy you today. But I'm quite bored and when I'm bored I speak even more." Nothing.

Ugh, this guy is insufferable.

I decide to watch the rain pouring and ignore him like he is ignoring me but then, from the corner of my eye, I catch part of what he is drawing. It's the same monster of yesterday, but now he's adding more details and background. A forest, a dark creepy forest and the moon is shining full in the sky. The drawing is wicked, I don't have another way to describe it. Well, wicked and creepy. I doubt that's part of any brief, this has to be a personal project or something.

I don't realise how I shift until I'm dedicating my full attention to his work, seeing how it comes alive and for a moment I think it will come to attack me and kill me. What gets my attention the most are the eyes. They have no colour but for some reason I swear they are yellow. I don't know why but that's like the feeling I get and they seem so alive that I even pull back a bit, putting distance between the wolf and I. I know it can't harm me, but still. It's like a reflex.

"You have some talent there, son," I say still watching him drawing. "I wish I could draw with such detail, especially from my mind. I can, you know, draw something that I'm watching so it's like copying, but when I try to draw directly from what I see in my mind it turns out worse than an amoeba. It's a sad story, I know," I muse.

I'm like hypnotised with the way his hands flies all over the page and what is more impressive is that he manages to draw without getting his hand dirty, without touching the paper with ink. He keeps it suspended and that must hurt a lot later from all the effort he is putting.

"I like photography. I think I'm good at that. Then again, I can't be sure. I do know I enjoy that very much."

I don't know why I'm even telling him that, it's not like he's going to reply or anything. It's clear he doesn't want to talk to anyone.

Then he flips the page, carefully, fanning it a bit and puts another piece of drying paper and starts drawing in the next page, making a square, like a vignette. And then he starts drawing inside, a different setting, a young girl, against a very dark, dark background. I think.

"What are you doing? Why aren't you making her as big as the monster? Is it because she is a girl? Why so misogynist?" I demand but he doesn't reply, he does nothing and I get angry. "That's discrimination. A girl is as important as your monster from before."

Angry, I stand up and leave. It's not like I want to be his friend anyways so I don't care.

I leave the library and it has stopped raining so I head to the E block and decide to scare people because I'm that bored. When I'm walking by the lockers I just slam the doors shut and then run before someone makes me pay for what I've done. People scream and jump and it's quite fun, but I don't hurt anyone. I could be mean and push them against the lockers or something, but I don't.

See? Good person over here.

Then the class arrives and I know everyone finds the lectures boring, but I don't. Everything is fascinating for me no matter how many times I listen to the same thing. I enjoy all the little details so I don't even notice what the others are doing, I just listen to Rick go on and on.

When the class is over I hear everyone groaning and even some shaking others to wake them up. I shake my head because they don't know what they are missing. I shrug and turn around to leave and I'm face to face with James, I almost bump into him. The surprise makes me gasp and take a step backwards. He doesn't blink, doesn't do anything. I calm down a bit and then wave my hand in front of him, but he doesn't blink. I think he is watching me, though, but when I'm about to poke his eyes, he puts the hoodie on and leaves.

"Weirdo," I mumble and follow him. "I'm also a weirdo," I add following him to our next classroom where we have textiles.

I can't ask him anything or annoy him, because Adeline is all over him. Apparently she's more clever than Roxi because she left first instead of staying back to stop him and have a private moment.

James groans and tries to dodge her, but she is quite a dense girl and doesn't get the hint that James doesn't want to talk to her.

Oh... I'm being the same, aren't I? Nagging him and not getting the hint that he doesn't want to talk to me.

Well, this really is a low blow.

I go to my seat and decide to leave James alone, I won't be like Adeline and Roxi. Plus, I feel sorry for him. I'm not hitting on the poor new guy, I'm just bored and trying to figure him out, but still, I'm not respecting his personal space and if I know something, it's that sometimes all what we want is to be left alone.

So that's what I do. I leave him alone but by the end of the class I realise I should apologise to him for bothering him this time. I want to also tell him I had no ill intention. It's the least I can do, right?

But does James Black -oh yeah, I learnt that is his surname and apparently the reason why everyone is assuming he is really some sort of bad boy and not just some asocial twat, which of course is idiotic because a surname means nothing but oh well, they are bored-let me apologise? Of course not. He leaves, almost running and I have to run after him. Really, why do I even bother? I don't know if he ignores me or maybe he is auditory challenged or something.

And it's raining again, so now he is running even faster.

"You're not making things easy, James. I just wanna apologise!" I shout from the door, deciding it isn't worth it anymore. "Fine! I'm sorry, I didn't mean to annoy you that much. Gosh! I'll never talk to you again!"

I stomp my foot and fold my arms, but then I remember that I also have to go home; I can't stay here so I just step forward and leave. What do I care about that guy? I'll just go home and forget he is even in the same group. It's not like it's going to be a challenge or anything. I don't care about him. I won't speak to him ever again. That is settled.

Chapter 4

I do end up talking to James again. And yes, to, not with because he doesn't reply, no matter how annoying anyone is. He really ignores us all, no discrimination whatsoever so I don't feel that bad. I don't talk to him because I'm hoping I'll be the only exception but because I'm always bored. When he ignores me, I don't feel it's because he has something against me but because he does that to everyone and I got to do something. Everyone else has friends and they spend time together. The only loners are James and I and I'd rather follow him around than watching what my other classmates do in their spare time.

It's been almost two weeks since he joined us and I think even Roxi and Adeline realised that no matter what they do, he will ignore them both.

Maybe, a tiny part of me likes him because of the way he keeps avoiding them. I think everyone who doesn't fall for the cheap tricks of those two is good quality.

The rumours keep following James as he doesn't say anything and has this mysterious aura around him which only makes it worse. People are getting more creative. I heard somewhere that James is a cover agent from Interpol and as almost no one has heard him speaking, they don't even think he is English. I'm sure James is not older than eighteen but people do think he's some twenty-eight guy pretending to be a teenager going undercover to get some criminals. Very much like 21 Jump Street.

I think the theory of James being a new version of Hannibal Lecter is more amusing, though.

The kid won't approach another human, though, so I'm not sure about those rumours. But he does have a liking for weird creepy things like monsters. He is writing a graphic novel —or I think that's it with those illustrations of his. He works mostly on that when he gets a bit of free time, which is not much as he is doing his best to catch up.

I talk a lot to him, as usual. It's me mostly ranting and telling him of all the rumours I've heard so far.

"I heard Alice and Chris talking about you," I tell him as he keeps working on his later assignment. The deadline is tomorrow and I think he's stressed. "I mean, they are always talking about you. They are these thriller addicts, you know? Always watching detective shows and stuff. They went crazy over Broadchurch. So don't take it personally, I think they just want to figure you out."

Once again, no response but I'm used to it by now. Talking to James it's like talking to a wall.

"Did you watch Broadchurch? I did with Mum and I swear, spoiler alert! I never imagined that Joe Miller was the murderer. Poor Ellie," I lament, remembering the show and how stressful it was.

It was the most animated I've seen Mum since Dad left her, engaging completely on something. It's hard to get some sort of reaction from her, it's like she's lost somewhere and all you get from her are some mumbles and nods. I honestly don't know how she manages at work. I guess that being a bank teller doesn't require much charisma or conversation skills and. As long as she does her job she'll be fine.

"Anyhow, they were saying that you're running from a murderer. You were a victim but managed to escape and now are trying to hide from everyone. You don't want to raise suspicious so you keep a low profile in case the psycho gets here and asks for you. If you don't talk to anyone and hide your face then people won't be able to spot you," I tell him, watching out of the window this time instead of seeing his work. "If that's the case, my friend, I think you should've stayed out of college. By enrolling you get in the system and anyone can find you like that... unless you stole someone else's identity! The other victim, perhaps?" I inquire, getting into the drama. "What is your plan, James Black?"

I don't get an answer. Not like I was waiting for one.

"Nah, bet you're just some boring bloke who doesn't like people, that's all."

I focus again on the view outside this library. It's Monday so we have the day off just to catch up on work and all that. Maybe I should've stayed home, with Luna. She's more responsive than James.

"Has anyone told you that you make great company? What a charmer you turned out to be," I mutter glaring at him for three seconds before heaving a tired sigh.

I hear him groaning and I turn to see what bit him. He is closing his laptop and collecting all his sketchbooks and other things.

"We're leaving? Do you need to use some studio or anything?" I ask standing up with him.

James normally spends all this time in this corner of the library or in the studios when we are in class or for something specific. I've noticed that when there's too many people he gets uncomfortable and ends up leaving, looking for a more secluded and solitary place.

"Did you finish? Are you gonna borrow some cameras? Are we going to do a shooting?" I keep asking, following him as he keeps his long strides. I hate that he has long legs; it makes me have to run to keep up with him.

We head to the E block and upstairs, I keep following him.

"You know that if you're running away from me, that ain't gonna work. I'll keep following you," I remind him, trying to catch up but now he's climbing two steps at the time. "If you had let me apologise when I tried, we wouldn't be here today. This is my way to punish you for being rude."

Lies. I'm just so bored.

He goes to Printmaking and then talks —briefly— to Nigel, our Printmaking teacher, for some help. As he is busy with his work, I wander around, not bothering him.

I wish I had a friend. A real friend. Someone to spend time with; someone who could reply and ask me questions. I wish it wasn't always me and myself, alone. I don't even know why I bother so much talking to James when I know he won't say anything back. No matter what, it's not like he'll turn around and suddenly be interested in whatever I'm saying. He won't even yell at me to shut up or anything.

I should just leave him alone, right? Why do I even come after him over and over again? He is not interesting. Yeah, mysterious and we literally know nothing about him, but he is not like in those films warning you.

Stay away from me if you know what's better for you.

Yeah, he won't even bother with that. He won't look at you and say he's not good for you.

It seems you can't listen so I guess I have no other option but to stay around. It seems I can't pull away either.

Hmm. Maybe I should start writing novels, cliché novels with some loser main character that has never been in love, or kissed or anything. And the fact that I'm exactly like that is just a mere coincidence. I wouldn't be like this if it were up to me. But there are things I can't control, like boys finding me attractive or anything.

First, I'm too awkward and it seems I have written loser on my forehead, so guys have always just looked down on me. Same with girls. And if I'm pretty I don't know how to make the best out of what I've got. I don't know how to wear makeup —seriously, that is like sorcery and the way they make it look so easy. Once I tried and I ended up like a raccoon— or how to do my hair. I can't even braid it! And it's short and curly and frizzy. I'm seventeen but I surely look younger. I've always been told I have a baby face.

I sigh, tired and resigned. When Mum used to talk to me and pay me attention, she said You're still in your cocoon. But you'll become a butterfly soon, don't get sad for what hasn't happened yet. It will happen. That was actually really comforting back in the day. Today it makes no difference.

I feel blue again, so I decide to focus on James better. When I'm talking to him I don't have time to think of myself or how things have turned out to be lately. Talking to someone —even if that person does not reply— helps me not to go crazy.

"What are you doing?" I ask approaching him, seeing the design he's working on. "Do you have a thing for wolves?" I inquire next when I notice what he has on the acrylic, which looks like a wolf pack to me, preying on you. "What does that exactly mean? Why did you choose this? Are you gonna connect it to another subject?"

He stops, and so do I, watching him before he heaves a tired and annoyed sigh. I watch him more carefully, assessing him before he goes back to his work.

As Nigel gives other classes in this same studio, James and I can't stay much longer and by the time we are leaving, I still don't know why he's doing what he is doing. Yet I still follow him downstairs.

"Is this connected to what you're drawing?" I inquire, hobbling down the steps, trying to amuse myself. "Were you perhaps attacked by wolves or saw something like that? It would explain your fixation with them. You know, a way to deal with the trauma is by characterising them. If that's so, then you're doing a lousy job 'cos they look absolutely terrifying to me. Or maybe you're just trying to get the fear out," I keep musing, practically talking to myself and I'm so engrossed that I don't notice him stopping until practically bump into him. "Oi! Don't just stop like that, mate. Not cool. I could've pushed you down stairs."

James turns around, his eyes cold and fierce. His brow is furrowed and I step back, going up one step so we can be at the same height. I swear he is looking at me, right at me and that makes my chest raise and fall notoriously. For a second he reminds me of the predatory look of the wolves and I get scared. But no, that's not possible. I'm just thinking nonsense again, he's not a werewolf or something. Those don't exist, right?

"Leave me alone," he mutters and I freeze. "I'm tired of your nonstop babbling. You're annoying! Leave me alone. I don't want you following me, I don't want you asking me questions or keeping me up to date with the bloody rumours. I don't care! Just leave me the hell alone!"

I gasp. My mouth opening but no sound comes out of it.

He is talking to me; he is really talking to me. His eyes are really seeing me. He is not ignoring me. This is really happening.

"You— you—" I choke on my own words, raising my hand to reach him, but he practically growls at me. "You can see me?" I ask and he frowns.

The rage and annoyance leave his features as confessions steps in. He blinks three times before his eyes widen in horror and he looks everywhere. I can't move, I can't breathe, I can't anything. I'm just watching him, too shocked that he is actually talking to me.

"Oh shit!" he curses and rubs his face with his hands. "Not this again."

"Can you see me? James? Can you hear me?" I ask, my voice growing frantic and desperate. It sounds like I'm about to cry, but I don't think I can do that.

He turns around and resumes. I react when he's turning around on the other set of stairs and run to catch him. "JAMES!" I shout, desperate to get to him but he is ignoring me again. I run even faster until I'm in front of him, my arms wide open, stopping him from going any farther. "Answer me, can you see me?"

He groans and tries to walk past me, but I move and stop him.

Oh God, he can see me.

"How? How can you see me?"

"Paige, please," he begs under his breath. "Just leave me alone."

"I can't! How do you expect me to leave you alone now? Do you understand what this means?"

He looks away and decides that going back is better than facing me, but I run to stop him again.

"You can see me!" I accuse him. "You can hear me."

"No I can't," he snaps but then closes his eyes, frustrated with himself. He's clearly lost his cool, that's why he isn't ignoring me anymore. He did for two weeks.

"You can... How? How is that possible? No one else can. No one else has seen me in so long. I'm dead! Why can you see me?!" I demand, raising my voice so loud I feel the whole building is shaking. He just looks at me with pity in his eyes and I feel like crying.

Someone can see me... someone can hear me. Someone.

Chapter 5

James looks everywhere, absurdly uncomfortable and before I can say anything else, or he gives a reply to my questions, he turns around and runs away and I'm too awestruck to move for three whole seconds, which gives him a lot of advantage.

"JAMES!" I cry when I finally react and run downstairs to catch up with him, the desperation making me clumsy and I almost trip once. Not that I care if I fall or anything, no one but James would see me and I can't die. Not again, at least. "Please, wait!" I beg almost reaching him when he's leaving the building. "Please."

Reluctantly, he turns around and looks at me with these pitiful eyes. It hurts, it hurts enormously but at the same time it's so thrilling because it's been so long since someone actually met my eyes. Since someone regarded my existence even if it was for a second. Oh God, how much I've missed this. I still can't believe it is happening.

James looks around, maybe making sure no one else is around. Then .he cusses under his breath. "Shit, shit, shit!"

"Don't run, please. I— I don't know why you can see me or why you can actually hear me, but I can't remember when I was this happy. Do you understand how—?"

My question is interrupted by him. "Please, Paige, leave me alone. I don't want to talk to you or anyone else. I'm begging you, leave me alone."

"But how can I—?" I try again but he shakes his head.

"Leave me alone. Don't you understand those words? I'm busy and contrary to you, I am alive and I need to do my assignments. I have deadlines hanging on me and I can't afford to flunk my classes," he tells me and I feel terrible. "I should've known better. No wonder why you never worked I thought you were just... ugh!" he groans before running his hands over his dreads. I notice they are shorter than the first time I saw him, which means maybe he cut them. I also notice his hair is lighter than I first saw. Not just plain brown but like dirty blond and now the dreads reach past his shoulders. He keeps them tied at his nape, with another dread surrounding them all like an elastic band. He's normally wearing the hood up or with a beanie, but with the frustration now he has pulled the hood down. I also notice his eyes today are bluer than usual and I wonder if it's because, miraculously, the sun is shining right now, although there are many dark clouds around and it's clear this won't last.

"I know but this... it's just that... don't you know what it's like having no one to talk? Ever?"

"I don't but I wish I knew. You seem incapable of under-standing that I don't wanna talk. Leave me alone!" he yells and I blink in surprise, trying to keep my expression neutral.

I can't cry. I feel like crying and all that, but I can't physically cry. I'm dead, after all. I'm stuck as I died, with the same clothes, the same hair and the same body fluids. I can't cry, I can't bleed, I can't anything. I just... exist. In a weird way.

"It's not nice," I mumble and he shakes his head.

"Let me know that! Ugh, just stop following me, okay? Stop talking to me. Leave me alone!"

This time he doesn't wait for a reply from me, he just turns around and leaves with long strides that increase the distance between us quickly. I don't move. I just wrap my arms around my own body, trying to pull myself together. So many emotions swirling inside of me, tackling me from every direction.

It's been so long since I died. I don't know how long, I don't even remember how it happened or when it happened. My memories are scarce and they merge, making it all confusing. I don't know if what I remember happening was when I was alive or when I was dead. The only thing I'm certain of is that the bullying stopped. That it was chaos and hell and then it was silence. No one looked at me, no one talked to me, no one answered me and I was all by myself.

Stuck. And I don't know why.

But for the first time in I don't know how long, someone heard me. Someone talked back. Someone looked me in the eyes and I can't stop shaking. For so long I've talked and talked but no one replied and now someone can actually tell me to shut up. Even that is glorious. Someone said my name without crying.

I laugh out loud, I can't help it. It didn't go smoothly and yeah, James yelled at me to leave him alone. But it's not like I'm good at listening to people or like I can let this opportunity slip from my fingers.

I step outside Block E just at the same time the clouds have completely covered the little bit of sun we had before and then a few drops start pouring. I look at the sky with the smile still on my lips and I laugh some more before I start towards my home.

I wonder why it is that James can see me. Is it only me or can he see others like me? Are there any others like me? If there are, I've never stumbled across one of them. Although I wonder if I could recognise one. I don't look any different from when I was alive. I'm not any paler or fainter, I don't smell like decomposition. I don't drag chains or float. I look exactly like I did before and I know it because I can still see my reflection. I've seen the same girl in the brown boots, dress and denim jacket for too long, with her light brown curls to her shoulders and brown eyes.

How could I recognise another like me, if there's someone else like me out there? James didn't know I was a ghost until I mentioned it.

Not this again, he mumbled at some point. Does that mean this has happened to him before? The whole seeing a ghost? Could he know more about ghosts than I do? Am I even a ghost? Maybe I'm something different, but I don't know what to call myself. I just know I'm dead. But I can still touch things and I have emotions. I don't feel the touch of things, but I know I can touch them, like opening doors or grabbing some other clothes to put on top and look at the mirror, pretending I can wear something else. I can also touch Luna and she can see me, but she's a cat. I think all animals can see me. I've touched people and it has different effects on everyone. Normally when I touch mum she cries. When I touch any of my classmates they shiver.

When I get home I have so many questions, things I never questioned or if I did I can't remember ever finding something about it. No one can answer my questions, no one could help me out and I've been doing the same over and over again. I never tried to investigate more about my state.

But now something is different and even if James wants me to leave him alone, I can't. I have to ask him! If he's seen others like me then he must know how to move on or something else. Maybe he can introduce me to someone else like me so I won't be alone for the rest of existence.

"Mum!" I call, my voice so cheery and loud that it wakes Luna, sleeping on the counter in the kitchen. Once again, Mum is already there, absentmindedly watching the telly with a mug of tea between her hands. "Mum, you'll never know what happened today!" I say, going to Luna first to stroke her fur and kiss her head, playing with her whiskers for a little while before I turn around and sit across Mum, covering the telly with my body but that doesn't seem to affect her. "Mum, someone saw me today!" I tell her, bouncing on my seat.

Luna jumps down and scrubs herself against Mum's leg and then against mine. I get distracted to grab her and sit her on my lap and then run my fingers through her fur. Mum can't see me because Luna is between the chair and the table and Mum's glance is fixed on the telly.

"Remember the new classmate I told you about? James Black? He can see me, Mum! And he can also hear me. Today he said something back to me. Well, he was mostly telling me to leave him alone because he doesn't wanna make friends with anyone, but that's irrelevant right now, the point is that he saw me and I talked to someone, Mum! I can't believe this actually happened I think I'm might burst out giggling again," I confess in a hurry and cue to my words I start giggling.

A little smile crosses Mum's features, although her eyes look as hollow as usual, as empty and almost teary.

I think she's been like this since I died, whenever that happened. I try to reach her every day, hoping she can hear me somehow or feel me. I want her to know I'm still with her, I didn't leave her or anything, but it doesn't seem to work. Although sometimes I think a part of her knows I'm here. Like how now she's smiling a bit because I'm laughing. Maybe she can hear that and remember of all those times I laughed at home.

Home. It was the only place where I was actually happy, where no one could hurt me and where I was loved.

Mum used to be such an optimistic and happy person. She always knew what to say to make me feel better, even a little bit. She would walk into my room with two mugs full of her perfect tea and would let me rant about college and how everything was so horrible. She'd let me cry and then stroke my hair, promising that after two years it would be over. That in uni people aren't that mean and immature and I would be fine. She smiled at me and told me I was a wonderful girl and it was my classmates' loss for not seeing what I had to offer, but she could and she was always grateful because I was her greatest blessing.

I've haven't seen her smile like that again.

I barely remember Dad, but I know that when Mum became like this he couldn't reach her. He was also mourning but he felt so alone and seeing Mum only made it worse. He left her. He left us.

"Mum, maybe James knows more about my condition and maybe he knows how to communicate with others. Maybe he can help me or teach me something. Maybe there's a way for you to see me and hear me, too and then it'll be the two of us. I'll always be by your side, Mum. I won't leave you, okay?" I tell her and that little smile quivers before she looks down, her eyes lost in her tea and I can see a tear falling in. I reach out to touch her, to grab her hands, surrounding hers with mine. "Mum," I call and she lets a sob escapes.

"Paige," she whines, more tears falling into her tea and I feel like crying, too, but I can't again.

You know that feeling when you know you'll sneeze and you are about to but you can't? And it annoys you and it hurts you? That's exactly how it feels feeling like crying, wanting to cry but not being able to.

"Mum," I say and she sobs more, taking her hands away from the mug and covering her face with them, muffling the sobs.

I can only watch her, not knowing how to stop this suffering. I want her to know I'm okay. Just lonely, but okay. And I'm with her. And maybe now I won't be this lonely.

"My baby girl... I miss you," she cries and I feel a lump in my throat, choking me.

"Mum, I'm all right. No reason to miss me, I'm here with you. Just... listen to me. I'm here," I try like I've tried another million times but it doesn't work, it only seems to make it worse.

Do I make it all worse? But I don't know what to do if I don't come back home. What would happen to Mum if I'm not around anymore? Who will look after her? Who would wish her goodnight and make sure she unplugged everything before falling asleep? Who could bring a blanket and cover her with it when she falls asleep on the sofa, watching old tapes of when I was a kid?

No, Mum needs me even if right now she is crying.

I'll ask James tomorrow what he knows and if he knows of someone else. Maybe he knows of a way to communicate with my mum, to reassure her I'm fine. Maybe there's a way and I'm closer than ever to changing something. I've been stuck for so long but maybe now something will change. I have a sliver of hope that I didn't have before and I'll hold on to this even if I annoy the living days out of James. Once he answers my questions then I'll leave him alone. I've been like this for too long; I can't let this chance go. I don't know if it'll ever present itself.

Maybe he knows nothing, but it's a start and that's better than nothing.

"It'll be fine, Mum. Don't worry, okay? Can you hear me? It'll be okay," I promise her, with more conviction than I've ever felt.

Chapter 6

"I wish mum could see me like you, Luna,"I comment once I'm in my room, petting my black cat.

I don't know how old Luna is; I just know Mum got her to cheer me up back in the day when I was brutally bullied every day. She heard that cats absorb negative energy and are of great help for depressed people. It's not recommended to have puppies around depressed people because they will also be affected and become sad. Cats can handle it better and help the owners, so Mum thought having Luna would help. I think it didn't.

I don't remember how or when I died. It all seems blurry. I think I remember a rope, but I don't know if I actually killed myself, wanted to kill myself, or something else. I do remember how people constantly told me to kill myself and I listened to them, but I don't know if I had the courage to actually do it. I've never been the brave type.

Many things are blurry in my memory, but I do remember how I felt. Happy with my family and miserable at school. I remember the desperation, the heartbreak and sorrow. I remember the frustration because I couldn't understand why people hated me so much, why they treated me in that way.

I've been doing the same thing for so long that I don't know how long I've done it; there's no cue in my body that tells me whether I killed myself or not. It would be helpful if it were like in films, where the ghosts remain as they did when they died. For instance, if I had shot myself I would have a whole in my forehead and loads of blood. Or if I drowned in a well then I would be soaking wet. But no, I look completely normal. I don't have a mark around my neck that could tell me I hung myself and my clothes are clean.

"If Mum could see me she'd be able to tell me what happened to me. Or you should talk like in Sailor Moon, Luna. That'd help, too," I continue talking.

What little I know is that all animals can see me but for some reason cats seem more willing to approach me than dogs or other animals. They can also touch me and don't complain about it. Luna seems to actually enjoy it and always purrs. I touch people and they seem to react, but I wonder what they feel.

That's another thing I'll ask James tomorrow.

I'm so excited for tomorrow, I don't think I can sleep. Not that I sleep. I don't feel tired or sleepy so I just lie in bed at night, with Luna and everything just blurs until it's morning and I leave the house.

I pretend to have a normal life. I pretend to be alive and do the things I always did when I was alive, although I can't even change my outfit. I've tried, but the moment I turn around after seeing my reflection, the clothes I put on fall to the ground and I'm back in the same dress and denim jacket. Summer, autumn, winter and spring, same clothes every season. But I still pretend every morning like I have a choice and I decide to wear the same outfit instead of feeling forced to do so.

Going to classes is...I don't know. I just go. It's like my body is dragged in that direction and I don't even fight it. What else can I do? Stay alone at home?

So that's what I do the next morning. I pretend I don't have anything better to wear so I go with the same dress and denim jacket. I pretend I don't have time to have breakfast and leave the house in a hurry after wishing Mum a good day at work. Once outside I take my time, walking slowly to college, getting distracted in the way per usual. I've never been known for having a large attention span.

Once in college I go immediately to our studio, hoping to find James alone but he's not around and other kids have arrived already. He only walks in two seconds before Nigel for our Printmaking class.

I realise something when I move to talk to him: he won't answer and he'll ignore me even if he can see me; not just because that seems to be his favourite hobby, but also be-cause we are in the class with everyone around and if he is seen talking to the thin air, then he'll be labeled as the mad new kid. He already has enough rumours without having to give them more ammunition to load the gun.

That is why I decide to stay away from him when people are around-and by away I mean I don't talk to him. It's not like I avoid him or skip class to give him some peace of mind,

I just let him be. I'll attack-I mean, talk to him when there aren't people around just to increase the chances that he'll talk to me. I should get some sort of reward for this, to be honest. It's bloody difficult, especially because I'm all itchy to talk to him, knowing that he can actually hear me. That fills me with excitement and I'm practically bouncing in my seat the whole time. I steal some not-so-discrete glances at him but if he notices he does not show it.

Once Art History is done and we are free to work on our assignments, I follow him to his usual spot: the library. The problem is that I didn't count with someone else following him, too.

"James,"Adeline asks him, looping her arm around his as he keeps walking and he doesn't even hide the fact that he is struggling to make her let go of him. "Why are you always avoiding us? Don't you wanna work with us? I know you're still catching up and getting used to the system. I can help you,"she offers.

I follow their trail, walking slowly behind them, with my fingers laced behind my back and making faces at the scene displaying in front of me.

"You're ruining my plans, Adeline. How rude of you. Didn't you receive the memo that I wanted to talk to James? I can't when you're around,"I complain rolling my eyes when she once again loops her arm around his. Can't the girl get it that he doesn't want to be touched?

I notice James tensing and I clasp my mouth shut with my hands because I forgot for a second he can also hear me complaining. He now knows I want to talk to him and I wait for Adeline to leave us alone. Oh, funny boy, now he doesn't fight to get free from the girl next to him. "Is that your plan, James? Are you gonna keep Adeline next to you so I won't talk to you?"I inquire and he doesn't reply, he kelps walking with the girl. I laugh. "At some point I'll just start talking and talking and she'll do the same. Is that what you really want?"

He stops on his tracks but Adeline keeps walking so she ends up jerking when the boy next to her ceases moving.

"Is anything wrong?"she asks and I smirk.

"Yeah, James. Something wrong?"I ask, walking until I end up at his other side. He doesn't turn to see me and I keep smirking.

"Do you wanna go somewhere else?"Adeline asks and he looks at her this time. She, mesmerised by the fact he is actually acknowledging her presence, smiles brightly at him. "Although it's better if we're alone, you know? That way no one can bother us."

"I beg to differ. I'll start dancing on the table if you don't leave,"I state bluntly even raising my hand.

James actually pinches the bridge of his nose and I can't help my smile. I think he isn't that good at ignoring me now. Or maybe I'm getting better at annoying the living days out of him.

If I were alive I would totally put that in my CV as uncanny talent: Paige Samuels, who manages to get a reaction from James Black.

"Hm..."James seems to struggle, looking at her but not say-ing anymore.

"Her name is Adeline,"I whisper, getting close to him.

"I know!"he hisses, making Adeline frown and I step back, raising my hands in surrender but fighting hard not to laugh.

"What do you know?"she asks with a confused expression and James just sighs heavily.

"Adeline,"he starts and I chuckle. I bet ten pounds that he didn't remember her name until I told him. "I don't work well with people. I'd rather be alone. And I'm capable of managing on my own,"he finally tells her and her eyes widen. I don't think it's because of what he said but because he actually said more than ten words to her.

Should I clap for this achievement?

"I'm just trying to be friendly,"she pouts and I furrow my brow. Is she trying to be sexy?

"I know and I appreciate it, but please, don't."

And that's all he says before grabbing her wrist and making her release his arm. Then he turns around and resumes his way, leaving a surprised and rejected Adeline behind.

"Next time don't pout like that. It makes you look silly,"I say waving goodbye and following James. I catch up with his long strands, my fingers laced behind my back again, my eyes locked on him. "That was an effective way to get rid of her. I congratulate you, mate. I was five seconds away to go all creepy-ghost-from-film on her."

He doesn't say anything.

"And we're back to ignoring, uh? Come on, James. I just wanna talk to someone. I swear to God that if someone else could hear me I wouldn't be bothering you but no one else can do what you can and I'm so lonely and I have so many questions. I need to talk to someone, please. I only have my cat and she can't answer!"I cry, reaching out to grab his arm and make him stop, but he moves faster and avoids me.

He stops walking and turns to face me, his eyes fierce on me and now they look dark blue.

"I've been ignored by everyone for so long that I can't even remember how long is that. It feels like an eternity since someone actually looked me in the eyes like you're doing now, even if it's to look daggers at me. Please, don't ignore me."

He still doesn't say anything but if I could feel physical pain, I'm sure his glare would cause me chest pain or something.

"James, I beg of you,"I try again, my hand reaching to touch him but he snaps and shoves it off.

"Don't touch me. Don't talk to me. Don't follow me. Do you understand? I don't care if you're lonely and desperate for a friend. I don't wanna be your friend,"he says in the coldest tone that actually makes me shiver.

"I know and I'm not asking you to be my friend, although that would be great because I never had a friend before and even less now that I'm dead but that's not the point,"I ramble. "I'm just asking you for a favour, James. To answer some of my questions and help me out."

He laughs. Not that, ha ha ha that's so funny type of laughter but more like ha! You're insane. Get out of my face type of laughter.

"You're all the same,"he mumbles and I frown, confused with his words. "But you're more annoying than anyone I've met before."

I look down, feeling hurt with his words, even if I'm conscious I'm being annoying.

"Can you blame me? It's not like I chose to be here today, stuck and all alone, isolated from everything and everyone. Talking like this, pretending to still have a life is all I have left."

"Go annoy someone else! Don't you understand? It's not just that you're a ghost, it's that you're the most annoying creature on Earth. Not even if you were alive I would want to talk to you. You're a stalker and you don't get the concept of personal space and the meaning of no. You do what you want and ignore what I want,"he snaps rather loudly and I look around, wondering if someone heard him. We're almost in the library but luckily for him, no one is around and no one comes out. "Get this, Paige. I don't wanna talk to you and I don't wanna see your face. You're fucking annoying and you just give me a headache. I won't help you and I won't answer any of your questions. Go and stalk someone else. Find another ghost or whatever. I don't wanna see your face ever again!"he cries out and I take a few steps back, feeling like his words are slapping and punching and kicking me.

I stumble and trip on my own feet, landing on my bum on the floor and James gasps but I can't react. I still hear his words echoing around me. He takes a step forward, almost as if he were to help me but then stops himself. I cover my mouth with my hands and start feeling like I'm choking. That need to cry eats me alive but that I can't fill it.

"Paige I-"

"You didn't need to be that-that cruel,"I stutter. I take a deep breath that doesn't help at all, but it's a reflex before I get back on my feet and then wrap my arms around my waist. "Believe me, if I had another choice I wouldn't be here. I'm sorry for bothering you,"I breathe out, choking on my own words. He looks remorseful, but I don't care. I'm feeling too hurt to care. "You're a twat."And with that, I turn around and run away.

Chapter 7

I'm angry. So angry I can't even be sad anymore. It's so unfair I can't cry and let out what I'm feeling, that I'm trapped in this frozen state and I can't even shed a tear when someone hurts me. The sorrow I live with is suffocating and I do what I can to ignore it and carry on, but I wish I could at least cry once and relieve a bit of the agony that lives within me.

James thinks he's so special and that he can just treat me like he wants because he's alive. I already went through hell when I was alive and I won't do the same now that I'm dead. If there's one positive thing to being dead it is that no one can bully me, no one can hurt me and humiliate me like before. James can't come now and remind me how miserable and insignificant I am and how no one ever accepted me aside from my family.

"Like I want to talk to you, you gigantic moron!" I cry out at the top of my lungs even if he cannot hear me because he's back in college whilst I'm just somewhere in town. "I just don't have another option," I add in a whisper, feeling low again.

I pull my legs upwards and I hug them, resting my chin on my knees.

Is it too much to ask that for once, one person, thinks I'm not a burden and would want to talk to me? Why is it that everyone rejects me? I've never had a friend and only my mum and dad ever loved me, but no other human seemed to even tolerate me. I just want someone who could smile at me and think I'm funny or nice. I don't need to be someone's best friend, just someone's acquaintance is enough.

Find another ghost, James said but where? Is there a community for beings like me? People that are stuck in the world of the living and can't move on, if the whole concept of moving on exists. Can I find a support group and meet every week to talk about our problems? That would be nice.

"Hello, my name is Paige Samuels and I've been stuck since I don't know when but I assume it's a lot. I can't really remember," I say out loud, imagining our meeting of Ghosts Anonymous. "This week I was insulted and rejected brutally by a living one. He's a total twat and has no compassion and he's super asocial. A real jerk. But he hurt me and my feelings and for a while it feels like I'm alive again, being bullied and hated by everyone for no reason. At least he told me he hates me because I annoy him. I know I do but still, he didn't need to be that cruel, did he?" I continue, hugging my legs even tighter. It doesn't hurt. Nothing physically hurts now. "I just wanted someone to hear me for once. Someone who could have an answer or anything." My voice breaks and I have to hide my face in my knees for some seconds. I want to cry so badly, I feel like crying but nothing happens. I'm stuck here.

"I wanted someone to look me in the eyes without mock or disgust. But I guess that was too much to ask, after all. Even when I'm dead people still hate me."

I start shaking. Once the frustration and anger fade the agony of what happened and what that means kicks in and starts chocking me. It feels like hands wrapped around my neck, squeezing and I can't breathe. I don't need to breathe but that doesn't mean I don't feel trapped and scared and horribly hurt.

"Am I really that horrible? That hateful? Maybe it is my fault that people treated me like that. Maybe there is something wrong with me that repulses people. I thought it was them being mean but if even when I'm dead people hate me, then I must be the one at fault," I whisper, thinking out loud and still wishing I could cry.

I take a deep breath and look up the sky, a sad smile on my lips as I try to calm down.

"I'd like to fill in a complaint. This whole not-being-able to cry business is a real scam. I want my money back. Not that I paid or anything, but I feel seriously ripped off right now," I rant, talking to the grey clouds above me as if these could have the answer or would send me a form to fill in with my complaint. "I'd also like to leave a complaint for James Black. I hope that when he dies he also gets stuck and learns what it feels to be all alone and to have people ignoring you even when you need them. That'll teach him." I feel immediately guilty after saying that. "Okay no, that's too cruel. I don't wish anyone to feel what I feel. Not even to James."

"Paige," I hear and for a moment I think I misheard or something because I can't say I'm used to hearing my name. Only mum says it from time to time but her voice is filled with sorrow and longing.

I look to my left just to find James standing there. Well, not standing more like struggling to stand. He bends forward, clearly having trouble to stand straight, his hands are on his waist and he's struggling to catch his breath. I just blink, confused to see him there. Did I summon him with my complaints?

Then it hits me. He came for me.

I move backwards, away from him, sliding on the bench I'm sitting and putting more distance between us. I take a defensive posture, waiting for the next blow do I can dodge it. I still keep my feet on the bench but I stop hugging my legs, instead I cross my wrist in front of my chest, shielding me.

"W-what are y-you doing here?" I stutter, narrowing my eyes at him, trying to figure out why he came here.

Didn't he have enough? Does he have to keep striking me? When I was alive the other kids used to follow me, saying all mean things, pushing me against the walls or pulling my hair, making me trip and more. They never left me alone. They never had enough. Is James one of them? Did he come here to keep insulting me?

"I get it. I understand. I won't bother you again. Leave me, please," I beg, closing my eyes as all what he said before echoes in my head, hitting me over and over again, making me feel like throwing up even if I of course can't do that.

I feel sick, dizzy and scared. I'm trembling. I don't want to hear more insults, more hurtful words. "I know I'm annoying. I'm sorry, okay? I'm sorry. I'm sorry, I'm sorry, I'm sorry, I'm sorry," I start mumbling, my voice shaking as flashbacks of when I was alive come to me, leaving me breathless. All those times kids followed me, even to my home, insulting me all the way. All those times they even threw pebbles at me. Maybe I should've apologised to them as well, instead of remaining silent. Maybe it was my fault and they just wanted me to apologise for my existence. That's why they kept telling me to kill myself, to just die because I was wasting air and insulting them with my presence. "I'm sorry, I'm sorry," I keep whimpering and now I hug my legs again, hiding my face and willing myself to disappear. I just want to disappear once and for all.

"Paige," he calls again and I shiver violently.

"I'm sorry, I'm sorry, I'm sorry," I keep repeating, my voice rising a bit more every time.

"Paige, I'm sorry!" he shouts louder than me and I freeze. "It's me who's sorry. Stop repeating that."

Hesitantly and scared, like a newborn bird peeking out of the nest for the first time, I look up to see him in front of me, closer than before, at the other end of the bench. He looks desperate but honest, he also looks remorseful and flustered. He is still breathing heavily but it doesn't seem it's because he's angry or ready to kill me.

"W-what?" I blink, confused. Those words sound so foreign in the mouth of someone else. Almost like a language I can't understand.

"I'm sorry," he repeats looking a bit more calm now and as I keep watching him as an exhibition on display, I notice the remorse in his expression and worry. "I went overboard when I told you all that. I was cruel and I'm sorry. I just... I lost my temper, okay? I didn't mean to hurt you."

I blink, trying to process the words I'm listening to.

I look everywhere, looking for another soul for whom these words are meant to because he can't be talking to me. I'm just in between. There's someone behind me and he's talking to that person. He's not apologising to me. People never apologised to me for all the things they did and the world hasn't changed that much since I was alive. James hurt me, why would he apologise now?

"What are you doing?" he asks but I keep looking for the person he's talking to. "Paige?"

"I'm looking for the person you're talking to and apologising to. It can't be me," I think out loud.

"Paige!" he exclaims, clapping his hands to get my attention. I snap out of it and watch him with wide eyes, trembling a bit, scared. I don't like loud and sudden noises that catch me off guard. When I'm the one causing them it's different. "I'm talking to you. I'm apologising to you, Paige."

"You're apologising to me?" I ask, repeating his words because it still doesn't make sense to me.

"Yes. That's what I've been saying the whole time. I'm sorry for what I told you before. I didn't mean to hurt you," he says and I take five seconds to process his words.

"But you meant your words, you didn't mean the harm they made. Is that it?" I question him and he blushes, looking away and scratching his head, burying his fingers under his beanie and touching his dreads that he hides there.

"Well, not exactly like that but-"

"That makes sense," I mutter. "I think," I add as an afterthought.

I am annoying, he hates me and he doesn't want to see my face but he just feels bad for hurting me that badly with his words and being so cruel. He still hates me, he's just decent enough to feel bad after what he did.

I'm still hateful and something he wishes he couldn't see.

"I'm sorry for you," I say next and this time he looks confused. "That you can see me. I'm sorry," I say again but this time I don't repeat it like a broken record. I can control myself. "I know you don't want to see my face again. I'm sorry."

"Paige," he repeats, almost like a plead and I stand up.

"I'll try to stay away so you don't have to see me. I won't follow you or anything. I get it," I tell him next, fixing my dress after being in such a position. I bet he saw my underwear. I appreciate he didn't mock me for that.

"Paige, I'm sorry for what I said, really. You don't have to-"

"I won't annoy you anymore. I'm sorry I can't disappear. I don't have control over that anymore and I can't kill myself to help you. I'm sorry." My voice is cold, detached and I guess I sound more like a ghost than ever, one that brings nightmares upon you and wants to drive you crazy.

"What? No. Don't say that. Paige!"

I turn on my heels and start waling away, feeling emptier than ever. Just a vessel. This feeling of wanting to disappear because you know that's what everyone wants is too familiar to me. I lived with it for so long and I didn't think I would feel like this again when dead. I didn't think I would feel something when being dead. Isn't it supposed to end with death? Why do they cheat us like that? Death isn't the end. It's all a big fat lie.

"Paige, wait!" he calls but I don't obey, I keep walking.

I don't wanna see your face ever again! he shouted. I hear that louder in my head than the words he's screaming.

"Paige!" he tries again and I guess he ran to catch up with me because he walks past me and stops only when he's in front of me, facing me, his arms spread as to stop me.

He didn't touch me. He didn't grab my wrist or anything and he makes sure to keep distance between us. He is careful not to touch me. I notice that.

"I'm sorry, okay? I never meant to make you feel like that or say something like that. I'm really sorry, okay? I take back all I said."

"You don't mean that," I say and he groans, I see him rolling his eyes."I'm annoying you again."

"Paige, please. I'm trying here," he whines, lowering his arms until they touch his sides.

"You don't want to talk to me, you don't want to be my friend and you don't want to answer my questions. You just don't want to feel guilty, isn't that?"

"No, it's not that-"

"Then you wanna be my friend now? You wanna answer my questions? You wanna help me out? Is that correct? Did you have a change of heart?" I insist. I feel cold, like I'm ice.

I feel like ice is coming out of my mouth, not words. I don't remember ever acting like this.

James doesn't reply, he looks away and I take that as my answer.

"See? I accept your apology and don't worry, I won't annoy you anymore. Goodbye, James."

And with that, I walk away, embracing myself and trying to feel warm again or at least more like in my body instead of just an empty shell. I hate this feeling. I hate it so much. I want to go back to my normal self. I hate this. I hate it. I hate it so much. I hate it.

Chapter 8

When I get home it's already late because I've been wandering around town. I haven't done anything productive or seen anyone at all. To be honest, I don't even remember what I've been doing all day since I left James, I'm not aware of the track of time, I just know it's late because Mum is on the sofa, sleeping. Luna greets me with a soft meow, rubs herself against my legs and then goes back on top of Mum and then back to sleep.

I kneel by Mum's side, trying to curl next to her kind of like Luna is doing, but I'm too big. Mum is sleeping peacefully, her breathing's even and slow and I try to imitate her. I close my eyes and I just stay like that for a while, sleeping with Mum but of course, I can't actually lose consciousness.

I don't know if I lose consciousness every once in a while. Maybe I do, considering all those lapses of time I can't recall. Maybe it's because I just- disappear. Maybe it's not that I can't remember, maybe it's just that there's nothing to remember.

"Mum, why am I stuck here?" I mumble, with my eyes still closed. "Why am I so alone? I just want to reach to someone and understand a bit, you know? If I'm going to stay like this forever, I want to at least understand what this is."

Mum doesn't say anything, of course she doesn't, not only because she can't ever hear me but because she's sleeping and I won't wake her up.

"I really feel bad now for annoying James all this time. At first I didn't think he could actually hear me and was willingly ignoring me. If I had known I don't think it would've ended like this," I muse, trying to picture the situation in my mind.

It would've ended sooner, I realise. It doesn't seem he likes people at all, alive or dead, and especially dead. He would've barked at me to leave him alone the first day if I had approached him telling him I'm dead. True, I wouldn't have annoyed him for two weeks. But he wouldn't have been more willing to be my friend than he is today, because he is completely against befriending the ghost girl.

"Well, at least I apologised. I guess that being dead made me more inept to dealing with people, don't you think, Mum? I guess there's no way to find out why I'm still here and how to tell you to be okay because I'm fine. I mean, not counting today and how I suddenly I felt again like when I was alive, I'm pretty good. No one bullies me anymore."

Positive, be positive, was something I always told myself, hoping to believe it.

It turns out that when you're being constantly attacked it makes it hard for you to be positive or to ignore people. Adults and others will tell you: ignore them, they just want a reaction. I guess that indeed that is the real solution, but ignoring them requires a certain degree of strength and the problem is that the constant bullying drains said strength away.

But now that I'm dead and I don't have people constantly hating on me I can actually have a more positive attitude. To be honest, it's the only way to carry on otherwise I don't know what I would do. It's not like I can actually leave and look for a better future because there's no future for me. I will never get a job or even go to uni. I'll be forever stuck at seventeen in this town.

So... if James will not talk to me and won't help me out, then I'll just have to continue the way I was until now. I did quite well, for someone who's dead and completely alone, in this world but not allowed to be part of it.

"I'm sorry, Mum. I really wanted to try to talk to you, at least once." I sigh and open my eyes to see her still sleeping peacefully. "As a ghost I should be able to get inside your dreams. I would always give you happy dreams, Mum."

She smiles in her sleep and I don't think it's because she can feel me next to her or anything. If she felt me that would probably make her feel sad. I have that hunch. But I do think she's having a good dream. Maybe a memory of when we were a happy family.

"You should smile more, Mum," I say next. I then stand up and go for a blanket to cover her up. I can't carry her to her room but I can at least make sure she won't catch a cold tonight.

Luna follows me to my room where I stay until the next day. When I got down and before I do the whole pretence of running late, I do take a look at Mum in the kitchen, preparing her breakfast. She's humming this morning, very softly and along to the song in the commercial, but humming, nonetheless. She looks a bit better, a bit more alive.

Sometimes I wonder who's the real ghost, my mum or I. She normally looks more like one than I do, as in the typical ghost we expect to see in films: pale and with hollow eyes. I look quite alive, if I say so myself. At first I didn't even know I was dead. I don't remember much of that time, I just remember the shock of realising people couldn't actually see me or hear me and I was all alone. Especially when I got home and found Mum crying and crying and Dad trying to comfort her.

I wonder if the person who started with the whole creepy ghost idea actually saw a ghost. Who was that person, by the way? I should maybe pay him a visit. Or her. I don't know.

When I arrive to college I leave behind all my internal rambling and I decide to cheer myself up. Over the night I decided that I'll pretend James is just like the others. He can't see me or hear me and he never rejected me like that. However, I won't talk to him because he doesn't like any being near him and even if I'm dead, I'm still some entity and that also bugs him so I'll leave him alone. He won't talk to me or even look at me so it won't be difficult to forget he's different from the rest for some weird and unknown reason-my crazy theory is that he is a werewolf but I won't go spreading rumours-, plus, I do have a horrid memory anyways. I'll surely forget him like I forget most of the people I see.

What I do to cheer me up is to be a creepy ghost. What's good in being completely invisible if I can't haunt people and make them scream bloody Mary?

On my way upstairs, I take the top book in a pile a boy is carrying, holding it up for two second and then I drop it, making the boy go completely pale and the girls next to him to scream.

"What the fuck was that? Did you see it? Oh my God!" the girl screams as the boy can't even utter a word.

I giggle to myself and hop my way up the stairs, like a real bunny. I touch some people and they normally shiver or even react and look back, but they can't ever see me standing behind and that creeps them out.

Have you ever feel like someone is breathing in your ear? Maybe it's someone like me doing that. I do breathe into peo- ple's ears, just to freak them out sometimes, even whispering things, just to see them going pale or shivering.

If I'm going to be a ghost forever, I might as well act like one, right?

By the time I'm in the printmaking studio, some students are there, James included so I stop my whole ghost behaviour and I just quietly sit as far away from him as I can. I focus on other kids and their conversations but I don't speak. I don't pretend I am part of the conversation and that they can hear my inputs and instead decide to ignore me. I just listen to them, nodding at some parts and shaking my head at others. When I'm about to get bored, Nigel walks in so that means it's time to start the class. I, of course, don't do anything, I just listen. If I decided to use the materials and create something, everyone would collectively freak out and next thing I know a priest is brought to throw holy water at me chanting the power of Christ compels you!

I can't help myself, at some point I take a look at James. I think it's just too soon for me to completely pretend he does not exist and to forget he can hear me, but I'm working on it. I just take a quick glimpse to see him working on his own art, fully concentrated and oblivious to everyone around.

I don't know if he can feel my stare or if I just have the worst timing to decide to look at him because he stops moving for a heartbeat before he turns to meet my eyes. I'm sure he's making eye contact with me and I just draw a sharp breath in surprise, frozen on my spot. He doesn't look away and his expression starts to change, to look pitiful and that makes me confirm that he is in fact looking at me.

I'm the one to look away and ignore him this time.

And I ignore him when we have Art History, too. At some point during that class I can actually feel his stare on my shoulders. I guess it's that because I have no idea how that really feels, but it's like something creeps up your back and makes you feel all weird. Like you're being watched. And I don't even have to wonder who could be because out of all people in my universe-because I don't know if there are more people like James in other parts of the world-he is the only one who's seen me since I died.

For the past weeks I've gone with James to the library to talk to him and watch him working so I guess I grew accustomed to that. I find myself at the doors of the rec building when I realise I'm heading to the library.

"Darn it," I spit, angry at myself. I just wanted to leave the room as soon as the class was dismissed. I didn't think where I was going, I just moved.

I turn around to leave and find another place to spend my time instead of going back home this early, although maybe that's the best I could do. I could spend all my time playing with Luna, petting her, making her purr and more. That is actually quite a warm plan.

But the moment I'm facing the opposite direction, someone is blocking my path.

His eyes are on me, his hoodie up, his hands shoved inside the pocket of this. "Paige," he whispers and then his eyes dart to our surroundings. Making sure no one is watching him, I presume. "Can we talk?"

I consider this for three seconds. I weigh my options in my mind. One, to accept his offer and delight myself in the opportunity to actually talk to someone. Two, to ignore him and pretend I didn't hear him like he did for two weeks. Or three, to make use of all my pride and reject him like he did.

I go for the worst of my options: I ignore him.

I try to walk past him, but he moves to block my path again. So I dart to my left and he blocks me again. And when I go back to my right he does the same and for a frustrating second I actually consider pushing him until he falls on his bum. Like kids in the playground.

"Stop that!" I shout, stomping my feet and all that. I even hold my breath, making my cheeks all puffy. "I'm trying to ignore you and you're making it hard for me. I'm not used to this! Why aren't you cooperating?!" I finally burst out, groaning for failing. "Don't smile!" I shout next when I notice the small smile that play on his lips. "Is this amusing to you? Uh? I thought you wanted me to leave you alone. I'm trying!"

"I'm glad you're not sad anymore, that's all," he says and I snort, blowing the hair that's come to my face as I throw my tantrum.

"You want me angry?" I ask, folding my arms over my chest, trying to look intimidating. I bet I'm failing.

"Not exactly, but it's better than what you looked like yesterday," adds James and that makes some of my frustration go away. His voice sounds different, concerned. "I was an arse, and I'm really sorry for the way I treated you. It's true I do not want to be your friend or help you. Believe me, I do have my reasons for that. But I don't want to make you feel miserable. I don't know how your... um, life is, but it's not my goal to make it worse. I'm sincerely apologising, Paige."

This time his words don't make me feel worse and maybe it's because I was frustrated before he apologises this time that I don't feel hopeless now like I did yesterday. My whole disposition to his apology is different and I can now see I was also unfair to him the day before. He apologised and I just made him feel more remorseful to the point he sought me out today.

If I really want to leave him alone and pretend he does not differ from the others, then I guess giving closure to this argument between us is the first step. If I don't hold grudges, then I can move on.

"It's okay," I tell him. "I'm sorry I didn't accept your apology yesterday. I just... I was fighting ghosts of my own, pun intended."

He laughs, he really laughs and my eyes widen in surprise. His whole face lights up when he laughs and his eyes kind of sparkle, becoming bluer and I'm just awestruck.

"Can we leave this behind then?" he asks and I just nod, even smiling to him.

"It's behind," I agree and I hold up my hand for him to shake.

He looks at my hand but does nothing. When his eyes meet mine again I know he's sorry for what he's going to say. "I'm sorry but... I really don't like touching ghosts. It's too uncomfortable."

I ball my hand and I try to take it back in the less awkward way possible, but it doesn't work. "I get it. And well... I'm leaving then. Be well, James. And don't worry, I will keep my word and I won't follow you anymore. I'll stay away."

"Okay, I guess. So... then... bye, Paige."

I give him a quick nod and finally walk past him and away from the building, away from him, the only person who can actually hear me and see me. Away from my last conversation with someone. Everything is solved and settled, no more bad blood between us but why do I feel so miserable?

Chapter 9

I wonder, I wonder... I wonder what does it feel to be alive and to touch a ghost. I imagine it must be creep, but could it be uncomfortable or even painful? I remember that when I was alive I randomly felt like jabs of pain. I didn't know why, they lasted a few seconds and were completely out of the blue. It was like someone had hit me in, for instance, the ribs. But then it was gone I just carried on.

So what if every time I felt like that it was because a ghost touched me?

Nah, it can't be that because I've touched Mum the most and she's never complained or made an exclamation of pain. Yes, she does cry when I do touch her and goes pale and other things, but she doesn't seem to be in physical pain. So I guess that theory must be discarded.

James said he didn't like touching ghosts because it's too uncomfortable, which has led me to the conclusions that he has indeed interacted with others like me and he has actually touched them, which means I'm not fully alone-unless even among ghosts we can't see each other-, and the other conclusion is that touching ghosts for living people is not pleasant. But what exactly does it feel like? Is he exaggerating or did he say that just to reject me in a way that wouldn't make me feel miserable just after we cleared up the problem between us?

I will go with the option he's just exaggerating because that's easier to cope with and gives me the option to continue being creepy and scaring some people when I get bored. That is why I decide to follow Roxy and Adeline.

I'm doing this for mere scientific purposes. I just want to figure out what it really feels and as I can't experience it myself I need to observe and take notes of subjects' reactions to the stimulus to draw a conclusion.

Uuhh, I made myself sound fancy and clever, didn't I?

"Oh, Roxy! My dear," I call when I see her walking a bit ahead, next to Adeline. "Wait for me, friend!" I keep calling, waving my hands and in an overly dramatic tone.

Of course, no one sees this and they don't even react to it. What a pity, they are missing my great acting.

I finally catch up to them and decide to test them so I jump forward and clasp my hands on Roxy's shoulders as I scream, "Boo!" just because it seems fitting.

"AAAAHHHH!" she screams, stumbling forward and breaking the contact. She starts rubbing her hands all over her body like when you think you have a spider on you and you just freak out. She shivers and keeps struggling and looking back, but there's no one she can see.

"What happened?" Adeline asks her, following the direction she's looking at but she can't see me there, wiggling my fingers and smiling sheepishly.

"S-someone touched me," she mumbles. "Grabbed my shoulders."

"There's no one there, Roxy," Adeline tells her and I gasp.

"Rude. I'm standing right here," I say, offended but I receive no comment whatsoever.

"I know! That's why I screamed and I-" she shivers again. "It was so cold and creepy." She looks at Adeline with pleading eyes, as if she could help her and offer her a rational explanation.

So it's cold and creepy. "Like a dead person is touching you maybe?" I ask out loud, pondering. That would make sense, I'm dead after all, but it's not like a corpse is touching her, my body must be rotting somewhere because if I had my real body people would see me. They would freak out because a zombie is walking among them but they would see me and scream when they see me.

Truth be told, I think I would prefer to be a zombie than a ghost. Maybe there could be like a treatment to keep me from eating brains, like In The Flesh. Speaking of, I should go to the producers of that show and make them regret cancelling it after that massive cliffhanger.

For a dead girl, I watch many shows even on my own. What else can I do? I don't sleep and Mum leaves the telly on most of the time.

"It was nothing, Roxy. Let's go," Adeline tells her, cutting my mental ramble, completely belittling what happened and practically dragging her friend.

I stay there, waving them goodbye. I shrug when I realise that they just left me there without saying goodbye. I turn on my heels and just look around, at the people who resume whatever they were doing before a girl screamed in fear and horror.

I spend the rest of the day scaring-I mean, touching people and seeing how they react. Most do it in the same way Roxy did: jumping and shivering as if something cold touched them. They feel creeped out and uncomfortable, as James described but none exactly tells me what it really feels like. Although, I know they all react in a negative way. All of them feel my touch but none can see me. I wonder, however, why is that Mum never screams when I touch her. Could it be because I'm more gentle with her or because my intention when touching her is different? Or maybe she's just used to it.

I think my next mission should be to find another ghost. As James will not give me answers or help me out in any way, I need to find them myself or at least try. I have all the time in the world after all, so might as well do something with it.

Maybe the cemetery is a good place to start. However, I've never gone there or felt drawn to that place but maybe other ghosts do. I do feel drawn to college every day, even if it was a living hell for me, I still go every day and I don't understand that, it's really irrational and against my better judgment.

Whatever, it's a starting point and I must begin some-where. Otherwise I'll keeping doing the same until the world ends.

On my way out I walk past the rectory and for a few seconds I wonder what James is doing, if he is still inside, working or just minding his own business. I bet he is enjoying the silence and solitude now that I've left him completely alone. He got his wish and now I got work to do.

Ahead of me I see a group of students and I'm about to walk past them when a word catches my attention: haunted.

"Yah really think it's true?" one of the three kids asks, her face shows she is really scared whilst the boy who is being asked keeps a smirk, looking confident. The other guy looks bored.

"I dunno, but the rumours is going around and you know weird things happen. Like today? Did you hear of all the people jumping and saying they felt cold hands on their shoulders? I bet the Strode Ghost touched them," the boy replies, almost whispering and the girl clings to him.

"Those are just stories, you're tryin' to scare me!" she whines but she doesn't let go of the boy's arm.

"That's what I've heard, it's not like I know. I've heard that most things happen in the studios for the Art students, yah know? I bet the ghost was an Art student, too," he muses and I blink, listening to them carefully.

I didn't know there were stories about me or that people actually talked about college being haunted.

"I'm popular!" I squeal before I burst out giggling. I even bounce and clap my hands, finding delightful that people are actually talking about me but not in a hateful or insulting way.

"I dunno but if it comes to haunt me I know I'll crap my trousers," the girl says and the boy laughs out loud.

A smirk comes to my lips and I start to reach out to touch her and give her the shock of her life, but before I make contact I hear a hiss calling my name.

"Paige!"

I stop immediately because no one says my name and so close. I mean, there are other girls named Paige but this sounds like someone is actually calling me. So I look back and I see James there, trying not to look at me but his eyes dart in my direction occasionally.

"Don't. That's mean," he whispers next, without even parting his lips. I just stare at him in shock.

I tilt my head to examine him more closely, wondering what's happening. As I've stopped moving, the trio is now walking away from me and the opportunity to scare the girl is completely gone. But James is still next to me, pretending he is just standing there, waiting for something instead of whispering to me.

"You talking to me?" I ask just to make sure because he was the one that barked to leave him alone.

He presses his lips in a tight line and looks at me for two seconds before looking away. "Yes. To stop you. You wanted to scare that girl, knowing she would freak out and probably cry."

"I was hoping she'd crap her trousers, as she promised," I say offhandedly and he looks at me with his brow furrowed.

"What have you being doing today?"

"Science," I smile brightly and innocently and I see him rolling his eyes. "You said you don't like touching ghosts 'cos it's uncomfortable but I don't really know and I got curious so I went around making experiments to see if I could come with an answer on my own," I tell him shrugging to lessen the importance of what I did.

He looks around before sighing and adding, "And by experiments you mean you went around scaring people?"

My sheepish smile is all the answer he needs. He actually pinches the bridge of his nose and I don't know why I find that amusing.

"But why are you talking to me? Because you talked first. I didn't even see you until you called my name," I question next, losing the smile and frowning.

He looks away and I notice his cheeks blushing. "I just wanted to help that girl, that's all. I was leaving when I saw you."

I look at him suspiciously, even approaching a bit and he reacts immediately, taking a step back and keeping the distance between us.

"Why do you care?" I interrogate him and he looks even more embarrassed.

"I don't but it just seemed like the right thing to do," he answers but my frown doesn't disappear.

"I thought you didn't like people, Mr Antisocial. Could it be that you're just pretending to keep all that mysterious aura around you but you're just really lonely and want to make friends?"

I honestly don't believe that, I'm just teasing him and I get paid off when I see his shocked expression. Wide blue eyes and mouth agape.

I laugh at him and step back, putting even more distance and just shrugging off what I did. "Anyhow, I wont take more of your time. You saved the girl and now I'll leave you alone. Adieu!"

I turn on my heels, ready to keep walking and leave him alone as he asked me to do, but then he calls my name again. I look back at him over my shoulder. "Are you gonna keep haunting people?" he asks and I shrug.

"Maybe. I might find someone else who can see me and answer some of my questions if I keep doing this," I reply, which is something really thrilling when I imagine it. Who knows? Maybe someone else can see me and I haven't found him or her. I just need to widen my horizons.

James groans and I shrug. Whatever is going through his mind I won't ask him about it. I got the memo that he doesn't want me around the first time and I said I wouldn't annoy him anymore, so it's time to leave.

"Come with me," he says then, surprising me. I freeze on my spot and I can't even turn around. "I don't know how much I can answer, but I'll try."

My head snaps in his direction, my eyes as wide as his before. "Are you kidding me?" He shakes his head. "Why now? Why are you gonna answer my questions now?"

He can't meet my eyes when he says, "I just do. Isn't that enough for you?" I can only blink, still expecting him to say it's a prank or something. "Don't you want to know anymore? 'Cos if that's the case then I'll-"

"I do!" I practically scream and I can see a little smirk on his lips. "I'll follow you. Lead the way."

Chapter 10

I follow James like a little duckling without saying a word. I'm still too awestruck to even form coherent thoughts. I can't really believe this is happening because I had just accepted he wouldn't cooperate and I would have to deal with finding answers on my own. But here he is, leading somewhere, ready to answer whatever I have to ask him. I don't know if he really knows the answers but he must know more than I do. I've never cared to find out anything or figure things out. I just kept going, repeating the days over and over again.

I am not scared of what he might do. I don't think he'll take me to a dark alley and kill me because he can't do that, right? Can you kill a ghost? Is there a way to get rid of my type? Maybe I should ask that before I keep following him, but if I do he would realise I suspect him and lie to me so he can actually kill me.

Aaaaand I'm rambling in my head again.

I don't think it was like this when I was alive. I don't think my mind drifted like this and I think it's because for so long I've only had myself to talk to. I didn't speak much when I was alive, I think. At least I don't remember me being like this before, but maybe that was because of the constant bullying. I just wanted to disappear so they wouldn't see me and attack me and for that I needed to be quiet. Maybe I've always been this talkative but I was repressing myself.

"Can you kill a ghost?" I ask anyways, risking to get discovered. Maybe if I catch him off guard he'll tell me the truth.

James stops amid street and I almost bump into him but I manage to stop before we collide. I look around, making sure no one is paying attention to the boy that suddenly stopped and that then turns to look at me over his shoulder.

"What?" asks James incredulously. His eyebrows arched and his expression confused, almost offended.

"You know, just asking. In case you decided to lure me to follow you so you can finally get rid of me," I explain and he just blinks. I shrug to make me look nonchalant, but deep down I think I'm scared. This theory is growing stronger.

"If there's a way, I swear I don't know about it. I don't think you can kill something that's already dead," he replies and I have to acknowledge his reasoning.

"You can kill a vampire, though, and vampires are dead," I remind him and he presses his lips tight in a line. I'm not sure if he's amused or annoyed.

"Vampires are not real," he reminds me and I take a step closer, my eyes narrowed and my finger pointing at him.

"How do you know? Ghosts are real, why not vampires? Maybe you're a vampire and you're just hiding your secret from me."

"Your imagination knows no boundaries, does it?" he says and this time I do see the little smile on his lips when he shakes his head. "I won't hurt you, okay? If there's a way to get rid of a ghost, I'm not aware of it so you're safe. I'm probably in more danger than you are."

"True that. I might just start poking you as you don't like being touched," I suggest and his eyes widen, sheer horror written in his face.

"Don't do that," he says, coldly and the engines in my head start working.

"Uhh, is little James scared of a ghost?" I tease, wiggling my fingers threateningly as if I wear to tickle him and he steps back, raising his hands to shield himself. "You're scared!" I laugh at him, stepping back to give him some peace. "Rest assured, I won't touch you. That's my way to pay you back for answering my questions. I'm not that bad of a person slash ghost."

James sighs and shakes his head, but I also hear him chuckling softly to himself before he turns around and keeps walking. I keep following him and soon I notice he's taking me to church.

"I assume you don't want to marry me so what's your purpose on taking me to church? Do you want a priest to exorcise me or something so I can cross over or whatever I have to do?" I ask out loud.

I hear James chuckling again but this time he doesn't stop nor he looks at me. "None of the above, Paige. I just know a quiet place there so we can talk freely without having to pretend I'm on the phone or anything. It's not so bad that I look like I'm talking to myself, it's more about the fact that

I'll be talking about ghost and other things that could make people lock me in an asylum."

"That makes sense. I thought the bigger problem was you talking to an invisible being but you're right, what we'll be talking about is worse... I guess. I'm not even sure how much you'll share and I'm still confused, I don't get why now you've decided to help me out."

"I have a conscience," is all what he says and now I'm the one sighing.

In front of the church there are some benches and true to James' words, no soul is around. It looks quiet and solitary so I guess it's a good place for us to have our conversation. I don't even know how long we'll be here but it's okay. I follow him until he takes a seat and I do the same, making sure to sit as far away as possible. I would sit on the other bench but then that would make him raise his voice and even if I can't see anyone, that does not mean there isn't someone around.

"Okay, so... what do you wanna know first?" he starts, looking at me and when he does, my mind goes blank.

There's so much I want know that I don't know where to begin. I don't know what to ask first and no matter how much I try, I can't come up with a first question. My eyes widen because I start to grow desperate. I can't miss this chance and what if he gets tired of waiting and leaves? You snooze you lose, right?

"Where are you from?" I ask, blurting out the first thing I could come up with even if it has nothing to do with what I really want to know.

He frowns and I close my eyes, knowing I asked the wrong thing.

"I don't see how that helps you out," he mutters and I know he's just going to tell me to bug off for not taking this seriously. "I'm from Winchester but I haven't lived there my whole life. I've been in many places. Before I moved here I lived in Bath."

Now it's my turn to blink in surprise because he actually answered that. I didn't expect that and for almost ten seconds I can't utter another word, too surprised to even think of a next question.

"W-why did you leave Bath?" I ask, deciding to follow the line I already started.

"That's connected with you... well, not you but your type. There was a ghost back there that wouldn't leave me alone and it got out of hand so I had to leave. Ghosts can't leave their homes and its surroundings, so moving was the solution," he explains and my mouth forms a big O, learning something I didn't know.

I never tried to leave Street but now I know I can't.

"Why can't ghosts leave and, for instance, follow you?" is my next question.

"They are bound to the place they died in and well, their homes as they spent most of their life there, I assume. For what I know, they're always roaming the place they died in," he keeps explaining, calmly and smoothly.

"Every time you move out is it because of escaping a ghost?" I inquire next, and immediately add: "Is that why you don't like ghosts?"

"Yeah, it's always been because of that. I'm not sure if it's a ghost thing or I'm just unlucky but all the ghosts I've dealt with are annoyingly stubborn." He gives me a glance that is both mocking and amused.

If my heart were beating and I had actually blood to pump, I bet I would be blushing because I do feel embarrassed. What if my insistence makes him move out again? That would make me feel so guilty.

"I'm sorry. In behalf of every ghost and for being so annoying," I say, looking down and he doesn't say anything, so I decide to continue. "Have you always been able to see ghosts?"

"Since I can remember. When I was a kid everyone thought I had just many imaginary friends. Around seven I learnt that my imaginary friends weren't a product of my imagination and were something else. At nine I learnt they were ghosts."

He looks away and his expression looks sorrowful, a bit tired, as well. I don't know what it would feel to be constantly surrounded by ghosts, especially if they are all so stubborn as he mentioned before.

"Have they ever hurt you?" I ask next, softly and a bit scared myself.

He stays silent for a few seconds and when I think he won't answer, he finally says. "Yes."

He doesn't expand on it and I don't dare to ask more because his tone and the look in his eyes make me know it's not a topic he would like to talk about and I don't want to push him too much today. I don't want him to leave me now that I'm finally getting some answers and understanding some things, like we can actually hurt people. As a ghost, I could hurt someone. I know that it isn't much different from when I was alive, I could've hurt someone back then, but I guess it's just creepy that something you can't see can hurt you.

"Do you know why you can see ghosts?" I look at him carefully, examining his expression to know if the weight on his shoulders that my last question caused has lifted. It has not yet.

"I have no idea. I've never met someone else who can see ghosts, either. It's just something I can do," he explains and I nod, following his words.

"Does someone know about this ability of yours? I don't know what else to call it. What about your parents?"

His expression turns distant and guarded again, his eyes avoid me and I notice how he lifts his legs until he rests his feet on the bench and hugs his knees.

"They don't care enough. They are somewhere in the world, I don't know where right now. I'll know when they send money again," he says and I frown, completely confused. He looks at me and laughs humourlessly. I bet my face is asking the questions instead of me. "They are professional photographers so they are always travelling the world. To be honest, I don't even know my parents. I don't think I've spent more than five months with them if I put all the days I've seen them together. They send money every fortnight and when I was a kid they hired someone to look after me, but they have never been parents. So no, no one knows about this... ability.

And I had the common sense to know people wouldn't react nicely to the news a kid can see ghosts."

My chest aches for him, for this lonely boy in front of me who has parents that choose to stay away instead of raising their own child. I feel so sorry for him and I want to comfort him, but I stop myself from touching him because I know he doesn't like that.

I'm not sure what to say and how to proceed after this, after this confession he's made. I start fidgeting and break my skull to find the words to utter.

"I... I'm sorry, James. That... that sucks," I lamely say and he just shrugs.

"It does but oh well, I'm used to it already. I can do whatever I want so that's cool," he says and I see he's smiling, but it doesn't look like he's honestly doing it so. It looks more like he's trying to fool me and himself by saying he's okay.

"Isn't that lonely?" He loses the smile and looks away. "Is that why you don't wanna make friends? You're afraid they won't like you and leave you alone like your parents?"

His expression becomes stoney, cold and hard and I see him closing up to me. I notice his fists clenching and the veins in his neck popping up.

"No. It has nothing to do with that. The reason why I don't like talking to people and I want to be left alone is to avoid people like you. I can hardly tell when someone is a ghost and I've never had a good experience with one, so I rather avoid them to spare me the trouble. If I ignore everyone, then I don't risk a ghost finding out I can see them and nagging me until I have to move again."

His words are cold and filled with rage, a rage that only felt when he snapped at me before. When he looks at me again his eyes are blue ice cold and I actually shiver. I don't know what's going through his head right now, but his eyes are stormy and his expression severe.

"I don't know what I was thinking. I should just stay away from you," he says, his voice low and raspy, angry.

"James, I'm-"

"I lost my mind momentarily, that's what happened. This was a mistake. I should leave," he mutters and I panic. I've barely managed to ask him a few things. He can't leave now.

"James, wait!" I try to stop him, but he's fast and is on his feet before I can even move. "Don't leave yet," I plead but he doesn't look back at me.

His posture is tense and unapproachable and he doesn't reply or add anything else, he just starts walking. Long strides take him away and I don't move. I don't follow him because I know now a bit about him, I understand a little bit about his personality and actions and even if I'm not sure what I personally did wrong, I just don't want to push him and be the reason he has to move once again. So I just watch him leave, feeling just sorry for him.

Chapter 11

"Ugh, I forgot to ask him about what it feels to touch a ghost. Why didn't I ask him that first?" I ramble, walking into my house, face palming myself for not starting with what I was most curious about.

I learnt about him and a few things about my type, but not enough and I ended up hitting a nerve, without meaning, what ruined my chances. Still, I should be grateful for what little more I know now, like the fact I can't leave this place even if I want to. I wonder if I died here at home and that's why I have to come back every day. It's not like I'm obliged to do so, but I do feel the urge to come back every day no matter what happened or didn't happen. I'm here every night when I could easily spend my time anywhere else in town, instead I come back. But then, why do I even leave hime every morning? Why do I go to college? I don't have good memories or even a good feeling from when I was alive. I remember how I didn't want to go when I was alive, then why do I keep going when I'm dead and free from that obligation? Did I die at college? Did something happened there that's made me roam that place?

Why can't I remember how I die? Is that something normal for all ghosts?

Argh. Now I have even more questions and I know James won't answer them. I won't push him no matter how much I'm dying to figure things out. I know it's annoying and I don't want to be another of those ghosts that have left bad memories in his life.

I actually feel very remorseful for annoying him so much back then, but I honestly didn't think I was annoying him. I just thought I was, per usual, talking to myself and pretending I was just being ignored instead of remaining unseen to him, but turns out he could actually see and hear me. If he had reacted from the first moment things would've been easier for him and he would've avoided two weeks of constant nagging.

It's conflictive. A part of me feels guilty for what I did, but then he also has his share of responsibility so I don't think I should even feel like this. I apologised already and learnt my lesson. I should move on from this. I just don't know why that seems so difficult.

Was I always this stubborn or is it because I'm a ghost now?

I should honestly write down all these questions in case I have another opportunity like today-not with James, of course, I know that-so I won't end up with even more questions and a few answers that don't really help.

"I'm home!" I call, trying to push all these thoughts aside and walking up to the kitchen, where I know I'll find Mum. "How was your day?" I ask even if I know I won't receive answer. I watch her, with those hollow eyes and the sempiternal dark bags under them. She keeps losing weight and I wish I could do more for her, to get her to properly eat or something. "Mum, today James talked to me. Yes, he talked to me, not the other way around, and answered some questions. Sure, I didn't really ask the questions I wanted but it's something, right? I shouldn't be that ungrateful."

I sit across from her, watching her wrap her hands around the cup and with her eyes lost on the telly.

"Apparently, I can't leave this place, I'm bound to it. Also, ghost can hurt people so I'll be more careful with you, Mum. I don't wanna make things harder than they already are," I promise, wishing she could hear me and know how concerned I am. "But you know what worried me the most? James," I continue, speaking the utmost truth.

After he left I stayed there at the bench in front of the church, thinking of the things he told me about himself. His lonely life, painful and haunted. It surely wasn't easy to grow up like that, not only without parents but also with ghosts nagging him, desperate for some company. I do understand why ghosts would follow and haunt him the moment they realise James can actually see them, but still, I feel so bad for that little boy he once was.

Was it scary for him?

"He grew up without parents, even if they are alive and doing well. They just choose not to be part of his life and I find that lonely, Mum. He never had a mum to read him stories at night or a dad to teach him to play football, or someone to run to on stormy nights. How sad is that?" I question out loud, trying to imagine a little boy with big blue eyes and short blond hair, all alone at night even when he was scared, with probably the only company of a ghost. That must've been terrifying for him, even if he didn't know that the creature next to him was a ghost at the time. "Why would adults decide to bring a child to this world but not raise him? Why would they be so cruel to a poor infant who didn't even ask to be born?" I keep the rhetorical questions, getting mad at James' parents for doing that to him. Such a lonely boy, whose only friends were ghosts. "He must carry so much sadness in his heart, Mum. I feel so bad for him."

I heave a tired sigh, feeling unease and restless. It's like I itch everywhere but I don't know exactly where to scratch. Is it because I want to help him somehow? I mean, I'd like to take some of that loneliness away, but he wouldn't like me to do that. He can befriend any living person, it doesn't have to be me. I just wish I could do something, even if it is to improve a bit his experience with ghosts.

"Did you know he's been hurt by ghosts?" I continue telling my mum. "I wonder if he meant physically or emotionally. Maybe both. What if they actually did something horrible to him? I mean, if evil people die and become ghosts, they will still be evil ghosts and keep hurting people." That thought is something I never contemplated before and it terrifies me. There are so many horrible people in the world, like murderers, psychopaths and rapist. What if they become ghosts? What would they do? Would they keep their MO? That's too horrible to even keep thinking about it. "I wonder if ghost have left scars on him. I can't blame him for being wary of me. For all what he knows I could just be one mean ghost that's come to ruin his low-profile life. Mum, what can I do?"

I don't receive an answer and that feels like hands around my throat, choking me. I miss so much the days when Mum gave me advices and helped me solve my problems. She's always been so wise but now I can't reach her and seek for her assistance. And I doubt I'll ever be able to do that. James was born with the ability to see ghosts and he's never met anyone else. It doesn't seem to be something that can be learn and it's clear Mum doesn't have that talent so she will not be able to see me. Ever.

"Mum, I really need one of your advices. Tomorrow I'll see him again and I don't know if I should pretend I don't see him or at least acknowledge his presence. I won't talk to him but should I at least smile at him and greet him? Will that annoy him? Will that make him hate me even more? Ugh," I groan.

I literally hit the table with my face, causing this to jump and startle Mum. I don't feel pain, no matter how hard I hit myself, but the furniture reacts and that scares my mother. She screams and draws back with chair and everything, almost falling back. I jump and try to catch her, but I bump the table again and that makes my Mum scream even more.

"I'm sorry, Mum! I didn't mean to scare you!" I cry but I stay still, afraid that if I move I'll only startle even more.

Mum is still on her chair, hands clutched to her chest and breathing heavily, her eyes are wild and wide, watching at the table as if there were something else there but her spilt tea.

"P-Paige?" she asks, her voice so shaky and my breath gets caught in my throat. My hands tremblingly try to reach her over the table, but then I see her trembling more than I am and her eyes become even wilder but at the same time, emptier. She blinks and blinks, tears falling down her cheeks and then she starts hyperventilating. "My girl... my girl... are you here... my girl..." she cries, barely getting the words out.

"Mum, I'm here. Please, calm down," I try but I can't move. I'm scared I might make things worse if I touch her.

Her breathing keeps picking up and her body is shaking more violently this time. I feel dread fill my body and I'm scared, so scared.

"PAIGE!" Mum screams, startling me, making me fall back with chair and everything. I try to get back on my feet immediately, but by the time I do it, Mum has also fallen from the chair and is unconscious on the floor.

"Mum!" I shout, rushing to her side but not touching her. "Mum, wake up! Mum!" I keep trying, watching her intently and sighing relieved when I see her chest falling and raising.

She's still breathing, she just fainted.

"Mum... I didn't man to scare you. I'm sorry," I whine, my voice breaking and that burning sensation because I want to cry but I can't.

Still, I manage to touch her, stroking her hair and caressing her cheeks, wiping the short brown curls from her forehead. Tears keep falling from her eyes even if she's unconscious and I know it's my fault. I know it because this has happened before because of me. When I grew too desperate and made some noise to get her attention Mum always collapsed. The shock, I assume. I don't know, I'm not a doctor. I just know it was my fault. And I've done it again.

"I'm so sorry, Mum. I'm so, so sorry. I should've been more careful. Mum, please..." My voice is so shaky and fragmented, almost as if I were crying but I'm not. My hands tremble as I take her head and rest it on my lap, trying to keep her in a better position. I also try to put her feet on the chair because I think that's good for when people faint.

Mum doesn't wake up, not even when I manage to drag her to her room and lie her there, covering her and making sure she's comfortable. When she wakes up she'll think she had a dream and will process the events like that. It's what her mind will feed her with in order to cope with the shock. She can't manage the thought I might still be here, even as a ghost, so her mind will provide the theory she can't handle.

I go back to the kitchen, feeling so miserable, but I still clean everything and put things back to where they are supposed to be. Only then I go back to Mum's side and watch her all night, even when she wakes up at some point, looks around confused and seems to think about what happened. I know the moment she accepts it was only a dream and goes back to sleep after putting her pyjama on. I just watch over her all night, remorse eating me alive.

This helps me to make a decision, though. I won't even acknowledge James at college, that will only hurt him even more and make him hate me more. I don't know if it's just me or because I'm a ghost, but I think my presence is toxic and I don't want to make things worse for someone who already has enough. I'll just stay here, as I've done until now, but more careful not to scare Mum again.

So that's why I don't even look up when I go to college. I keep my eyes on the floor, avoiding everyone. I tortured enough people yesterday, I don't need to keep doing this, no matter how bored I am. After what I did to Mum, I don't want to scared anyone for the time being.

I get into the studio and I avoid everyone. I don't even look up at the teacher when they talk. I don't move. I don't anything. I stay on my chair, hugging my legs and trying to block all the noise around me. I should've stayed home but I found myself walking towards college before I even realised it and I'm here again. Maybe due to all what happened here, all the bullying and strong emotions I felt during my living days here I'm bound to this place. Maybe I'm being punished to relive the same routine but without having to go through the hell from the past but a new one instead. A hell that can't touch me but it feels as asphyxiating as the one before.

I don't even notice when the class is dismissed and I'm left all alone behind. I don't even feel like moving. I could stay here. It's not like I need to go to the next class or anything. It's not like I need to work on any assignment. It's not like I have I life. I just come here to haunt this place, to see others live because I can't do that anymore.

"Paige?" someone calls and I freeze. Slowly, I look up just to find James there. I look everywhere around in the studio but no one is there, so I frown. "Are you okay?" he questions next and I just blink at him surprised.

"You're talking to me," I state. Not a question, just a fact. He notices my confusion because he is, once again, talking to me on his own free will without me nagging or following him.

"I... yeah," he confesses, looking flustered. "I just... noticed you were kinda... well, feeling down and I wonder if it's because I left like that yesterday." I don't reply, I just keep staring at him and that allows me to see the light blush in his cheeks. "I just want to clarify that I don't have anything against you in particular. I just don't like ghost in general."

"I know," I say without venom or anything. I don't judge him for that. I wouldn't like ghosts if I were him either.

"Okay. So you're not like this because of me?" he wants to make sure so I shake my head. Still, his expression doesn't change, he looks unease. "Then... why don't you come to the library with me until Photography?"

"What? Me? Do you want me to go with you?" I can't help the incredulous tone in my voice.

He blushes even more and looks away, his hand scratching the back of his neck.

"Well... yeah. It's too quiet now that you're not around and ... yeah," he says in a whisper and I swear I can't react for ten seconds, I can only stare at him. He looks so uncomfortable and embarrassed and at that a small smile comes to my lips, a bubbly feeling setting in my tummy.

"Okay," I agree, smiling radiantly and he meets my eyes again, looking relieved now. Then he smiles back at me. "Let's go."

Chapter 12

Once in the library it is complete silence, which is extremely weird for me because I don't tend to stay quiet. But as I sit across from James and watch him do his work, I don't know what to do. I don't want to disturb him or annoy him in any way and I'm scared that if I open my mouth he'll get angry and ask me to leave. Now that I know he can hear me I don't really want to bother him. If he were like everyone else I would be rambling, per usual.

I'm not sure why he asked me to join him, it's not like we are friends or like he enjoys my company. Maybe he just felt sorry for me and said that so I wouldn't be all alone. It doesn't make much difference though because we are the only souls in the library, or at least this part of the room. James is quiet and focused so I might as well be on my own.

I watch him carefully but when he looks up-which doesn't happen that often-I look away, pretending I've been engaged watching out of of the window the whole time. He probably notices I'm just pretending anyways but if he does, he says nothing and I'm glad for that.

James hasn't told me to keep asking my questions or even mentioned to keep helping me out so I'm assuming what we talked in front of the church is all what we'll ever discuss about the topic. I have certainly learnt my lesson with him and I won't just go rambling or pushing his buttons just to get my answers. He's had enough of ghosts and I don't want to be another bad experience in his life. If possible I'd like him to look back at his life in the future and say: yeah, all my experiences with ghost were bad... except for one. I once met a nice ghost.

If I can do that I think I could say I actually accomplished something important during my life... or no-life. Whatever the proper term is.

He works diligently on his assignments, editing his photographs on his computer. I see him working with an ease that is foreign to me but it seems second nature to him. His fingers move so fast and he clicks here and there and uses a pad and I get a bit dizzy. I'm not on friendly terms with technology. It changes so fast and I can't keep up with it, plus, it's not like I get a chance to try it for myself; I can just see how others use it.

Story of my life, only seeing how others live whilst lamely staying behind.

"You're oddly quiet," comments James, his eyes not parting from the screen. "I thought you couldn't shut up. Are you really feeling well?"

"I'm being cautious," I reply, narrowing my eyes as if like that I could actually figure this guy out and find out exactly what he is planning.

"Cautious?" he echoes, this time his eyes dart briefly to meet mine. "Why?"

"'Cos I'm not sure how to proceed with you," I honestly answer. "I don't wanna make you angry again or bring up a subject that might make you uncomfortable. Plus, I don't want to annoy you anymore. I know my memory sucks big time and I forget many important things but I haven't forgotten how much you hated my constant babbling."

His eyes show a bit of embarrassment and remorse so he looks away, what makes me frown. It's not like he did something wrong, it was me the one annoying him. Fine, he made me know if the cruelest way but it's because I drove him to the edge. I accepted that already. It was my fault.

"I learn from my mistakes. I'm clever like that," I say in a lighter tone so he doesn't feel bad anymore. I even wink and give him the peace sign in my best attempt to look nonchalant.

"So you won't say anything unless I ask you to?" he tries and I think about it for a few seconds.

"That seems the safest and wisest option and although you don't know how to get rid of me, I can't underestimate your ability to find out or bring a priest," I explain and I see him pressing his lips in a tight line to keep himself from laughing. I can see the amusement in his eyes that look like a sky in a summer day... before the clouds gather and it rains again. "If you don't feel like talking, however, you can submit your questions on a sheet of paper and I'll answer them. Preferably multiple choice."

This time he can't hold it anymore, he laughs out loud and the corners of my lips curl up in a small smile at the sight. He looks quite nice when he's laughing, so much more approachable and kind. I like how he shuts his eyes so tightly these become two fine lines and how he covers his mouth with his hand, almost as if like that he could trap the chuckles.

"Do you always say whatever is in your mind?" he asks next and it feels weird that I'm the one being questioned.

"I wasn't always like this but if I had some filter I think I lost it when I died. I don't think social filters are that lasting, to be honest. I got used to say whatever is in my mind. Talking out loud or in my head is the same to me," I explain, shrugging to add the feeling of normalcy.

"You also mentioned your memory sucks. How so?" he asks next, this time he puts his laptop aside and I can notice how his full attention is on me.

I feel weird, a bit paranoid and unease. I look away and this time it's not to check no one is watching, but looking for a way out. To my mind come flashes of when people cornered me, when they approached me with intent looks but bad intentions at heart.

I bet that if I were alive, I would start hyperventilating right now, under James' scrutiny.

I gulp before answering. "There are many things I don't remember. It's like the are blank spaces in my head, lapses that I feel should be there but I can't recall. From when I was alive and since I became what I am." My voice shows I'm nervous, it trembles and it is an octave higher.

I shut my eyes closed and count to three in my mind, trying to calm down. James won't do anything to me, I tell myself.

He's not one of those kids who bullied me. He didn't bring me here to torture me... did he?

"Have you always been like that or is it since you became a ghost?" he asks next and I open my eyes again. His expression is curious but also worried, it seems he senses there's something off.

"Not that I know of. I'm not sure if it's because I don't remember or because I just stop existing or something. What do you know about that?" I ask this time, trying to deviate the attention from me.

"Hmm, not so much. When I used to talk to ghosts on more friendly terms I was really young so I didn't ask things like those. Then I just avoided them or just did what they asked so they would leave me alone," he explains and I nod. "But it seems to me they remembered quite well, although they always seem fixated with something."

"I don't even remember how I died," I blurt out and this time he frowns.

"You don't?" he repeats and I shake my head. "That is peculiar. Not all ghosts share their stories with me, but most of them told me how they died. It's what they say the moment they tell you they are ghosts. Especially those who died in unfair circumstances," he muses and I try hard to think back and how I died. "How long ago did you die?"

"Hm, I dunno," I reply again and his frown depends. "Told yah, my memory sucks. I think a long ago, but then maybe it was a month ago and the monotony of this new life has made me feel I've been like this for eons. However my mum is still alive and living in the same house so I guess it hasn't been that long."

"That is peculiar once again. You don't feel the track of time?"

"More like I don't care about that. I just... keep going. I keep coming here and going back home. I repeat, repeat and repeat. I pretend I'm alive and all that, I guess to cope so I don't feel so depressed and start bawling and making people shit themselves at night, you know?" he chuckles again and I bite my lower lip in my own attempt not to smile so wide for making him laugh.

"Well, I don't think you died too long ago, either. You don't look that much out of place, just like someone who hasn't realised it's winter," he adds and I can sense his lighter tone in an attempt of humour.

"Perks of being dead: you don't feel the cold!" I cheer, throwing my arms in the air and he laughs. "Rain doesn't bother me either or any weather. That's the biggest perk, I must admit it."

"Sounds quite good, especially here in England where it rains all the bloody time," he agrees and the smile doesn't leave his lips.

He leans a bit closer, resting his elbow on the table between us and then cupping his cheek. He has taken off his beanie so his dreads hang loosely around his face and as I look at him I start to think that dreadlocks actually suit him and he looks really handsome in a very relaxed way.

"I like your hair," I blurt out again and my words surprise him, I can notice that. He blinks quickly at me and pulls back just a little bit, cheeks blushes as his eyes focus on something else. "It's wicked. At first I didn't know what to think when I saw it but now I think I like it."

"Th-thanks," he says but he can't meet my eyes.

"How do you keep them? Is it hard? Do you wash them? How often? Is it uncomfortable? Does it hurt to get them? Do you think I'd look good with dreads?" I practically bomb him with questions, all in a rapid succession that make him blink quickly in surprise once again, but that takes away the embarrassment of my compliment.

"It's not that hard to keep them once you get them. Once in a while you need to do something 'cos your hair grows, right? But it's quite comfortable. And yes, I do wash my hair constantly but with a special kind of shampoo. It doesn't have to have so many chemicals." He stops for a second, to recall what else I asked him, I assume. "It hurts a bit when you're getting them done 'cos they pull your hair but totally bearable and I don't know how you'd look. I do think you look good with your curly hair, though" he says and now I am the one to get embarrassed after that small compliment. "Can you even get dreadlocks, by the way? Aren't you stuck the way you died?"

"True that. I tried to put my hair in a ponytail but the elastic band fell off the moment I looked away and my hair was back to how it is. I can't have anything... real? on me. It just falls off and I'm back on this clothes and style," I explain and he nods, understanding.

"At least you died in nice clothes and looking good. It would've been sad if you died in your pyjamas. Can you imagine that?" he says and I try to think of my usual PJ. Yes, that would've been humiliating and sad. "I sleep in my pants. I can't imagine staying in that until I cross over. I would hurry the hell up to finish my business here."

"Is that what ghosts do? We have to cross over? How do we do that?" I ask him, seeing a chance there to know a bit more.

"Yeah, most do that. Some just stay forever. It's a choice, basically. Not everyone who dies become a ghost, I've noticed, but every ghost has free will to choose once that opportunity presents itself," he explains next and I nod. I think it's good not everyone becomes a ghost, otherwise it would be quite crowded.

"Why do some become ghosts? Is it a punishment or something? Did I do something wrong when I was alive to be stuck like this now?" My voice has an edge and he sense it because the smile disappears and his eyes look at me carefully.

"I don't think it's that. I assume it's because there's something else they have to do. Cliché unfinished business? Pretty much that. Once they are at ease they can cross over. I haven't ever seen what they do at that time, but I have seen ghosts just disappearing and saying goodbye. They all seem to react to something, so I assume they see something."

"A door like in Being Human?" I question and he looks at me with curious eyes, surprised that I can make that reference. "What? Can't a ghost watch telly?"

He laughs again, shaking his head a tad bit. "Maybe. I don't know. Maybe they just see the light or the Grim Reaper. I really don't know and I haven't asked."

"I'll tell you what it looks like when I see it so you can go to all those writers and tell them what really happens. Or add it in your graphic novel," I continue, keeping the light tone and he chuckles softly. "If I ever see it," I add, this time in a more depressing tone.

"I guess if you really wanna cross over you'll see it," he says with a slight shrug. "Every ghost sees it at some point. Whether you decide to cross over or not, that is your choice, but you'll see it."

"What if it never shows?" I question, my voice low and uncertain. "What if I'm stuck here forever?"

His eyes show so much pity before he opens his mouth, and to worse my sorrow, his answer doesn't help. "I don't know then, Paige. I don't know."

Chapter 13

I look away, outside the window as what's there is the most fascinating thing in the world. There's fear in the pit of my guts, paralysing fear and I even have to hide my hands under the table because these are trembling and I don't want James to see that.

It's not that the possibility of being like this forever didn't cross my mind before, it's more that now it's a confirmation that the possibility exists, even if it's by choice. Somehow it has become real and that scares me. It's already difficult enough to exist like this, then what do I do when Mum passes away? What do I do when the world keeps changing and I'm still stuck? It's like seeing the world and everything that's happening but not being able to actually touch it. It's as if I were locked in a glass cage. But can I even stay in that case forever? What do I do when the world that was mine completely disappears? When there's nothing else left that once was mine?

"You must have something left to do," James says, his voice soft and careful. I chuckle but not because I'm amused, it's more of a cynical laughter.

"What? Are you willing to help me find my unfinished business now?" I turn to look at him and my voice is cold and lifeless... like a corpse. "I don't remember how I died or why or when. I can barely remember when I was alive and I don't even know where to go. I am stuck. I repeat. That's all I do. What unfinished business could I have? Finishing college? I can't do that, no matter how many times I repeat this diploma. Form a family? Fall in love? How? With another ghost?" I laugh again, that cynical and hateful laughter. "What can I do to help me cross over? I have no clue, I don't even know where to begin."

"There must be a reason why you're stuck," he continues and I shake my head.

"I'm not only stuck, I'm completely alone. I don't have answers, I just have questions, even about myself." I look down for a few seconds, focusing on the pattern of my dress and heaving an exhausted sigh. "I don't even even feel compelled to do anything. Do I even have an unfinished business?"

James doesn't reply because if I don't know it, how could he? I don't feel dragged to anything. I didn't leave anything behind that worries me or anything.

"Is it normal that ghosts don't have a clue what is holding them back?" I ask because he doesn't seem unwilling to answer this time so I might as well make use of this chance.

"I've never met one that didn't know until..."

"Until you met me," I complete for him and when I look up to meet his eyes I can see pity in his. "It seems I'm not your average ghost, then."

I stand up, suddenly feeling very suffocated inside this library. I just want to go out, take a breathe even if this won't change a thing. I want to let at least the wind touch me. So I turn on my heels to leave but before I actually take a step away I remember something I need to know before leaving James.

"May I ask another question? The last one, I promise," I say, not turning to face him or anything.

"Go ahead," he replies.

I wrap my arms around my waist and take a deep breath before I fire away, "What does it feel to touch a ghost? Is that unpleasant?"

He doesn't reply for many seconds so I think he won't. I turn to look over my shoulder and find him watching me carefully, his eyebrows furrowed and the dreadlocks framing his boyish face. I feel a tug in my chest when I meet his eyes, something inside of me that makes me feel even more sorrowful than I already do.

"Very," he replies, a mere whisper but I hear him in this quiet room and that simple word hurts. "It's not painful, but it feels like cold hands are running down your skin. You feel cold to the bone and so sad and lonely. It's like that when they touch you they pass on all the sorrow they carry and I have never met a happy ghost." A little smile plays on his lips when he pauses. "You're the most cheerful ghost I've met."

"I try," I sigh and his smile widens.

"But even you carry so much sadness with you. I'm afraid of what I might feel if I touch you. You seem in so much pain when you stop putting on a smile," he says and I take step away from him immediately. It's not like I'm going to touch him or anything, but he's scared and I don't want to make it difficult for him.

"So every time I touch Mum she feels all the pain and concern I feel?" I ask but I fear the answer and he knows that because he looks away and that's all I need to confirm my fear. "I've been hurting her even more without even knowing it. I've been making it worse for her." An incredulous chuckle escapes, choked and desperate; the only sign of that asphyxiating pain in my chest, growing and growing. "I'm horrible, after all."

"You didn't know," James tries to comfort me and I guess he acts by instinct because he takes a step towards me, holding up his hand as if he were to reach for me but I take a step away from him. "It's not like you did it on purpose."

I know he's right, it's not like I willingly hurt Mum, but still, I should've figured it out because she cried every time I touched her. I saw the pain in her own face. It's me then, it's me the one who's been holding her back and keeping her from moving on. It's all my fault.

"Th-thank you for answering me," the words leave me in a strangled tone and I shut my eyes tightly, wrapping my arms even tighter around myself. "And thank you for talking to me today."

I turn around and walk towards the door, only wanting to leave and disappear right now. I don't even want to be alone, I just want to cease existing. I want all this to stop right now.

"Paige!" James calls my name but I don't stop. "You don't have to leave. You can stay here," he adds and this time I stop but I don't turn around. "I know you don't wanna be alone, especially right now, and to be honest I think I got used to your rambling."

I can feel the smile in his words and I wish I could cry or do anything to expressed how moved I am by his actions. No, I don't want to be alone, but I don't want to annoy him. To be honest, I don't want anything. I don't want to be alone but I don't want to be with anyone else. I just want to stop. Once and for all.

"It's okay, I'm used to be alone by now. You don't have to do this. If this is your guilt moving you or anything else, it's not necessary." I turn around to look at him over my shoulder again and I make sure to smile brightly at him even if I feel like there's a storm inside of me. "Aren't we even already? Do you want me to owe you? I annoyed you for two weeks and you hurt me. I think we are even. Let's leave it there, okay?"

"Paige," he calls my name but his voice carries a tone I can't read, it sounds almost as a plea.

I smile brightly at him, even wider than before and I even give him a peace sign before turning around and running outside the library. I keep running and I don't stop. I don't get tired, I don't need to catch my breath or anything, my muscles don't burn and I feel I could run forever. But as I get away from college to the borders of the town I start feeling weak. No, weak isn't the right word. I feel less real, as if I were losing myself, as if all the energy in me were leaving me. It's not because I'm tired, it's different. I just feel less corporeal.

At some point, when I've run so much that I think I've left Street, I can barely hold myself. I don't even feel like I'm here. Everything spins around and I feel lighter, almost as if I didn't weigh a thing. I look at my hands and these are so pale, almost white, almost transparent.

Is this why ghosts can't leave the places they are bound to? Because they start to fade? Because they lose energy? What happens if I can keep walking? Can I even keep walking away?

I try it.

I take another step away, closer to the next town but I can barely move. My whole body is shaking and I can't control my own limbs. I can't take two more steps before I collapse on the grown. But even then I try to crawl away, pushing myself to the limit no matter how dizzy I feel. I can't even see what's ahead, it's all blurry, but I keep trying. I push and push and push until it's all black.

I open my eyes and I'm back in college, on my desk in Art History. The desk that has been scribbled over and that looks so old and mistreated. I actually wake up here and that confuses me. How did I end up here? Why did I wake up? I don't sleep, I never did something like that before. I pretended to sleep many times but never once I lost consciousness and woke up somewhere else.

What happened?

I jump from my seat, pushing the chair with me and causing this to fall with a loud thud but that's not the worse part. The worse thing is all the screams and chaos that arises in the classroom, all the startled kids holding on to one another and looking in my direction and... and not seeing me. They just see the chair on the floor and the desk a bit farther from where it should be.

"Oh my God, oh my God, oh my God. It's her... she's here, she's haunting us!" someone cries but I can barely register that. I'm still confused, trapped in a different bubble, one that makes everything blurry around me.

"H-how did I get here? Why are we here?" I ask because we have Art History only on Tuesdays and last time I checked it was Wednesday. "What happened?" I ask even if no one is going to reply.

"Stop playing pranks," Regina shouts. "Don't disturb the class."

"It wasn't any of us, Regina!" Roxi replies back, completely freaked out. I can hear it in her voice even if I'm not looking at her. I'm still frozen on my spot. "It was her!"

"Ghost don't exist!" Regina refutes. "Don't be kids and stop these games. You're old enough to know better," she scolds everyone and they all complain in mumbles and still trembling whispers.

There isn't calm for Regina to resume the class, but she tries. I can't move, I still watch my desk a few steps from me, then look around, utterly confused. I don't know what's happening now. The last thing I recall is me trying to get away and just... blacking out. How did I get from there to here? Did someone carry me? Who?

I turn to my side, looking for James and I immediately meet his eyes. His are surprised and confused, startled like everyone else's.

"Was it you? Did you bring me here?" I ask in a shaky voice and he shakes his head no. "Then how?" I ask out loud, not exactly at him.

My head feels stuffed, overwhelmed and I feel dizzy again because everything is spinning. I don't know what's happening nor how I ended up here. I don't know why it's Tuesday again. I don't know if I passed out or fell asleep. I have no idea.

I run away because I don't know what else to do. I storm out causing a ruckus again and making the kids and even Regina scream when the door slams open and then slams shut as I leave the classroom. I run downstairs, away from the building but I don't leave the campus. I don't know what happened but I know I don't want to do it again.

I don't stop until the benches near the rectory and only then I allow myself to sit down and curl up, hugging my legs and hiding my face, counting to ten in my mind trying to calm myself down. I'm scared and confused and so lost. What did I do? Can someone even answer me this time?

I start shaking and I want to scream because I can't cry and I need some sort of release for all what is swirling inside of me.

"Paige," someone breathes out and I freeze again. I slowly look up, still feeling disorientated and confused, but I find James' blue eyes watching be carefully and sure. Then he holds up his hand, palm facing the sky and I frown.

"What?" I ask and he just nods, kind of pointing to his hand, he even moves it closer to me when I pull back.

Hesitantly, I hold up my own hand, reaching for his even if I'm not sure this is what he means. I do it slowly in case he wants to stop me or correct me but he doesn't and once my hand is like five centimetres away, he grabs it and pulls me, making me rise to my feet and I can't even process what's happening because next thing I know I'm in James' arms.

Chapter 14

I can't react and I'm frozen, I can't even blink and I'm holding my breath as I feel James' arms tightly wrapped around me, pulling me against his body.

I've touched many people and things. At first I couldn't do it, I remember how I went through everything but then I learnt that I just had to concentrate and managed to succeed to be more... corporeal, I think. And since then I learnt that I've always kept that concentration. It's basically all I can do and a way to fool myself to think I'm not just a creepy ghost. I rather open a door than just go through it because that is just creepy. By now I'm so used to keep my mind focused that it comes naturally. Like breathing for a living person or even myself. I don't have to do it, but I do it unconsciously.

Even though, I have never been touched before by another human being. At least not since I died.

It feels... weird. Too warm and solid, it's electrifying and it makes me tremble. It's also shocking and all that anguish I felt before he hugged me disappears. I stay limp in his arms, I don't react, I just stare at the horizon over his shoulder but he hugs me even tighter. I also feel him trembling and soon after I hear something that's not right.

Is James crying?

I pull away before I can even get used or comfortable in the embrace, just to check on him and he is pale, his lips are a light shade of purple and he's clearly shivering, but he is also crying and his expression shows the most heartbreaking ache I've ever witnessed.

"A-are you okay?" I ask. Whatever worry I had before is gone when I see him. He looks terrible, ill and about to faint.

Naturally, I reach to grab his arm to guide him to sit but when I do his expression shows even more pain and his body kind of spasms so I retrieve my hand immediately, almost as if I touched a hot surface. Did my touch cause that on him?

"S-sit down, James. You look ill," I say, but my voice is trembling and I have a bad, terrible, horrifying feeling sinking in the pit of my guts, eating me from within.

"I'm f-fine," he says but his voice sounds shaky, betraying him completely. "I just need... a few minutes. That's all," he adds and slowly moves to sit on the bench.

For the first time I look around to see if someone else is passing by and saw him basically hugging himself. A boy is staring at him with a confused expression but then just gives James a what-a-freak look and resumes his way, leaving us alone again.

I focus on James one more time and I keep seeing tears falling down his cheeks, sorrow furrowing his brows and a grimace that tells me he is in pain.

I'm about to ask him what's wrong when he speaks first. "H-how... how do you go on with... with that much pain?"

For a few seconds I don't understand what he is asking and I'm about to request him to rephrase that when I remember what he told me before about touching ghosts and how he didn't like it because he could feel all what they did, the sorrow and pain. He hugged me, which means he felt all what I feel and now he is... he is crying, like I can't do. He is crying because of me. I did this to him.

My hand flies to my mouth, covering it as my eyes widen in horror. He rubs his face with his hands and wipes the tears way. It seems the colour is coming back to his skin but he still looks awfully pale and sick. And even if he brushes the tears away, these keep falling.

"There's so much... so much pain," he keeps rambling. "It eats you alive. So much fear and loneliness." He looks up to meet my horrified eyes and I can see in his expression all what I always feel and push to the back of my mind. "So much ache," he whispers. "How can you even smile when you feel like that?" he asks once again, a new tear falling down his cheek and I feel tempted to brush it away, but if I touch him I'll cause him more pain... and he'll get colder. It's winter already, no need to make things worse.

"Why did you do that? Are you mental?" I spat instead of answering his questions. "You said you don't like touching ghosts then why did you hug me? You don't even like me why did you do this to yourself? Why?!" I shout, getting angry because I can't even control my own emotions.

James looks at me with confused eyes but that's better. Part of the loneliness and sorrow are gone and that's good.

Those aren't his emotions, he shouldn't suffer for them. They belong to me, they are my struggle.

"I can't understand you. You told me to leave you alone and I did, I apologised for what I did and obeyed but then you came after me. Time after time. Why? And not only that but you also hug me! You hugged me when you know better than anyone what that feels. Why did you do that? Are you a masochist?!" I keep shouting, pacing from one side to the other and getting more frustrated by the second. I know James' eyes follow me but I can't stand still.

"I— I was worried," he mutters and that makes me stop. I stare at him with wide eyes in disbelief.

"Pardon me?" James looks down and a bit of a blush comes to his cheeks that he tries to hide from me.

If ghosts could have a headache I'm sure I'd have a migraine by now.

"How couldn't I? You disappeared for a week without notice. You just left and then I couldn't find you and you didn't come the next day or the day after that. I was worried!" he raises his voice this time, but then takes a deep breath and continues. "I thought that you stopped coming because of me and I felt so guilty because you don't have to do that. What I said that day was just in the spur of the moment, you can't take it that seriously."

"I— I disappeared for a week?" I echo his words, completely confused and suddenly feeling like everything around me is spinning. My knees give out and I end up crouching down, my eyes keep watching him, though.

"You didn't know?" he asks, as confused as I feel. "Weren't you at home or avoiding college?" I shake my head because words fail me. "Where were you then?"

"I— I don't know. Last thing I remember is leaving the library," I start to explain, recalling what happened—a week ago. "Then I just ran until I reached the town limits and tried to keep going. I remember feeling weaker with every step and then I just blacked out. Next thing I know I'm back in Art History, on my desk, in the middle of the class with no recollection of how I got there."

Saying all that gives me a nauseating feeling but it's not like I can throw up, I just feel sick. What did really happen when I reached the town limits? Did I pass out? But then how did I come back? Is that why we can't leave the places we are bound to because even if we try we are back to them?

"What happened, James?" I ask him but he looks as lost as I do. "How?"

"I don't know. Is that why you were so surprised in the middle of the class?" he asks and I nod. "I was surprised too because I never saw you get in and I arrived first."

"I just... woke up there. I... for a moment I thought you brought me back but... Argh, what's happening?!" I shout, frustrated and mostly scared. I ruffle my hair, leaving it in a horrid mess but I don't care. James is the only one that can see it and it's not like he will mind.

"That is certainly weird. I never knew of something like that happening," he muses and I sigh heavily. "I knew ghosts were bound to places and were always lingering around them, but I never thought they couldn't actually leave. Something dragged you back, I don't know what, but it happened and it took a week."

I shiver at his words, wondering what and how that happened. Is this some superior being's doing or is it just how energy works? What am I made of? What am I? Is this like magnets, that the more I pull away from a place the stronger it pulls me back? And why was I out a week? Well, technically six days as I passed out on Wednesday and it's Tuesday now. Where did I go during that time? What happened to me during those days?

I heave a tired sigh and rub my face again. My head is so full of questions I can't even utter them out loud and I'm sure James doesn't know the answers. And even if he did, I don't want to bother him anymore. Being held in his arms was... nice. New and different, but nice nonetheless. At least for me it was. It felt warm and alive, but for him it felt like death. I know for sure one thing and that is that I can't ever touch James again, even by accident. the more reason now to keep my distance and not only from him but from anyone else.

Oh God... No wonder why Mum cries every time I touch her. Every time I did she felt my pain, she felt death touching her and that surely reminded her of losing her only child.

I can't breathe and I'm chocking again. I hit my chest with my fist several times as if like that I could relieve some of the ache there, that claustrophobic feeling but nothing happens. It's still there, in the centre of my chest, suffocating me.

"Why?" I ask in a whisper, feeling terrible for what happened to James because of me. "Why did you follow me? Why did you hug me?"

"I came after you 'cos I knew you were upset and something happened, plus I wanted to apologise. It seems that's all I do," he muses and his ashamed tone makes me forget a bit about the chaos in my mind. "But then I saw you so... lonely and miserable here and I just... I dunno, I just moved before I could even think of what I was doing."

"That was a stupid move," I declare flatly and he chuckles. "But thank you. Still, you're a fool for doing that. It only caused you pain," I remind him, looking into his blue eyes that still look a bit watery.

His face has recovered some of his colour, but he is still cold. I can tell by the way he snuggles inside his hoodie, making himself look smaller.

"It's your pain, though," he comments and that makes it worse, so much worse because it means I gave him that ache. "How do you do it, Paige?"

"I'm used to it. It's my pain, you shouldn't even know about it. You shouldn't have done that, James. No matter how guilty you feel, you don't go doing things you hate and are uncomfortable for you," I remind him and he actually shrugs. "And seriously, what do your really want? Why do you keep coming after me? If it's guilt, I told you already it's okay, you don't have to do that."

"It's not guilt," he says and I blink in surprise, my lips slightly parted in a small O.

"What?"

He chuckles as if my reaction amuses him, which only adds points to the theory he lost his mind.

"At first I thought you were like every ghost," he starts explaining, a little shrug to make it sound more casual. "But then when I told you to stay away you actually did. You didn't insist anymore when I told you I couldn't answer your questions or that I didn't want to help you. Every other ghost has pestered me until I give up and that's why I hate them. They don't know the meaning of no and they just ruin my life. But you stayed away despite the way I treated you." He smiles kindly at me and I can only blink. Any other reaction is something I can't accomplish. "You're the loneliest ghost I've met and after touching you I can say for certain that I've never met a ghost that feels so much pain as you do. And even like that, even if you're constantly suffering you still left me alone when I asked you to."

"Because you asked for it," I say as if that's the most obvious thing.

"Exactly. No other ghost did that, you're the first. You didn't force me to help you, you gave me the choice and respected my decision." His smiles widens a bit, become more endearing. "That makes you a special ghost. And I think it's remarkable you manage to look so cheerful when you feel like you do."

"I don't have another option," is all what I can say.

"That's why I want to give you another option," he continues, confusing me again.

"How do you plan on doing that?" I question.

He leans forwards, closer to me and that startles me, so I pull back but as I'm crouching down, I end up falling on my bum. His amused expression disappears and it's replaced by concern, so I hurry back on my feet and step away from him. His eyes follow me so I just smile widely to make him know I'm okay.

"So... how do you plan on doing that?" I repeat to distract him and his smile comes back.

Looking up to meet my eyes this time, he says, "On my own will, I'll help you, Paige."

Chapter 15

"**I**s it April's fool? Did you lie to me and instead of a week I was out for months and now it's April and you're just teasing me?" I blurt out because that's the first thing that comes to my mind.

I heard all the explanation he just did and me asking this probably sounds dumb and repetitive, but I can't help it. Call me slow because that's how I feel right now. I can't process his words and the meaning of them because to my mind come flashes of that outburst he had the time I learnt he can see me. I also remember his tortured expression when talking about ghosts and his past experiences. I understand his reluctance perfectly, better that his newfound will to help me out this time. Whether his actions are guilt-driven or not, I think he is going too far. Considering his past record, the most logical thing is that he stays away from me and I wouldn't blame him for that.

Why did he change his mind? He can't be that guilty. We've cleared that up already many times, he can't be that dense.

James chuckles but I keep looking at him with wide eyes and blank expression because I still don't know how to react. "No, I haven't lied to you and this isn't any type of joke. I really mean it, Paige. I want to help you," he explains again and I just blink. "It's not that hard to understand, to be honest," adds James, shrugging with one shoulder only.

"Yeah, it is. First off, you already said no and I don't resent you for that, you have all the right to refuse and all the reason to. Second off, why now? Why did you change your mind and decide to help me? Can you even help me? How? I don't even know where to go first. With or without your help I'm still clueless and you would be only wasting your time," I rant, raising my voice a little bit by the end, a sign of desperation and frustration, I assume.

James looks down, avoiding my eyes for a few seconds and I use that chance to take a deep breath and calm myself. I'm overreacting, I can't just raise my voice because I can't understand the reasoning behind his words.

"I judged you harshly at first. I thought you were like every other ghost but you're not," he mutters without looking up and meeting my gaze. "You ask what changed my mind," continues James and this time he looks up and his blue eyes show an intensity that takes my breath away. We stay in silence for five heartbeats, just staring into each other's souls and it seems to me the air is charged with electricity. I can't move and I don't even dare to blink. "You changed my mind."

I can't reply, or move for what matters. I can just look at him as a weird feeling I can't describe goes up my body, from the tip of my toes to the top of my head, and it leaves me buzzing.

"If you changed your mind and don't want me to help, I understand. I just don't... I guess I don't want you to be alone," he explains next in a softer tone, almost like a caress.

"I-" my words get stuck in my throat, although I don't even know what words because my brain isn't working. "It's not that I just-" I sigh and finally break eye contact. I think that's what is not letting me think. "I'm just confused and I'd like help but I don't really know how you can do so. You've answered many of my questions already. I don't think there's more to do. And even if I appreciate you not wanting me to be alone, I don't want to cause you any sort of trouble. I am okay, I'm used to this already. You really don't have to do this." I briefly look at him to show him my sincerity.

I hate being lonely and not having anyone to talk to. I have to admit that these past few days-the ones I've been conscious of-have been like fresh air after being locked up for so long, despite the incredible high amount of angst. But even if I'd love to be around James and be able to talk to him, the idea of causing him pain or any sort of discomfort makes my chest tight and like a heavy weight is hanging from my shoulders. I rather be alone forever than causing him discomfort, even if he's willing to endure it.

"I'm very grateful to you, James. For talking to me, for even hugging me before even if it was so horrible for you-"

"I wouldn't say horrible," James interrupts me and I shake my head.

"Uncomfortable. Whatever," I correct myself. "The point is that you've done more than you should already. Don't bother yourself."

"It's not a bother," James states, shrugging and keeping the little smile on his lips. "I want to do this. Maybe I'm curious, too. Maybe it's in my nature and it's part of the reason why I can see ghosts. I'm not forcing myself or anything of the like. And despite how things started I find you quite... comforting. Your company is soothing somehow."

My eyes widen at his words, even if he says them so casually and not even meeting my eyes. I have to look away and touch my cheeks, almost covering them. I know I can't blush, but it's a natural instinct and I think like that I can hide a bit how flustered I am.

"I don't know how I'll help you but who knows? Maybe we'll find out how you died or even figure out what's your unfinished business. And if not, then we can keep each other company," he adds with another shrug. "If I can't help you cross over, at least let me be by your side so you don't feel that lonely anymore."

My hands fall slowly from my cheeks to my sides, hanging limp as I watch him carefully. My emotions swirl furiously inside, making me feel a bit dizzy and enhancing the buzzing feeling from before.

"Would you really do that?" I ask, my voice a mere whisper.

James smiles brightly and genuinely, my chest feels tight again but not in the same way as before, this is different, it touches a different part in my soul.

"I would," he replies and for a few seconds I can't react, I'm still letting those two words sink in my mind. Once they do and I finally understand what's happening, the first giggle escapes.

I hurry to cover my mouth to muffle the giggles but it doesn't help much because after the first one more escape and soon I'm full-time giggling, feeling all giddy and deliriously happy. My reaction amuses James because his own smile widens and although my mind knows that I should refuse and just let him be in peace, I can't fully pay attention to that warning in my head. The thought that I won't be alone anymore more is too intoxicating and glorious to let room for anything else in my mind or heart.

"Of course," he speaks again, trying to be heard above the noise of my giggling fit. "I don't want to be labeled as lunatic and sent away, you know? So we'll have to be careful about that. I think using headphones is the easiest way to pretend I'm on the phone instead of talking to someone they can't see, but only if we're in a crowded place."

I nod enthusiastically. If we are really going to spend time together and all that, I want to minimise the problems I'll cause.

"Of course. And I'll be careful not to touch you again so don't worry about that. And don't stress over helping me or not, okay? It doesn't matter if you can or can't find the answer to why I'm stuck here. You're doing more than enough already," I hurry to add. It's better if we draw the lines now to avoid any kind of complication in the future. "And if at some point you get tired and want your space again, feel free to tell me. I won't take offence or anything."

"But touching might help you to lessen the burden you carry, Paige," he mentions.

I shake my head. "I won't make things harder for you, James. After I saw the effect that touching me had on you I can't make you go through that again, not even accidentally. At least let me do that," I plead, using almost the same words he did and I know the moment he agrees because he heaves a resigned sigh.

"Fine. I also think that the library is the best place to hang out. It's quiet and warm and I can work on some of my assignments, as well." I only nod, completely agreeing with his idea. "And during class I have to pay attention so don't distract me," he says that with an easy smile and light tone. "By the way, why do you go to class? I mean, you don't have to so what's the point?"

It's my turn to shrug and this time I sit on the bench with him, making sure to keep a safe distance between us. I pull up my legs and hug them, resting my chin on my knees and looking into the horizon.

"I honestly don't know, I just go. It's not like I have anything better to do. I don't even question it I guess it's part of the whole pretending-I'm-not-really-dead thing." I shrug again. "At least there are people around and, incredibly, by listening to the teachers or even seeing the kids work time passes by faster."

"Have you even tried not to come to college? Are you bound to this place?" he questions next and I shrug once again.

"I'm not sure if I'm bound. I just come here, it seems natural, like I have to. Same as going back home every day. To be honest, it's almost an unconscious things. I sometimes find myself going to college before I realise what I'm doing. And to your other question, I have never tried. As I told you, I don't even question it."

From the corner of my eye I can see his concentrated expression. I see how he also pulls up his legs and is sitting the same position as me. I turn my head a bit, resting my cheek on my knees now so I can fully watch him now. He does the same and when our eyes meet I see the little surprise in his eyes before he smiles.

"I think you're bound to this place," he speaks again. "I mean, you 'woke up' here after you passed out, so I think there must be for a reason. Maybe that's a clue to find out how you died but first, do you really want to know how that happened?"

His question confuses me and for that reason I frown, which must be enough for him to know the effect of his words so he explains further next.

"Maybe you don't want to remember how you died and it's not that you can't. You pretend to be alive to cope, right? Maybe not remembering is part of it, that way you can pretend more easily," suggests James and that actually makes a lot of sense. "Maybe you don't even want to cross over and you haven't even realised it yet. So why don't we figure that out first?"

I think about it, pondering this theory in my head and seeing how much sense it makes. It does sound plausible and very like me, taking in consideration my MO as a ghost. I don't question things, I just act and I don't even like thinking about being a ghost. Since James said something to me the fact of being dead has been a constant thought and I've been feeling quite more miserable due to that. If he hadn't shown up I wouldn't even think about my death or anything like that. I would be pretending I'm still alive and just being ignored.

Do I want to remember how I died? Or even when I die? Maybe it was horrible and traumatic, a shocking accident. Or maybe I killed myself. Or maybe I was murdered. Maybe knowing exactly how it happened will be too much and it won't allow me to ignore the fact that I died at some point. And what if I died long ago? What if it's been years instead of months or days? How will I feel when I find out for how long my body has been rotting? Will I be able to handle that?

The questions are too many and they make me dizzy, but James doesn't push me to answer. He just watches me carefully, probably reading my face expressions to figure out what I'm thinking. Can he see the fear I'm feeling? The anxiety making me uneasy?

"I'm... I'm a bit scared," I confess and his expression doesn't change. "But I'm also scared to stay like this forever. I don't think I can play to be alive until the end of the world." He shakes his head as his way to show me he agrees with me. "I think I should know and if the chance to find out presents itself, then I should take it." Besides, James won't be by my side forever and possibly no one ever again will ever again try to help me, so this might be my only chance to cross over I ever get.

"But you're still scared about it," he voices my feelings so I just nod. "I guess that's very normal. I'd be scared, too. So what about taking it slowly?" I frown a bit so he knows he has to explain himself. "Like no need to go all crazy detective over it, instead to just pay attention to the clues until we run into the truth. Does that make it more manageable for you?"

I think about it and I realise that's the best approach.

"I think that works." I offer him a hesitant smile with my words.

"For now we know that we should start with college. Maybe asking the other students about this ghost rumour. How does that sound?" he suggests, his smile is kind and comforting and it does help a lot to easy my worries.

"Still scary but it's a start. Let's go with that," I agree, trying to smile like him. "Let's start with our finding-out-how-Paige-died plan then!"

Chapter 16

"So," I drag the word, looking at James intently.

We've moved to the library when the rest of the kids started coming out and it began, as usual, to rain. We've come to the farthest corner where no one can see us or definitely hear us. It's warm and nice. Until James came to college I barely set foot in this place, now I can really see its charm and I really like it.

"So," he echoes my words, a little smile on his lips that make me know he's amused.

It's such a delightful change. It seems like yesterday when he wouldn't even acknowledge my presence and just completely ignore my rambling, now he doesn't exactly meet my eyes as he decided to work on his graphic novel, but at least reacts to my words and his expression is friendlier.

I've been watching him draw for like twenty minutes. I just find it so fascinating, how he creates a story out of nothing. And yes, I have been watching him work in silence-until now-, mesmerised with every stroke and even the story, although it does not make much sense to me yet. I want to ask him if he'd let me read it once it's completed but I think it's too soon.

"So," I say again and he chuckles. "How do you plan on finding more about the rumours? Are you gonna socialise and ask the kids?"

His hand stops drawing and his expression becomes serious. I keep resting my head on my hand, but I tilt it a bit more, watching him carefully. He looks up to meet my eyes, hand still holding the pen. Did I mention he is left handed? No? Well, he is.

"Um," he mumbles and now I'm the one chuckling. "I guess?" It really sounds more like a question so I shake my head. "Not sure how I'm going to approach it. Maybe I should just ask people from other programs. What do you think?"

I think about it seriously, wondering what's the best option for someone like James but then I remember something he said before. "You said you keep distance so that way ghost can't bother you, but if you talk to someone you know is alive for certain, then you shouldn't be in risk... although hanging with me might be a high risk already," I start rambling, my mind drifting off a bit. "So I guess all your efforts are for naught but then again we can just hide here or something so no one else, not even other ghosts, if there are other ghosts around which I doubt 'cos I haven't met anyone and if there's anyone else like me that one is quite rude. I mean, we should be friends, shouldn't we? We only have each other. Damn you, ghost-I'm-not-sure-exists!"

"Paige," James calls me name and I stop. "You're rambling again. Focus."

"Oh, sorry," I apologise, feeling embarrassed. "I'm just... so used to talk and talk. It's just a stream of conscious with me."

I stick my tongue out in a sheepish gesture. He just shakes his head. "Where was I going with that?" I ask to myself but James shrugs nonetheless. "Ah right! Well, the thing is that you just have to make sure to talk to someone who's alive."

"Well," he begins and his voice sounds awkward. "It's not like I'm the most social guy around. I've never been, well, a people person. Not sure it it's because of the I-see-ghosts thing or because I'm just socially awkward. The ignoring thing started because of ghosts, but I've never been good at talking to people. Dead or alive," he confesses and my lips part forming an O. "That made it easy to just ignore everyone."

"So even if you know the person is alive, you'd still have a hard time talking to them?" He nods to my answer so I keep thinking. "Then maybe we have the wrong approach."

"Maybe," he agrees. "But it's not impossible. Plus, I think it's good to know how people 'see' you and what happened to you and it'll help us to know if you actually-died here or not," he says, hesitating a bit on that verb, his expression even showing discomfort. "I guess I can try asking someone. Maybe Roxi? She'd be happy to tell me," he adds in a light tone but I don't find that funny at all.

"Any other kid would be happy to tell you, as well. It does not have to be her," I reply but my voice sounds grumpy.

I know that out of all the kids in the diploma, Roxi is the one I hate the most. I'm not even sure why, I just do. But the mention of her name makes me even angrier today and I don't want her a slightly bit closer to this plan we are designing with James.

"Woah, okay. No Roxi. Adeline maybe? She's always trying to talk to me, too," he continues and I keep frowning. Those two are one of the same kind. I don't like them. "I'll take that as a no. Okay."

I look away, feeling in a bad mood for no good reason. I fold my arms and I fight hard not to pout, but I can almost feel my lower lip sticking out.

"Paige, are you okay?" I hear him asking but I don't turn to look at him.

"Perfectly fine," I reply, but it sound more like a snap.

"Are you upset? Because I mentioned Roxi and Adeline? Do you hate them that much?"

"Why would I be upset because of them?" I continue and even I notice that my voice betrays my words so I turn to look at him this time, huffing and grimacing, especially when I notice his amused expression.

"Why do you hate them?" he asks and I shrug.

"They are mean," is all I say and he sighs. His amused expression slowly disappearing and a more serious one shows up now.

"You think they did something to you when you were alive? That they are connected to your death somehow? Maybe it's not that you're bound to college but to someone and that's why you keep attending all the classes of the program," James proposes and I can almost see how the pieces start fitting together in his head.

"I'm not sure," I blow up his bubble, though. "I... Okay, it's mostly Roxi and it's from the pit of my guts. I just know I have to hate her but I can't tell you exactly why, although I'm sure

I have a good reason. I just don't... remember. Maybe you're right and she was one of the ones who bullied me."

"Bullied you?" he repeats my words and I realise I've never told him my story from when I was alive.

I notice his expression changing again. He is now concerned and even his body language expresses it in the way he leans closer. He drops the pen and rests both hands on the table between us, but these kind of reach out to me. Of course, I'm sitting opposite to him, just to keep safe distance even if the seat next to him is empty.

"I-I remember more things form when I was alive, but still they are kind of blurry. What's vivid is what I felt during those times," I start, breathing evenly to keep myself calm as I dive into my past, that horrible hell I went through day after day, without someone who could help me. "At home I was okay, you know? Happy kid with parents that loved me and everything, but it seemed like no one else could accept me outside my family. Since I was a little girl the other kids bullied me, but it got worse during secondary school and almost unbearable during sixth form. It wasn't just verbal abuse, you know?" I look into his eyes, trying to stay calm by staring into the blue of them. It's working so far. "They hit me, tortured me, humiliated me and were always pushing me to the end. And no one cared. Most people bullied me and hose who didn't stayed quiet, which I think it's worse than actually bullying me."

"It is," he agrees and I take another deep breath.

"They pulled my hair, cut it, pushed me against the lockers, threw disgusting things at me, vandalised my work, pulled down my trousers, punched me, played pranks on me in front of everyone so I could become the laughing stock and well, the constantly reminder that I was worthless and I should be dead. Sometimes they even followed me home, just to keep insulting me or picking on me. When I was a kid other kids used to throw rocks at me," I tell him and a choked laughter escapes me. I know that I'd be crying if it weren't because I just simply can't. "More than once I had to get stitches, you know? Once someone even pushed me down stairs. I broke my leg then."

"That's horrible! Why didn't anyone help?" James almost shouts, his eyes wild with concern and shock. His hands tremble a bit and I bite my lower lip.

"My parents tried to make the school responsible, even talked to the parents of the other kids. It was to no avail. Things just stopped for a few days but soon they started again so it was basically pointless. The school couldn't make them stop, their parents couldn't make them stop. And after a while I even tried to hide it because I-" I have to stop to take a deep breath. I'm shaking already so I try to hide my hands and hold them tight so they'll stop. "Because I started to believe it was my fault. Why else would I always be picked on? It wasn't just one kid, it was almost everyone. It had to be my fault. I made them do that to me. It was my fault. I did it. I'm responsible for it. I drive them to treat me like that. I force them. It's all my doing. My fault. My fault. I'm sorry, I'm so, so sorry. I'm sorry. I'm sorry. I'm so-" I choke on my words, I can't even continue. I'm breathing heavily and shaking violently as the memories take me in their arms, crushing my bones and suffocating me. I can't escape and I'm hurting, but I'm trapped.

"Paige. Paige!" I hear but I can't answer. I keep shaking and everything is blurry. I just see faceless kids, shouting at me, cornering me, hitting me, hating me and I can't stop. "Paige, it's over. Paige, listen to me. Paige!"

Hands grab my shoulders and shake me, but they release me immediately after a loud cry of pain and that gets to me. It's like a bit of sunlight through a small hole somewhere and I can focus on that in this complete darkness.

I shake my head and fight to get out of here and once I manage that I can see James. He's gasping for air, almost lying on the table, shaking and with lost eyes.

"James?" I ask, confused, my voice weak. I try to put the pieces together to make sense of what I'm seeing.

I was telling him about my life and then I- I got lost in the pain of it. He was the one calling me, right? Did he try to-?

"JAMES!" I shout, as loud as I can because no one but him can hear me. "You touched me. Why did you do that? Oh my God, are you all right?"

"That- that was horrible," he mutters and I feel terrible for causing that to him.

"I'm so sorry," I start but he shakes his head. "You shouldn't have done that."

"I had to, you were... gone. It was so scary seeing you like that, in so much pain and traumatised. I never saw something like that, so intense." He pulls back, sitting back and taking deep breaths. Then his eyes find for mine and I can still see pain in his. "Then I touched you and it was like someone kicked me in the guts. That was... horrible. You lived with that? You still live with that kind of pain? How?"

"I- I don't know," I reply. "I normally just shut it out."

"I'm even more impressed you can even smile and have this bubbly personality after all that. It's so... terrible, Paige. I'm really, truly, deeply sorry."

"It's not your fault," I tell him and he sighs.

"I know, but someone has to apologise for what happened. You shouldn't-no. No one should ever go through what you did. That's not even human. What they did to you... that's... I don't even have words. And if Roxi and Adeline or anyone here actually did that to you then I- I don't even know what I'll do." He really looks angry and I see him clenching his fists as if he were getting ready to get in a fight.

"I'm not sure if they were. When I look back I can't really see faces. There are so many and they blur together. I don't know if Roxi bullied me or whether I hate her because of that. I can't be sure."

"Well, of one thing you can be sure, Paige." I look at him expectantly, waiting to know what that thing is. "It was not your fault. What they did to you wasn't your fault and you don't have to apologise, okay?"

"Then why?" I breath out, my voice weak and small, like I feel right now.

"I don't know, but I know it wasn't your fault. I also know we'll find out what happened and whether our current class-mates treated you like that." He then grabs his pen and shoves it back inside his pencil case. Then he closes his sketchbook and shoves everything back in his backpack. "Let's go. We'll go and ask people around about you and how you died. I'm determined now, more than ever."

I just blink, looking at him with big surprised eyes as he stands up. "Now?" I ask, sounding like a fool.

"Yes, now. Let's go. Hurry," he confirms, holding up his hand for me in an invitation. I don't take it but I do stand up and walk up to him., still keeping safe distance between us. He nods and smiles before adding, "We'll find out the truth."

Chapter 17

"What about her?" I propose, standing next to James—but not too close that I might accidentally touch him—, watching some random girl walking down the hall towards the cafeteria.

"I've never seen her before," he mumbles, barely moving the lips. He has the headphones on but he still speaks lowly so people won't pay attention to him.

"That's the point. You probably won't see her again so it doesn't matter if you sound crazy for just asking her about the ghost stories and so," I reason but I can see the reluctance in his face and I feel both sympathetic and amused at the sight.

We've been at this, trying to find someone to talk to so he can finally ask what we want to know, for like fifteen minutes to no avail. He always finds an excuse to stay away and that is proof he really isn't a people person. His anxiety is evident when people are around and when he knows he is supposed to interact. All his determination went away when we saw the first person. I should probably tell him it's okay, he doesn't need to do all this, but I can't help myself, I'm actually having fun seeing him like this.

I know he ignores everyone because that way he doesn't risk replying to a ghost—what he did with me but that's just because I annoyed him—but without that knowledge he just comes off as a rude person when in reality he's just awkward. I think that knowing that makes me like him better.

"James?" someone asks, catching me completely off guard so I scream and jump, turning around raising my arms in a defence posture, ready to go all karate kid on whomever approached us. James reacts pretty similar, minus the whole scream and karate pose, but he is equally surprised.

When we turn around I realise it is Roxy the one that spoke and she is watching James with a confused expression. I get why she could be confused, considering he was hiding behind the corner, watching creepily the other students walk by. But even if she saw James hiding a body she shouldn't approach and just keep walking, especially when she's alone. It makes me angry that she is here, looking at a nervous James that was caught off guard and hasn't pulled himself together yet. I want to push her so she can give him space, and if in the way I manage to make her turn around and leave James alone, even better.

"What are you doing?" she asks instead and I feel about to snarl and show her my teeth like an angry dog.

James should pull one of his moves and just ignore her. Stand straight, shrug and walk away. But he doesn't and I'm too focused on glaring at Roxy to see what his face looks like.

"Looking for something," he replies instead and my eyes widen because he is talking to her.

Before I turn to look at him I can see Roxy practically beaming because James's talked to her and that makes me so angry, but I still turn to stare at him with my most bewildered expression. His is cold, though, tense and a bit angry. Almost like when he yelled at me and was that cruel and that is somehow relieving. I have to admit I don't want Roxy to see James' smiles or more approachable aura.

"Can I help you instead? I'm free right now," she offers and I clench my fists.

"No," I reply for him, stomping my foot to give emphasis. James' eyes dart to me for the briefest second before watching Roxy again.

Is it wrong that I want to stand between them and block his view? Even if I'm shorter than her and it would be useless? I just want her away, very far away from us right now. I've always disliked her but right now she's annoying me and I don't even want her near to mock her or something like I've done before.

"Maybe," replies James instead and I feel like someone punched me in the guts.

"What?" I say at the same time she says "Really?"

I swear I would make a scene and start asking James what's wrong with him if it weren't because I don't want him to look like a mad person in front of her or anyone else. I don't want him to look at me or even say something when there's someone else around. But I want to, so badly!

"About what happened today in Art History," he begins and I feel personally offended that he is actually asking her about it after what we talked in the library. It doesn't matter that his expression is cold and kind of disgusted right now. "I've noticed people talking about her. Who is she?"

"Oh," Roxy mutters and I can feel her disappointment. What? Was she hoping for something else? "I guess even you would get curious. To be honest, I don't believe the rumours 'cos they're silly, but who am I to judge?"

"Ha!" I snort when she says that and I roll my eyes. James, on the other hand, does not even make a reaction.

"But people say there's a ghost haunting college. Can you believe it?" she laughs and I just fold my arms.

"Yeah, totally. I'm standing right here. Hello, let me introduce myself, I'm Paige the ghost!" I practically shout but she can't hear me.

I don't even know why I'm so annoyed. I can't even stand still and I just want to grab James' wrist and drag him away from her and this stupid plan. We can manage without talking to her or any other living person. Maybe we should go to a medium or someone of the like.

"Weird things happen, like today in the class, but I'm not sure that means it's a ghost." I laugh again because I'm sure she believes it, she's just trying to sound cool in front of James right now. I've heard her making reference to me so this is just blunt lies.

"And what's the story behind the ghost rumour?" he asks instead of agreeing with her. I watch her and I can see her confused expression. Roxy clearly didn't expect James to ask that, she was hoping he'd agree and laugh along.

"I'm not so sure. Some girl that died in college. You know how rumours are, changing all the time so you can't really know," answers Roxy, shrugging to make it look less important. "To be honest I've heard so many versions I don't even know which one is the original. All agree on one thing, though; that it's a girl."

"You didn't know her?" he asks in a voice as confused as I feel because as I listen to her my anger and annoyance start to fade and a cold feeling sinks it. Dread and fear, I recognise. She is talking about me but she makes it sound as if she never knew me. As if I were a distant rumour she never paid attention to.

Was I really that insignificant to her that she can't even know the ghost is me?

"Me? Of course no," Roxy laughs. "It's just my first year here and I can't see ghosts, so I haven't met her... if she is even real," she adds like an afterthought, as if just now she remembers she's playing cool by not believing in ghost stories.

"So she didn't die recently?" James' voice still sounds confused, as much as I'm feeling.

I start stepping back, away from Roxy and her now confused expression, like she can't understand why James could possibly ask her that when the answer is obvious. I don't know why I'm feeling so scared and cold as I watch her and why I have such a bad feeling in my guts. I'm trembling as I wait for what she might say.

"No. That rumour is basically a urban legend. I don't know how long, but she died long ago. I think it was a huge deal back then but today unless something weird happens, no one remembers her. I don't even know who she was," Roxy says, shrugging just to make it even more clear how insignificant this is for her but her words have the opposite effect on me.

I feel like even the ground under my feet is shaking and I can't see properly, everything is blurry and I feel sick to my stomach. I don't even know how is that I can feel like that but I think I could throw up right now. my ears are ringing and I can't even hear what she is saying now or if she's speaking. It's a high pitched sound in my ears, like the type you hear after a loud explosion or noise, one that makes your head hurt and your teeth clench. It gets louder and louder and I can't hear anything else.

I keep taking another and another step away from James and Roxy, completely shaking as my head tries to process what I just heard and what it means.

Long ago. So long ago that no one remembers my name. Longer than what Roxy has been here. I died long ago.

I gag because I feel nauseous. I know I can't throw up and I won't, but it's like an automatic reaction from my body because I can't cope with this piece of information. So I cover my mouth with my hands, muffling the sounds I make and then turn on my heels and run away. Outside from the building and where there's fresh air that won't make a difference but that at least will give me open space. I run even if I can barely stay on my feet, I tumble and trip many times, but I stand up again and keep running.

I'm so distracted, with my mind everywhere that I can't focus on anything else so I end up running into someone. Or better said, running through someone.

The first time it happened I learnt that I could never let this happen again for two reasons. One, it is a reminder I'm noting but incorporeal substance, that I don't even have a real body. And two, it's the most agonising pain I've ever felt. It's burning cold, consuming me, freezing me and killing me all over again. I don't even know what the other person might feel because I can only feel my pain.

I scream.

I burn alive.

I fall down and break into pieces.

I'm pulled back together just to keep screaming.

I cry for mercy and to stop, but it doesn't.

It's like every piece of me is torn apart and pulled in every direction, leaving me open and exposed, hurting and crying out. I can't even move, I can only cry out in pain but no one can hear me. The world around isn't even black, it's red and yellow, like flames but it isn't hot, it's ice cold. So cold it burns. And it seems the seconds drag forever and the pain will never stop. I don't even feel whole. I don't feel here at all. I am nothing but pain and ashes right now and my screams won't lessen it.

How can someone who's dead be in such pain? Why can't I pass out so it'll stop? Why did I let this happen?

I can't stop screaming, hoping someone can hear my cries for help and do something but no one does. I'm dead and I'm dying again. And again. And again.

"H-help... someone..." I cry, my voice shaky.

I think I'm on the floor but I can't be sure, I'm not conscious of my own body, but I think I'm crawling as more cries of pain escape me. I feel like the pieces of me are being pulled together again, but too slowly and it still hurts, but I'm getting back to be one thing.

Why did I run away? I should've calmed myself down before doing that. I should've been careful. For so long... I've been careful for so long so this would never happen again.

Long... I died long ago. I've been a ghost for a long time. How long? What is of my body now? What's of my remains? Is there anything left? What happened to my body?

I scream once again, louder and in more agony. I just want it to stop, to stop forever. The pain, the loneliness, the aching in my chest. I want everything to stop once and for all.

But then the burning pain stops when I'm collected and wrapped. All the pieces pulled together once and for all, although it doesn't feel like pieces but more like dust. Like ashes collected and piled together. I don't feel dispersed anymore and that helps me collect my mind as well, and to focus. I focus on myself and my body... or whatever that I have.

I slowly start to feel my limbs again and I'm aware of myself and my surroundings. I can see again although it isn't very clear. I also start feeling warm, the cold that burnt me before slowly disappears and I can stop shaking.

I finally take a deep breath, still shaky and a bit achy, but better now. I look up and find James' face, practically pressed against mine and his is constricted in horrid pain, tears slowly falling down and laboured breathing. My eyes widen in horror at the sight when I realise he is the one holding me tight, pulling me together... and suffering the consequences.

"James," I breathe out, struggling to get away from him even if I'm weak and I can't really control my body. I need to get away from him, to stop this; but he doesn't let me. He stays crouched down, holding me in his arms, pressing his forehead against mine and biting his lips tightly to bear the pain. "James, let go of me," I beg and he shakes his head ever so slightly.

"It's okay... I've got yah."

Chapter 18

"It... it hurts you. Please, James," I stammer, trying to pull away from him but he's either too strong or I'm too weak.

It's probably the latter.

Until very recently I couldn't even feel my body and I felt like ashes. I'm just now becoming whole again but I don't think I'm quite myself just yet. I don't know where we are, how is that he is holding me or what is actually happening. I barely remember what happened last time I walked through someone, I just remember the pain and that I never wanted to feel like that again. The big difference, though, is that back then I felt hot. Burning hot like I was caught up in flames. But today it was burning cold, as if I was exposed to absolute zero temperature.

"I can... endure it," he replies between gritted teeth. I can feel him shaking and it's probably due the pain he is feeling.

He knows so well what it feels to touch a ghost. He has touched me before so why is he doing this again? Hasn't he had enough for a day? Is he a masochist or did he just lose his mind? I can't understand him and his behaviour. He keeps confusing me and even if he is doing something to help me,

I want him to stop. No matter how warm and comfortable it feels in his arms, he is hurting and I can't allow that. I can't let him suffer because of me.

"Stop. Stop now. I'm okay, now," I speak, trying to make my voice sound firm and sure.

I concentrate hard to push everything to the darkest part of my mind, where not even I can reach them. All the agony and misery away. I focus only on James' warm arms around me and the beat of his heart. I focus on his laboured breathing and the way he rocks me back and forward. I concentrate on this living boy and push every bad feeling of mine as far away as possible. I have no idea if that helps or it is a futile as a wingless bird trying to fly, but I have to try.

It seems it works because his body stops shaking that violently and it's more like shivering due to cold. His breathing also evens and he doesn't hold me that tight. His heart is still racing, I can feel it under my palm. I continue pushing my feelings, blocking everything, shutting myself out and just paying attention to James.

"Let me go," I whisper, closing my eyes because if I open them I'll lose my concentration and bring all the agony back. I can deal with it, but I can't let him feel it again. "I'm fine now."

Reluctantly and hesitantly, his arms loose up around me and I'm slowly released until I can put at least ten centimetres between the two of us. I open my eyes and the moment I do that all the agony that lives within me comes back and for a second I can't even breathe or move. Black clouds start to blur my vision and my hearing becomes muffled. I blink once then another time and another until I can see properly again and the emotions settle down. An eternity later I can take a breath and release it. Only then I can see James properly again and he is on his knees, breathing hard, sweating and completely pale. Drops of sweat and tears stream down his face and even his lips have adqsuired a blueish colour. My hands itch to reach his face and wipe these away but I can't forget I'm the reason why he's like this, looking so miserable and exhausted.

"Are... are you okay? For real?" he asks and I sigh with a slight shake of my head. I can't believe he is asking that.

"Take a look of yourself. I'm sure you look more dead than I do," I reply, trying to make my voice sound lighter so he doesn't worry more. "I'm fine. Thank you," I add next with a smile that hurts my heart. "You didn't have to do that," I tell him and now he is the one shaking his head.

James pulls back, sitting down and crossing his legs. He takes deep breaths and wipes his face with his sleeves, then he takes his beanie and lets the dreads fall lose.

"Yeah, I had to. Paige, you don't understand how heart-breaking your screams were. It was like someone was being murdered and tortured. I couldn't just call your name until you listened so I grabbed you and dragged you away," he explains and only then notice we are in a small empty room. "And even then you wouldn't stop screaming."

He looks at me so intently that I feel a hot wave going down my body, leaving me all tingly.

"It would've stopped eventually," I say, looking away because I can't hold his stare.

"But I couldn't take that," he says and my chest feels weird, like something alive is in there. "I couldn't bear seeing you in such pain and like... I dunno, Paige. It was like you were gonna just disappear. I didn't think, I just held you."

"You... you felt it, right? The pain," I explain, looking at him from the corner of my eyes because I can't meet his eyes just yet.

James nods and that's all I need to feel worse because I know how agonising and paralysing that pain is and the thought he also experienced it makes me feel like I'm going to throw up.

"What happened, Paige? Why did you feel like that? It wasn't like before. It wasn't emotional pain, it was physical... like..." he frowns, trying to find the words. "Like you were being pulled apart and burnt at the same time."

"I..." I don't even know how to explain things but I know he needs to understand. There are so many questions that I feel like we are drowning in them, so if there's at least one thing I can explain to him, then so help me God, I will tell him. "I walked through someone. I wasn't paying attention. I normally can avoid people so I don't bump into anyone. And I'm not sure why but when I do that it's like... I lose my body and it's painful, so painful. I don't know if dying felt like that when I did, but I can't describe it any other way: it feels like dying. Like being burnt alive. You know when you like feel your hands and legs and, well, your body? I just feel like ashes."

I finally look at him, his serious glance greets me and I take a deep breath that I don't need but that it feels like I should do. His brows are furrowed and a grimace taints his expression. He still looks tired, but colour is coming back to his face.

"Paige... were you cremated?" he asks and I just blink, his words bouncing in my head.

"What?" I ask because even if his question is quite simple, I just can't process it.

It's something I never thought about and that leaves me numb. I always pretend I'm still alive and I try not to think of my body and where it is resting. But only now that James mentions it I think that maybe there is no grave and I was cremated. Maybe that is why I have never felt dragged to the cemetery and why I feel like ashes when I walk through people. Maybe that is why I feel like being burnt, because my body was literally burnt.

Oh boy, I feel sick.

"You know, cremated. It feels like being burt so maybe that's why," he explains exactly what I just thought of.

"I-I don't know," I reply, my voice shaky and I have to close my eyes and take deep breaths to stabilise again.

"Because if not, then we should find your grave so that way we can actually see when you died. It can't be that long ago. I know it was a shock for you, Paige, but it's impossible you've been dead decades. You mentioned your mum so she's still alive and your style isn't from the nineties or before," he keeps thinking out loud and I'm just struggling not to scream.

"Cremated... ashes... my body is..." I mumble and James stops speaking to stare at me with worried eyes. "There's no body. Not even a skeleton. Just... ashes." I laugh, this incredulous fit of laughter that just makes you look like you lost your mind.

I think I'm losing my mind, though.

"It's a theory, we don't know that just yet, Paige," he tries to reassure me but I keep laughing.

"I don't even know if ashes is better or worse," I breathe out. "If my my remains aren't ashes, then it's some rotted mess and it means worms and other things ate my decaying flesh. It means what's left of me is six feet under." Another fit of laughter escapes me. I think I even look mad by now. "I believe that's worse now. It's more disgusting and slower."

"Paige..." James speak but I stand up and take a few steps away from him.

"I prefer the cremated theory, to be honest. I don't even want to think what it would feel after walking through someone if my body disappeared the other way." I shiver at the thought. "The problem is that without a grave there isn't a gravestone with my name, right? Then how can we know about my death? And where are my ashes? You think Mum scattered them?"

James also rises to his feet and he looks considerably better. In his left hand he keeps his beanie, tightly squeezed. "I don't know. She's your mum, what do you think she did?"

I think about it and try to imagine what my mum would've done with my body-ashes. Considering I died before her and when I was still seventeen, and if she decided to cremate me then she probably did it to keep me close somehow. She has kept my room intact for how long I've been dead, so that means she doesn't want to erase my presence.

"At home," I speak out. "She has my ashes at home. Some-where. I don't know. Maybe her room?" I try to think harder of a vase or something where she could've have my ashes but I can't exactly remember one. "I need to check. What time is it?" I ask out loud next and he seems confused.

James takes a look to his wrist watch before he replies, " Twenty past two in the afternoon."

"We're going to my house," I blurt out. "My mum won't be there until five so we have time. We'll look around until we find my ashes," I explain the plan and James' eyes widen in surprise and disbelief.

"We?"

"Yes, we as in you and I. My house isn't that far from college, neither it is big so we'll find my ashes. And if we can't find them, then we'll go to the cemetery. I-" I hesitate a bit at this point but I think it's necessary, even if it is not appealing. "I will find out where my remains are."

James still looks at me with those shocked eyes so I just smile and try to look cheerful until he gives in. I notice it because he sighs and shakes his head but a smile comes to his lips.

"Okay, let's go. You lead the way," he says and my smile widens.

"Follow me!" I instruct and walk out the room.

We leave college in silence, none of us says a word until we are far from campus and James has his headphones on again.

"And what do we do if we find your ashes. Roxy couldn't even tell us since when the rumour of the ghost has been around so I don't think asking around will help us," James mentions and I nod in understanding, walking to him, keeping my hands at my back whilst James hides his in his pocket. He looks like he's cold but I can't tell.

"Not sure. I guess that we could look in old papers? Maybe there's an article about my death or an obituary," I suggest.

"Yeah, but without knowing exactly when you died it becomes too difficult to find that. We wouldn't even know where to begin or how to narrow things down," he reasons and I nod again because he's right. We would take forever looking through old papers until we find something.

"What about the Internet? In films they always find everything there," I suggest and look at James just to see him blushing.

"Well... the thing is besides editing programs I am useless with technology. I'm not sure if I could find an 'old' article on my own, but maybe we can try," he offers but he sounds defeated.

I step forward, walking past him and then turning around to face him. I notice as well we have arrived to my house already.

"We need to find the ashes first so let's focus on that for now. Then we'll see what we do with our poor technology skills because I such, too," I beam at him giving him even the peace sign. "By the way, we're here."

I turn around, motioning to my humble home and then run to the door, looking for the spare key buried in the ceramic pot next to it. It's been here since when I was alive. Mum kept it there because I normally forgot my set inside. So I use that to open the door and then wait for James inside. Hesitantly, he takes the steps towards me.

"Welcome to my crib," I say with a big smile and he chuckles.

"You watch loads of telly for a ghost, Paige," he says, still smiling as he takes the first step inside.

Chapter 19

"Wow, this is an old cat," James says when Luna comes running downstairs and looks at us surprised because I'm not alone and there's a guest in our house. No one ever comes. She overcomes her surprise pretty soon because next thing I know she is rubbing herself against James' legs, purring and making little sounds to get his attention.

I watch as he kneels down to pick her up and then holds her against his chest. She is delighted, purring and kneading his chest. James wears an adorable smile that captivates me and leaves me trapped in a trance I can't seem to escape from. His expression softens so much and his eyes seem to sparkle. I couldn't have imagined he'd change like that with a cat or that he would like one so much.

There goes the old theory of James' being a werewolf.

"Oh, aren't you a cutie one? And so fluffy," he talks, still too into Luna as to pay attention to the way I'm staring at him. "Oh, you like that?" he asks next when she purrs even louder the moment he starts scratching under her chin.

I chuckle, I can't help it and that seems to get his attention. He meets my eyes with blushed cheeks and an embarrassed smile.

"Her name is Luna," I tell him and his eyes are back on my cat, smiling widely again.

"Hello, Luna. It's a pleasure to meet you." I can't stop smiling as the scene unfolds in front of me. He looks just too cute for words.

"She loves you. When I pet her she never purrs that loud or seems that happy," I comment and he just smiles at me.

For a moment I can only look at this picture perfect but then I remember his first comment when he saw my cat, about her being old. So I lose my smile and look at Luna more closely, trying to see that. I saw her when she was a kitten and I guess she's grown but is she really old? I haven't really noticed that, but then I don't pay attention to many things. I just... go with the flow, almost automatically without a second thought. And I can't always remember how things are or were.

"Is she old?" I ask out loud. "How old do you think she is?"

"You don't know?" he asks and I shake my head. "When did she get here? Before or after you... got stuck?" The fact that he doesn't say the word die or ghost doesn't go unnoticed, but right now there's another fact more important than that.

"Before," I answer. "Mum got her to help. She heard cats are good when someone is depressed."

"Well, that's something good," he says, still petting Luna. "Cats live an average of fifteen to twenty years so that means you can't possibly have been like this longer than that," he explains and I understand he didn't mean that Mum's idea was good as I thought first. "That narrows things a bit. Now, looking at her I don't think she's twenty or that old, but she is several years old for sure," his voice loses strength as he speaks until it's barely a whisper. Even his hand stops moving through Luna's fur.

Several years.

I've been dead for several years. Even if it's one or two or three it is still a lot. So Roxy was right, it was before she got to college. I close my eyes and try to remember, to concentrate and think of other students before her. Maybe even my classmates! But all I have are faceless people in my memory. I can't really remember one single person before the classmates I have now.

How many years has it been? How many generations?

"Paige..." he calls my name so I open my eyes again and meet his blue ones. "When were you born?" he asks next and I blink.

Oh! That would help us know what would be my age right now and then do the math.

"In May," I reply but as soon as those two words leave my lips I realise how useless they are. I concentrate a bit more, trying to recall the day I was born but I can't even remember that, less alone the year. "I-I don't remember my birthday," I laugh, a chocked laughter that sounds crazy and desperate. "Of course I don't remember my birthday. Why don't I remember anything important? Why do I just remember the pain?"

James puts Luna down, who has to wake up because she fell asleep in his arms, and then he straightens up. I notice how he approaches before he can touch me so I can dodge him. I even raise my hands as a sign for him to stay put.

"I'm useless," I breathe out. "I can't even remember my birthday." The incredulous laughter is back.

"It's okay. We're at your place, surely we'll find something," he tries to reassure me but I shake my head. That's not comforting.

"And my ashes. We'll find how long I've been dead and stuck as a ghost." I notice how James cringes when I say those words, but I can't really dwell on it. "Okay, let's find them. Once and for all." I sound defeated and resigned because that's exactly how I feel.

All this mission is making me face the fact I'm dead constantly and that is extremely depressing. There's no way I can pretend I'm just being ignored and bullied in a different way. I have to acknowledge I died at some point, several years ago, and that there's no coming back.

I'm dead. I'm so dead.

I wish I could throw up. I would be doing that right now because I certainly feel sick. But I can't so I just turn on my heels and walk to the living room. I can hear James' footsteps behind me but other than that he's silent. I think even Luna is following us because she meows softly, trying to get James' attention, I presume.

Once in the living room I just scan everything, trying to find a urn. If I was actually cremated then that's where my ashes should be, if Mum didn't scatter them, which I doubt.

"Try to find a urn or anything where ashes could be kept," I instruct, my voice cold and detached.

"Paige..." James calls my name in that way I'm starting to recognise. It's tinted with pity and worry and right now I can't take it so I just step away from him, searching the shelves in the living room, above the fireplace but there's nothing, just pictures of my family when I was still alive.

"You were an only child," James comments. Not a question, just a statement. I look at him over my shoulder and see him holding another picture frame. Mum has many of those around. "You've mentioned your mum many times. What about your dad?" he asks next and I turn to look at the pictures in front of me. There's one of both my parents and I when I was like ten or something.

"Dad left... I don't recall much, per usual, but I know he left after I died. I don't know how much after. It could've been days, months or years, considering I've been dead for several." I really can't let go of that. "It was because Mum... she kinda also died. She was never the same. She's been mourning... for several years."

Until now, so selfishly, I have only been thinking of how I have been dead for many years and not even once I thought that Mum lost her only daughter at the same time and has been living with that sorrow for that long. She hasn't moved on. She is as stuck as I am.

"Mum..." I whine. "She's still crying every day. She hasn't moved on, for as long as I've been dead, she's been in pain. Oh my God," I choke on my words, covering my mouth with my hands because I just can't even take a breath right now.

"Oh shit," James curses under his breath and I can immediately hear his hurried footsteps towards me, so I move away, almost running from him.

"I really hope, and this time not for me but for Mum, that I didn't die that long ago. It would kill me again if Mum has been like this for so long," I breathe out, my vision getting blurry because everything spins around me.

My mum, my poor mum. She's been like a corpse for as long as I've been dead and yes, she's always been a concern of mine, especially since I became a ghost, but now I feel even worse about her.

"She needs to move on," I keep rambling, just saying all what's in my mind. "She can't stay like this any longer. She must be old now... and I didn't notice. Of course I didn't notice! I am that dense!" I scream. "I did not notice how my mum is getting old. I just assumed it was because she was sad! How can I be so despicable!"

"Paige, stop it! Paige!" he cries out, grabbing my wrist and holding me. I snap and get free of him, scandalised because he touched me again but also because he stopped me from digging my nails too deep into my arms. Not like it hurts anything, but I bet it's a disgusting sight for him.

"Don't touch me!" I shout at him. "It hurts you," I add in a whisper and meeting his eyes. He looks so miserable and I feel so fragile, like I'm about to break. "Don't..."

"Then don't hurt yourself," he negotiates and I shake my head.

"It doesn't hurt, at least what you stopped me from. I don't feel that pain... but my mum... that hurts."

I feel Luna rubbing against my legs, trying to comfort me and purring lowly. I just look at her with wide eyes, feeling my heart twisting a bit to just then feel a bit better. I chuckle humourlessly because it's almost as if she is taking a bit of my pain with her.

Maybe it's true and cats do absorb negative energy.

"What if... what if I talk to your mum?" James suggests, getting my attention away from Luna and back to him. "I could... maybe I could tell her I communicated with you and that you're fine and you want her to be okay, too."

"I'm not okay, though. You'd be lying to my mum..." I muse, taking my hand to my chest to appease a bit the ache in there but it doesn't help.

"Okay, maybe not that you're okay but that you want her to be okay for you. That she needs to move on... maybe that's holding you down, Paige!" he thinks, getting excited. "Maybe it's that guilt keeping you here. Maybe your mum is your unfinished business!"

I blink as I try to think about it. It can be that, considering what worries me the most is her and I just want her pain to stop, but could that be? Maybe James should talk to her indeed, try to explain things even if it's difficult just so she can finally move-

"You can't," I say and his excited expression changes to one of utter confusion. "You can't talk to her about me still lingering here or anything. You just can't. She can't take that," I explain but that doesn't help him.

I try to battle a memory that stays with me because it is frightening and because it's kept me from trying again to communicate with her. It's like the memory of walking through someone, something I can't really recall fully detailed, but enough to keep me from making the same mistake.

"I once... I once wrote her a note. I can do that and they stay. I told her I was still with her and looking after her... I told her that... I never left her... I told her..." I feel weak as one image tortures my mind, one horrifying scene. "She found it. I know that much. And when she read it she started crying and... and..."

"And what, Paige? What happened?" James asks, bringing me back to the present because it seams I'm leaving this place and getting lost in that painful memory.

"She... started convulsing and just... it was horrible because I screamed her name and she just... she was on the floor, hopeless, alone and I couldn't do anything for her. I tried holding her but it seemed to make it worse. Now I know why... but back then, I... I basically tortured. I thought... I thought I was doing something good. I was excited when she found the note then terrified. I couldn't call for help or anything." My knees give out and I end up on the floor, too horrified at the memory. "It was horrible, how she just shook violently on the floor... until she fainted but it seemed like three lives before that happened." I look up and I can barely meet James' horrified eyes. "I did that because I wanted to communicate. Because I told her I was still here."

"You didn't know that would happen..."

"But now I know and I won't let you do that. I won't do that to her again," I shake my head. "That won't do, James," my voice shakes. "We need to find another way. You can't talk to my mum."

Chapter 20

James' eyes are still as pitiful as they were five minutes ago, so I decide to leave the living room. I need to walk, to move, to be able to push all this agony that is choking me. I need to leave it behind. I need to clear my mind but if I keep seeing how James looks at me, as if he is desperate to do something, then I won't be able to activate my defence mechanism. So what I do is walk up to Mum's room. I haven't seen the urn in the living room so if she keeps my ashes, they aren't here. The only other place I can think of is her room, even if that is a little creepy but then again, Mum is depressed so maybe it's not that weird in her state.

I know he's following me, I can hear his footstep although they are not exactly stepping on my tail. He is close, I feel that. Somehow, I can feel his presence behind me. I don't say a thing, I keep walking until I'm in front of the door, only then I open my mouth.

"This is Mum's room. I think that maybe she keeps the ashes here."

"If you were cremated. We're not sure about that just yet," he reminds me and I turn to look at him over my shoulder with a blank expression. "Don't look at me like that. It's not that crazy. Maybe you're not even dead, maybe you're just in coma or something."

"I don't think that's very likely," I say but I can see in his expression how much he hopes what he's saying is true. I see that in his eyes, the intensity of it throws me off and makes me feel bad for blowing up his bubble. "If I were in coma my mum would spend all her time at the hospital, next to me. But she finishes work and comes here and never leaves unless it's extremely necessary," I explain to him but it doesn't seem like he wants to give up.

"Maybe she's not at work and spends all day with you at the hospital. You don't know if she actually goes to work. Or maybe she just can't be twenty-four-seven at the hospital, right?"

"Don't you think I would feel drawn towards the hospital if that were the case?" I ask but I really feel a lump in my stomach because I can see how his expression falls.

Why does it seem that this affects him more than it affects me?

"I'm sorry, James, but I really don't think that theory makes sense. I'm super dead and I'll find my ashes."

"Don't say it like that," he pleads but I just shake my head and focus on opening the door, ignoring that little jab in my heart that tells me to comfort him. Right now I'm not in the mood to do something.

Mum's room used to be bright and always smelled like roses, but now it's a room where someone sleeps at night. It feels abandoned and kind of broken. She rarely opens the curtains and I always feel so miserable when I'm in here. It's not a big room so James barely takes a step inside when I spot it. I don't know why I never noticed it before, but it's there.

An urn.

My ashes. I'm sure of it.

Where there's used to be just pictures of me now there's an urn with a picture of me when I was like fifteen. I am smiling in the picture, happy. I'm not sure when that happened but I think it was a day out with my family, escaping from here and everyone that hurt me. That was probably why I was so happy in that picture. And that is probably why Mum has that picture next to my urn.

I walk up to it, slowly and feeling scared because I don't know what will happen when I touch it. What if I cross over the moment I touch the urn? What if it hurts like when I walk through someone? That is why I hesitate in front of the urn, not sure of what to do. James even catches up to me, standing by my side. Instantly, I move a bit to the left, away from him just in case we might accidentally touch.

"You think this is it?" he asks out loud and I take a deep breath.

"Positive," I breathe out.

"But maybe it can-"

"James," I cut him off and turn to look at him. "It's nice what you're trying to do and I appreciate it, but it's not necessary. I've accepted I'm dead so now I have to do these other things. Figure out how it happened, when and then how to cross over."

He looks at me in a way I can't describe and that is just so intense, I can't manage to hold his stare so I look away, and instead focus on the urn. I feel that knot in my stomach, so I take another deep breath even if it doesn't help at all, it's just a reflex. I take a step closer and then raise my hand, trembling. I hesitate, pulling back when I'm about to touch it and then trying again but I just can't. I am too nervous to even try and I don't even know what will happen but my mind is creating the worst case scenarios.

Then I feel it. Someone touching my hand, squeezing it and it takes me three seconds to realise what's really happening: James is holding my hand.

My head snaps in his direction, horrified for what he's doing so I try to pull away immediately but his hold is tight. I can see in his face the pained feeling, it's evident in the way his jaw tightens and how he presses his lips tightly together, but he is fighting to look calm and fine.

"James, stop it," I command, still trying to pull away but failing.

"Right now you need it. I won't let go," he says, trying to sound strong but his voice is shaky due to the effort of controlling the pain. "If you want me to let go then stop complaining and touch it."Even if he says that I can only stare at him, moved by his words and actions, by the meaning of this. Such support from someone who's not related to me is the most foreign thing that has happened to me, and I'm a ghost so that's saying a lot. I feel so touched that even my chest hurts, my heart races and I can barely think of anything else.

James is enduring the pain to help me go through this.

But he's in pain so he's right, I need to hurry. With that in mind I turn to look at the urn again and reach out for it once again. My hand doesn't shake that much but I squeeze James' tighter and he does the same.

My index finger touches the urn first and I shiver but there's no pain. I don't feel anything just yet so I dare to press my whole palm against it and that's the moment the wave of desperation comes to me. Strong and unstoppable with the force of a hurricane, throwing me off with memories.

So much tears. So much fear and sorrow. So much loneliness and confusion. So much hatred and agony and it's choking me. I fall to my knees and I can't breathe but I fight for air I don't need. I struggle but it's to no avail.

I get memories. Memories of myself crying on a bed, my bed, begging for this pain and torture to stop. Begging someone could give me a hand. Wanting to just sleep and never open my eyes.

I also see myself locked in a room and banging at the door desperately. It's a small space, like a janitor closet and dark. I can't see. I feel like there isn't enough air and the tears are drowning me. I bang and bang but no one answers. I hear giggles at the other side but no one opens the door no matter how many times I beg for it. I fall to my knees, still crying but I stop calling for help. This will not come. I put my back to the door and hug my knees, muffling my sobs between them and shaking. It's cold and everything hurts. I remember hoping that this would be the end, once and for all.

"Paige!" Someone screams and it's hard to pay attention to that faint voice. It's hard to focus on anything but the pain and desolation I felt locked in that small space, the paralysing fear and the pain in my every muscle. "Paige, come back!"

I'm shaking... or someone is shaking me. I don't know. I blink once and then again and again until the voice calling my name grows louder and louder and I can finally see James crouching down in front of me, shaking me, worry written all over his face.

"James," I breathe out and he finally seems to take a breath as well. His shoulders relax and he ends up kneeling in front of me.

"God, you scared me. What happened? What did you feel?"

"Didn't you feel it?" I ask but he frowns.

"You pushed me and fell to the floor so I didn't. Then you were just screaming there, hugging your knees and trembling," he explains and I take a deep breath.

"I think... I think I saw my last memories," I explain and James' frown depends. "I was dressed like this and someone locked me in a closet. I cried and cried but no one helped me. And I remember I wanted it to stop right there. I think I might... I might've died there."

James' eyes widen in shock and I keep trembling slightly.

"It was probably at college, James. I could hear people laughing at the other side. They did it on purpose," I continue. "I think I died there."

"Are you sure?" He asks, his voice barely a whisper.

"No, but it looks like the last time I was still alive."He opens his mouth as if wanting to say something but nothing comes out. We just stare at each other with probably the same thought: they murdered me. Yes, it's likely they didn't intend to and it was just an accident but an accident they caused. If I really died there, then it's because of those people... and I don't even know whom they could be.

James stands up and I see him pacing in the room. I just stay on the floor watching him, feeling so confused and cold. So cold, especially now that James is not by my side.

He walks up to the urn and opens it, in just one movement that makes me gasp. He stops and seems to freeze when he sees what's inside: most likely my ashes. Then he closes it and takes the frame picture. He looks at it carefully and then turns it around to remove the picture inside. I furrow my brows, wondering what he's doing but I don't ask I just let him, feeling weird but for a different reason now, one I can't describe.

"This picture," he speaks out, still holding it in his hands and not turning to look at me just yet. He seems to be too focused inspecting it. "How old were you here, Paige?" He asks next, turning around to make me see the picture again.

"I'm not sure," I reply, shrugging. "Probably fifteen or something."

He gulps and his blue eyes are so intense on me."Do you realise what this means, Paige?" He questions next but I just keep furrowing my brows, confused.

"I was happy once with my parents and could smile despite everything?" I suggest but he shakes his head.

"No, it doesn't mean that although it is true." He finally approaches me and my whole body seems to react to him, trying to get closer faster. He then kneels in front of me and hands me the picture. "Read what's written at the back."

I do as told, turning the picture and finding mum's writing there with a few words.

"Finally seeing our baby smile honestly," I read out loud. "Cardiff, summer nineteen ninety-eight..." I continue but my voice fades and I hold my breath. I can only look at the date written there.

I remember the trip now. Dad offered to travel around the UK during summer, trying to put the best distance between us and Street. I think Dad was also trying to look for a better place to live, hoping I'd like another city more than where we already lived. I don't remember what happened after that whether we even really considered moving but I remember having fun and being happy just with them.

And that was seventeen years ago.

If I died at seventeen and I was around fifteen in that picture, that means I died fifteen years ago.I look up at James, my eyes wide in horror at the realisation. His own eyes are pitiful and worried but also ever so sad. He looks as devastated as I feel and for a second I want to reach him. Hug him to comfort both him and I, but I can't move.

"Fifteen..." I whisper, my voice cracking. "I died fifteen years ago, James. I've been dead for fifteen years. My mum's been alone for fifteen years. I've been a ghost and stuck here for fifteen years... oh my God."

Chapter 21

I choke on my words, dropping the picture and covering my mouth with my hands, shaking because I can't even cry. I feel like I'm going to start convulsing any minute because the horror of what this means, is too much for me.

Fifteen years.

Oh boy, I haven't even felt time pass by like that. I never imagined I had been like this more than a year. That means I've seen many generations go through college but I can't remember any of them, they're just blurry faces. I can only remember those I'm actually with but they'll also fade in my memory. Even those I seem to despise, like Roxy and Adeline.

Roxy was right. No wonder I'm like an urban legend, I've been fifteen years dead. Fifteen years haunting that college and all my classmates. All the generations I've had.

I know that if I could produce any fluid I'd be throwing up right now. And this is not even the worst part of it, I can cope with how many years I've been stuck and how everything seems to slip from my mind and nothing stays, but what is actually killing me all over again is the fact that I have been torturing Mum for fifteen years, my presence and constant touch bringing her agony and desolation every day. I have kept her in this depressed state for fifteen years, I have done that unconsciously but the harm is done nonetheless.

But my ashes are here and this is the reason why I keep coming back home every day, even if I might have died at college. I come every night because my ashes call me and Mum keeps them here. She should've scattered them. How do I convince her to do that?

And what happens to me if she does? Do I fade away like dust in the wind if she scatters them? That thought actually terrifies me. But if I have to disappear for Mum to get better, then I guess it's time. I'm already dead and maybe it's for the better if I do that. Who says there's actually something on the other side? Maybe we all eventually fade away regardless of how long it takes.

"Paige," James speaks and I look up to meet his eyes that watch me carefully before he kneels down until we're at the same level. He slowly takes the picture from the floor where I dropped it. "I know what you're thinking. You're feeling guilty because of your mum," he says and although I'm not exactly thinking of that right now, it is the reason why I'm having this train of thoughts. "Don't, okay? You didn't do it on purpose, you weren't even aware and now that you are you'll stop, right? You won't touch her again and you'll find the way to cross over. I'm sure the moment you do your mum will be better and will move on. Maybe she'll move from this house and start anew. Focus on what you can do for now, and that is finding out how you died and your unfinished business."

"But I... I have tortured her for fifteen years, James. How can I just ignore that?" I whine, wanting to hold on to him because I feel too frail but I can't hurt him anymore. Not again.

"I'm not telling you to ignore it, I'm telling you to do something about it. Dwelling on it won't get you anywhere," he says and although his words are cold his eyes are warm and sympathetic. "I'll help you, remember? Look at all what we've accomplished in one day." he tries to cheer me up, more energetically.

It's hard to believe all this has happened in one day since I woke up. We've discovered I was cremated, that my mum has my ashes in her room and that I died fifteen years ago, also that I might have been murdered or driven to my death in a janitor closet when a bad prank went wrong. And all this since I woke up in Art History after disappearing for almost a week.

It actually feels like weeks. I feel mentally exhausted. Plus, I walked through someone and that is already horrible on its own.

"I don't want to come back here," I blurt out and James furrows his eyebrows. "I want to stay away from Mum and this house and see if that makes a difference to her life. I want to stay like a week away and if Mum is actually doing better, then... just stay away, until the end. I need her to move on or I don't think I can even concentrate."

"And where will you go?" he asks and I shrug.

"I don't know. I'll probably stay in college or go around, testing my limits. But I won't set foot inside this house again." I declare with determination and he still looks at me uncertain.

"I'm not sure if that's good, Paige, but I guess it's worth a shot. But if you died at college maybe it's not good you're always there, so lonely at night," he ponders.

"Well, is either that or homeless and sleeping on a bench although I don't sleep but that's not the point," I ramble a bit and he chuckles lightly.

"Well, I live alone and unless you're scared I might do something to you," -he laughs but I don't find it funny- "you can come with me. At least until you figure out if staying away actually helps your mum. I promise I won't touch you."

"You better 'cos otherwise I'll just call you James the masochist," I declare and this time he laughs. "Is it really okay? For me to go with you? Are you sure you want to bring a ghost to your house? Willingly?" I question because the thought makes me too nervous, although it's good because it drives away the agony from the realisation of what I've done.

"You're not just any ghost," he smiles at me.

I feel weirdly touched and anxious, I can't even hold his stare so instead I just fix my eyes on my hands and how they fidget on my lap.

"So what do you say? Are you coming with me?" he asks, pushing me a bit and I have this urge to meet his blue eyes but I can't right now.

"Okay." I pause to take a deep breathe. "And thank you, James. Not just for this but for everything you've done so far. I don't think I would've ever found out all this without you," I say and this time I do look up and when I meet his eyes I feel my stomach tied in knots.

He only replies with a smile before standing up and holding up his hand for me but I just shake my head and rise to my feet on my own. He shrugs, knowing exactly why I have to reject his help and then he makes sure to return the picture and its frame next to the urn. He lingers a bit longer there, even touching the urn and I just watch him. I want to take those ashes away from here, away from Mum but if I do she'll panic and think someone robbed her and I don't want to cause her more stress.

James finally turns to look at me and gives me a small smile. "Should we go? I think your mum will be here anytime now," he reminds me and that alarms me.

"Right! Yes, let's go before she enters. If she finds you here it won't be pretty."

He just chuckles but the thought horrifies me so I guide him outside Mum's room and when we are getting near the door I hear it, the keys on the lock and I feel like my soul has left my body... or well, whatever I have. It's just an expression!

"Mum is here!" I tell James and his eyes widen with panic that wasn't there before, all amusement gone.

"Shit." he mumbles and I just nod frantically.

Oh boy, what do I do, what do I do?

"Upstairs! To my room. Fast!" I say, almost pushing him upstairs whilst I go and hold the knob of the door, giving him some time.

James practically flies upstairs whilst I feel mum struggling with the door, I can even hear her mumbles because it's not opening. Only when James disappears I let go and the door bursts open with Mum practically barging inside. I have to step back quickly to stop her from bumping into me and her confused expression has me on my toes. She looks around and at the knob, hoping to find what's wrong but there isn't anything. Then she looks around and only sees when Luna walks past her, rubbing herself against her legs before going outside. She just smiles sadly before heading to her room.

"Mum," I call but of course she can't hear me. "Good bye. I'll leave you alone now. Please, move on. Don't stay like this. I'm sorry for all what I did to you," I add anyways, apologising out loud even if she can't hear. At least I'm doing it.

I sigh deeply and hug myself before going to my room. I have no idea how I'm going to get James out of here but I need to think fast. I go upstairs to meet him and I carefully enter my room just to find him looking around. Now that I pay attention to my room I realise how ninety's it looks, like the band posters I have, like the Backstreet Boys, NSYNC and Spice Girls. I never paid attention to that but now that I know I died fifteen years ago it's so evident that I want to slap myself because I didn't realise sooner.

James is watching some pictures I have around from when I was a kid and some more 'recent' ones. I stand next to him and see them with him and even if I'm smiling in most of them you can perceive a change, how life seemed to be escaping me as I grew older. The dark bags under my eyes, the even messier hair, the shallow cheeks and extremely pale face, even some faint bruises. James is looking at what was probably the last picture I had before dying. It's a picture I took of myself when Mum and Dad gave me a Polaroid camera. I have a large bunch of those, some that I took, some that my parents did of myself and I guess I was really happy with my present. I've always liked photography. I have mostly landscape pictures and quite a few of my parents and Luna. As he goes through them I try to remember the exact moment I took them but it's too blurry and too long ago for me to succeed.

"These are great," he mumbles and even if he didn't even move when I stepped by his side he knew I was there. He then takes the camera and turns to aim at me. I automatically smile as bright as I can even if it might not work, I have no clue. It's just what I do in front of a camera. And then he snaps the picture and slowly the paper comes out. I can't believe it still has some. He grabs it and fans it until the image starts showing. To my surprise I do show up in the picture. Blurry, almost like a reflection, but that's me.

"It works!" I cry out, too excited to see that. "That's wicked!"

He just chuckles before getting very close to me but careful not to touch me and then snapping a picture of the two of us. I wasn't prepared for this and too shocked by his fast movement so I don't even look at the lens, I just look at him with wide eyes and that is how I show up in the picture when this finally reveals. James smiles at it fondly.

"I like this one. You look cute," he says nonchalantly and I feel like everything twists inside of me. "Who else can say they got a picture with a ghost?" he adds more cheekily, in a light tone that tries to make me smile. I do so, but it's still a very nervous smile.

"I think... we should go. You'd have to get out the window, though, unless you want to wait until Mum falls asleep."

"Window is okay," he replies and leaves the camera where I had it and next to it all the pictures. I go to the window and try to open it. It hasn't been open in fifteen years so it's almost impossible and James has to do it when he realises I just can't.

"I loosened it first," I say and he chuckles and rolling his eyes. "Make sure not to make too much noise and careful with the other windows so Mum doesn't see you."

"Will do. No worries, Paige. Do you need anything before we go?" he asks me, getting his body out of my window.

I just stare blankly at him. "James, I'm a ghost. I can't even change my underwear."

He blushes furiously and looks away before carefully climbing down. I follow him, making sure to close the window and taking one last look at my room, saying goodbye.

Once I'm on the ground next to James, Luna comes to us. Well, mostly James but I grab her in my arms and say my goodbyes.

"Thank you, Luna. For being my only friend these fifteen years. Take care of Mum, okay? Take all the sorrow away and make her happy. I trust you," I tell her and maybe it's too big of a responsibility and she doesn't understand, but she still meows and rubs her head against my hands and I feel my chest closing up. "I love you, Luna."

I let her go but she doesn't move, she just sits there, watching us. Then I look at James and he smiles encouragingly.

"Let's go. I'll show you my home now, and your now temporary one."

Chapter 22

I'm not surprised when we walk in silence. After all, if he just goes talking to himself in public he'd just get weird looks from the people passing by, but I still wish it wasn't like that. If I can't get distracted then my mind goes back to the few discoveries we've made today and the cumulus of emotions makes me feel disorientated. I'm used to the sorrow and loneliness, to the angst that preys on my mind, the worry and even that bit of resentment. But today every emotion has grown exponentially and I'm left raw. I feel that if James touched me, or anyone else, they would get knocked out because it's all so chaotic and destructive.

There's rage, so much rage that I don't even know what to do with it. All that resentment I felt before has evolved into murderous rage and it's not just because it's unfair I'm like this, it's because I'm like this after someone pushed me, someone drove me to this state. If those people had left me alone I'd still be alive. I'd be thirty-two years old and probably with a family on my own, with both my parents together. I'd be able to actually have a life. But that was taken from me.

Whether it was an accident or deliberate, someone pushed me until I fell off the cliff.

I'm not sure what exactly happen but I know it, I feel it. I know what I saw the moment I touched the urn were my last memories. That was the last thing I lived and it was horrible. I still can't remember the exact moment of my death but it was that same day, after what I saw. That was the day I died and my last memories were of fear, panic and so much pain.

No wonder why as a ghost I repressed those memories. It would've been even harder to exist having to carry the weight of those reminiscences with me. Having to go through fifteen years knowing I died like that would've probably driven me insane and I don't want to even think what I could've done. I'm invisible, I'm capable of hurting people without them even able to see me. I could've driven people to worse fates than mine.

I guess not remembering was my mind's way to protect not only me but everyone around. Grief and hatred make people do crazy things, and the more power you have, the more dangerous you become.

And now I remember, not fully yet but I know I need retribution. I need to make the people that did this to me pay. Someone who has done something this cruel to anyone needs to pay, they can't just go around, living their lives as if nothing has happened, as if they haven't destroyed lives. Even if they wrote apologies on my desk afterwards, they still took my life in their hands and squeezed it out of me.

They need to pay.

"Revenge," I mutter and James stops cold on his tracks.

"Pardon?" he speaks, his eyes fixed on me, a confused expression adorning his features.

"Revenge. That is my unfinished business, James. It's so obvious. For myself, for my Mum. Those people... the ones that locked me in the closet, they are my executers. They took me away from my family and caused all this pain to my mum. I'm like this because of them," I explain.

I can't actually focus on him, I feel my eyes are wild and lost. My hands are shaking and I probably look as insane as I feel. But I've been stuck for fifteen years, my mum has been mourning for the same time and my family broke in the year two thousand. I have the right to be insane.

"I need retribution. I need to make them pay for what they did, James. Only that would leave me at ease, don't you see? Only then I'll be able to cross over. I need to avenge myself and my family," I keep explaining. "I had repressed that memory but now that I know, I have to do something about it."

"Paige," he calls and his voice calling my name manages to make me focus a little bit, enough to see him and even notice the people walking by and giving him weird looks. He doesn't seem to mind, though. "I'm not sure that's correct, considering you're not even sure that's how you died. It could've been later that day, an accident. I doubt you died in a closet and if it was like that, I doubt college would be the place it is today."

"I died that day!" I shout and he takes a step back, surprised by my outburst. "Even if it wasn't there, even if it was a car accident after that, it happened because of it. You think I was able to even look to both sides after that? You think any human would be able to do that? You think someone would even want to live after all that?!" I keep shouting, that need to cry burning inside me, making me ache all over and feeling like I'm going to fall into pieces in any moment.

It hurts, it hurts so much. More than even walking through someone and feeling my body disappear. It hurts so much I can't even compare it to anything. It's pain, raw and only pain.

"Paige, calm down," he insists and I see his hands tried to reach me but I slap them away. He looks more hurt for my actions than for the brief contact. "We need to find out exactly how it happened and then decide what to do."

"It doesn't matter, I know it. I feel it, James!" I argue, hitting my chest as a way to emphasise my words. "I'm sure of it."

He looks so conflicted and can't even hold my stare any longer. He rubs his hands all over his face and even takes his beanie off, messing his dreads and just looking plain miserable. I only notice then, when I see the white flakes falling all over his hair and face that it is snowing.

I can't feel the cold or the heat, I'm always the same even if I'm only wearing a dress and denim jacket, but James must be freezing and I keep him in the cold. That realisation lessens the strength of my rage and makes me calm down a bit, enough to worry about him and stop focusing only on my pain.

"Fine. If that's what you have to do then we'll find a way, but first we need to find out what exactly happened to you and who are the people who did this to you." He takes a shaky breath, probably due to how cold he is. "You think you're the only angry," he laughs humourlessly. "I'm furious, too, Paige.

I can't believe people did that to you, that someone could be that cruel. It seems impossible and it is really tempting to seek revenge. But I'm holding myself."

Oh. So the shaky breathe is because of that? Because he's struggling to control his own rage?

"We can't just go around like that. We don't even know who did that to you and we can't just make everyone at college pay because they even weren't the ones that hurt you." He looks at me so intently, his eyes fixed on mine and for a moment I almost feel as if he's touching me, as if his arms are wrapping around me and keeping me close.

Almost.

"We'll find what exactly happened to you that day and if you need to make them pay, then we'll do that. We'll make them regret. But we'll do it properly, that I promise you."

I swallow the lump in my throat, unable to find the words my heart is urging me to tell. I can only nod, sucking my lips between my teeth and biting hard, but no pain comes. Not physical pain, at least, because the agony in my heart will not subside.

"Let's go now, okay? Once we get home we'll look up online and see what we can find with our limited skills," he says more calmly now, a little smile that tries to cheer me up. "And if we fail at that, tomorrow we'll look in all the old papers. We know it happened fifteen years ago so maybe some local newspaper covered it."

"Yes, let's go. You're cold and you'll get sick if we stay here any longer," I finally say and he smiles sheepishly.

"True that." Cue to his words she shivers violently. "Are you up for a run?"

I look at him confused for a few seconds before I understand what he means so I nod and then we get ready to sprint. To be honest, this is better than even talking about pointless things because it keeps my head busy on just following James that runs actually pretty fast.

I'm not sure why, maybe it's just the adrenaline of running as fast as we can, but we end up laughing. At some point James even trips and falls down, and we laugh even harder. I want to help him back on his feet but I hold myself and it doesn't matter, he can do it on his own. And he does it pretty quick because we're running again.

We run for so long, at least twenty minutes until we get to some new buildings, and James leads me to his flat. It's big although it has only two rooms and two bathrooms, but these are so spacious. The kitchen and living room are probably the size of my whole house and all the furniture looks expensive avant-garde. Only when I see where he lives I can fully appreciate the difference in social status. James looks anything but posh, but it's clear he has loads of money whilst I don't have anything and even when I was alive my family had only enough to make ends meet and have a decent life. Our house is small and old whilst his flat, where he lives alone, is at least twice as spacious as my home.

"Oh boy, that was a good run. I'm exhausted," James complains, his hands resting on his knees and he is still bent down, trying to catch his breath.

"It's far from my home. Why did you run? Why not taking a taxi or something?" I ask because but he just laughs.

"I thought walking, and well, then running, would help us clear our minds. I also needed that," he replies and I don't know how to reply. He stands straight and smiles at me. "Well, welcome to my crib, Paige," he laughs, using the same words I used when he entered my house. "I'm gonna take a shower and change so just make yourself at home while I'm at it, okay?"

I just nod and he smiles one last time before going into his room, and, I assume, to the bathroom that is connected to it. I stay there, in the living room with amazing and luxurious leather sofas, outstanding home theatre and a great view. That whole wall is just window and leads to a big balcony with its own set of sofas and chairs. Snow is still falling outside and it looks so pretty so I get closer to the window, just watching. It rarely snow in Street and I like watching when it happens. After a few minutes I keep wandering around, taking notice of the huge library with different films and graphic novels and the humongous computer on a big desk with all sort of printers. When I was alive having things like these at home was a rarity, or at least an impossible dream for me, and computers were big but in a different way, and they had more parts. This is just a big screen, like a TV on nowadays, flat and thin, and nothing else. It looks so fancy and shiny. I can only recognise the brand, though, mostly because the little bitten apple was the same back when I was alive and has perdured in time. Even if I used computers back in the day, I'm sure that I wouldn't be able to figure out what to do with this one.

I'm not even sure how to turn it on. I can't see a big button or anything.

I'm too mesmerised watching this computer, trying to figure out how it works when James walks in barefoot, in just sweatpants and new and larger hoodie that looks so comfortable. His dreads are loose and still a bit wet so he keep a towel around his neck and shoulders.

"Do you know how to use this?" I ask, instead of keeping my eyes wandering all over him.

"Barely," he replies with an embarrassed smile. "We'll try to use it for more than printing today, though. Let me get a snack, though," he says and I just nod.

He leaves to the kitchen and comes back a while later with a mug of hot tea and a sandwich. I look at it incredulously and he just shrugs. I keep my words to myself, it'd be too ironic if a ghost that can't eat a thing scolds him for the way he feeds himself.

He sits in front of the computer before bringing another chair for me and just moves the mouse, and like that the computer magically turns on. My eyes widen in bewilderment and I hear him chuckling softly.

"Okay, Google then. Everyone says this is magic but I always fail at it," he mumbles to himself. "You say your name is Paige Samuels," he continues and I smile. I only once told him my full name when I introduced myself to him. I didn't think he was listening back then, that he was even able to. It's nice he still remembers my surname.

"Paige Leonor Samuels," I tell him, adding my middle name and he looks me in the eyes briefly, a little smile on his lips.

"Okay then, let's type that,"-he says as his fingers fly over the keyboard-"and see what Google throws at us. I'm not sure how successful that would be considering it happened fifteen years ago and in a small town, but we have to try." And with that he presses enter and Google shows the first results to us. It's time to find out what happened to me.

Chapter 23

"Paige Samuels, Paige Samuels..." James mumbles, reading the results. "I don't think this is you. Do you have Facebook?" he asks.

"What's Facebook?" I ask back and he just mumbles some gibberish.

"LinkedIn?" I just stare at him with blank eyes and he chuckles. "Thought so. Twitter?"

"Is that like a virtual pet? Like Tamagotchi?" I ask and he laughs louder this time.

"No, it's a social network. But I think you... passed away... before all these were created so it clearly isn't you. Why do you have such common name, Paige? You're not making this easy."

"What? Would you prefer if I were named Petronila Leopolda Eustanaquia de las Mercedes?" Now it's James watching me with a blank expression. He doesn't even know how to react to my suggestion. "Mum watches Latin-American soap operas," I explain and this time he laughs out loud, almost losing it and I just smile sheepishly.

"I don't think that name suits you, but oh well, we need to keep doing this," he remembers and types again, this time adding my middle name but the results are basically the same. Other people's social accounts, even if I have no clue what these are and how they work. Furthermore, these are all recent results, people that are still alive.

"What if you add like the year I died?" I suggest and he tries that but the results aren't much different.

James tries other words, like 'Paige Samuel's death', or 'Paige Samuels bullying' and even 'Paige Samuels Strode College' but nothing shows up.

"In films it always looks so easy. They type what they are curious about and the first result is exactly what they need. What a scam," I pout, folding arms and everything because we've been more than twenty minutes at this with no results whatsoever. I have seen, however, many other girls with my name, and they all look so happy and young. Some others have lives and families and jobs, and here I am, a ghost. "Google isn't magic."

"I think we need something more specific to find an article that might or might not exist. I'm not sure if an article written fifteen years ago will be online, specially if it was covered by a local newspaper."

"I feel cheated. I will not believe what I see in films anymore," I continue and James chuckles again. I try to think how we can narrow down our research considering my name won't give us anything. And then I remember something. "I died at seventeen. I was still a minor, which means an article can't even use my name, right? They have to use my initials."

"Well, that certainly narrows it down, Paige," James says with a derisive tone and my head snaps to glare at him.

"Are you being sarcastic, James Black?" I ask, my voice dangerously dark and his expression changes completely to a more concerned, even embarrassed one, I daresay.

"No?" I can't help it, I laugh at his hesitant and careful tone, and for a moment I feel this urge just to bump shoulders with him, let him know I was just teasing him somehow, but I stop myself before I can make contact. "Anyways, if that's the case then we won't find anything using your name. Maybe focusing on college instead of you. Maybe we can't find exactly an article about your accident but another more recent that will connect with your case."

"Can you actually find that?" I ask because he's said many times his searching skills are very lacking.

"I can try," he replies with a shrug and I sigh.

And there he goes again, trying to find anything that can tell us what exactly happened to me. The best way would be to ask someone who was alive back then, like Mum or maybe the principal, if he's the one still in charge. But I'm too scared what might happen to Mum if someone suddenly came asking about me. So we have to try this, even if it's more futile than all the other things we've tried before.

James tries with different things like 'murder in Strode College', 'bullying in Strode College', 'accident gone wrong' and so many other options, but we can't get to anything concrete. He even adds my initials at some point but still we can't come up with one result that helps. All we ever find is an article from five years ago that mentions the new policies anti-bullying in Strode College and a faint mention that's always been a problem but they have always taken action regarding that. I would like to differ, but then I don't know what happened after my death. Maybe things changed or maybe they just covered it up...

Oh.

"What if they covered it up, James? If it was an accident or anything else, it happened in college and if it happened there then it would actually affect them negatively. It wouldn't be the first time something like this is covered up," I suggest and James freezes, his fingers hovering the keyboard and I just wait for a response.

"You think they could be that low as to hide something like this?" he asks, not meeting my eyes, his are still fixed on the large screen.

"I dunno. Possibly?"

James' hands fall on the keyboard, smashing it and his shoulders slouch, showing his defeated posture and I feel so bad for causing all this to him. I'm also impressed he's that invested in this. He decided to help me today and we've done a lot, but just now I notice how into this he is. What happened during that week I was out? What went through his mind to make him care so much?

"Or maybe we just suck at online research," I suggest, trying to lessen the burden he's feeling but he shakes his head.

"No, by now we should've found something already. So either it's not an article online or they covered it up. We could go and ask for the records of your death, but I'm not a relative and they wouldn't let me see them."

"Don't you have a hacker friend? Aren't those like super good at finding things in less than thirty seconds?" I ask next and he laughs humourlessly.

"Do I look like the kind to have friends, Paige?" he asks back but I can't answer that. For me it's obvious, he could have all the friends he wanted, but he refuses to even acknowledge his classmates. "The closest things I've had to friends are ghosts. And in my whole life you're the only one I haven't felt scared or angry at, I would even dare say you're my first friend."

I feel a lump in my throat when I hear him, and when he gives me a smile I get my breath caught in my throat and I don't even know what to say.

A friend. That's something I never had before, something that looked so foreign to me and almost like a dream upon a star. And here is James, telling me I'm his first friend and I can't remember when I've felt this happy. I have to press my lips together so I don't burst out giggling, but that's not even enough, I have to press my hands to my mouth but I guess my eyes are giggling already because James chuckles.

I guess I'm too drunk in this newfound happiness because I don't react when I see James moving his hands away from the keyboard and to my face until he grabs one of my hands in his. And because he doesn't show pain or struggle, I don't realise what he's doing after several seconds have passed.

"James!" I snap, trying to pull my hands away but he doesn't let me.

"No, focus on that feeling. That happiness!" he cries out, showing the first sign of pain. But instead of doing what he's told me to, I only get concern and I struggle to let go of him, to cease the pain I'm causing him and that only seems to make it worse. "Paige! Relax. Just focus on the happiness you were feeling."

His hands hold mine tighter and I get frantic, so scared for him but I try to obey and do what he's asked me for. I close my eyes and focus on the happiness I was feeling, the fact I'm someone's friend and I finally have a friend, but it doesn't work. I can't. I can only think of James, suffering.

"Ugh," he sighs, finally releasing my hands and I even stand up, taking a few steps back and putting distance between us.

"Why did you do that?" I demand, slightly shaking because I'm just so concerned.

"You were so happy, you looked so damn happy that I thought maybe it wouldn't hurt," he explains, taking deep breaths and then looking up to meet my eyes. "And I was right. At first, you were so happy and that overpowered all the other negative feelings and it didn't hurt, Paige. When I touched you, it didn't hurt... until you realised what I was doing and lost focus."

I don't know how to react and what to say. My mind is still processing the information and this new discovery.

I didn't hurt him-at first-because I felt happy. That means I don't always bring pain and sorrow with me. I just transmit what I'm feeling, but more powerfully. So if I'm in pain, I share pain, but if I'm happy, I share happiness?

I want to touch James again, I even take a step forward but then stop myself. I'm still scared and concerned I might hurt him this time. The happiness I was feeling before was overwhelming, I wasn't thinking of anything else, and that's why I could transmit that. That feeling was stronger than any other before, but now it isn't. Even if I think of what he told me, I can't feel equally happy. And if I don't feel like I did at that moment, then I might hurt him now.

"You see? It's not always bad, we've learnt something new again. We just need to give you more positive feelings," he says and the first smile after what happens comes to my lips, a bubbly feeling being born in my guts.

"You think that once I solve my unfinished business I won't have so much sorrow inside me?" I ask as if he knew everything about being a ghost and crossing over.

"Maybe. That would make sense. And it'd be a good way to know if you actually finished that and can cross over," he comments. "But do you realise what this really means, though?" I look at him, confused. "It means that you can touch people without hurting them. There is a way for... us... to touch without hurting the other."

I stare at him, trying to calm my heart and everything that is twirling and spinning in my chest. I can't even take a breath, I just look at him, feeling something I can't even describe, something I've never experienced before. It's not exactly what he says but the way he looks at me that carries so many meanings I can't pick up. His words are just a few but what's between the lines is so much more and I can't read all that.

He stands up, still locking eyes with me and takes a step forward, closing the distance between us, and without even allowing me to blink, he takes my hands again, lacing our fingers together.

For a second my eyes dart to our hands. "Paige!" he calls, making me meet his blue eyes again, these are so intense that my breath gets caught in my throat.

I see a bit of struggle in his eyes, but not enough to make me panic. He's also smiling and seeing him like that makes me smile back, feeling even happier because I'm not bringing misery to him right now. Even if there's a bit of pain, it's bearable. It is working and the result of this experiment is making me deliriously happy, and I think James is also feeling that because his smile widens and even a small chuckle escapes his lips.

"The happier you feel, the less painful it is," he tells me before releasing one of my hands just to cup my cheek ever so softly. I see him flinching a bit, but not enough to make him stop or make me react. "It's possible, you see?"

I nod. That's all I can do, because he is touching me. This... it's been so long since someone touched me like this, with care and almost love. Only my family touched me like this before, and now James. And it's so different now because I don't have a body to actually feel, it's not on my skin and nerve ends, but I feel it. All over me. I feel his hands as if they were touching my very soul, and I think that's exactly what he's doing.

I close my eyes and lean into his hand, feeling like my whole body is tingling and I sigh in delight, feeling calm and happy at the same time, blessed and accepted.

We didn't learn how I died, but we found out something even more powerful and important: my touch isn't always pain.

Chapter 24

"Are you sure you'll be okay?" James asks me for the nth time and I just smile, nodding.

After our failed attempted to find an online article about my death, and the amazing discovery I don't always give pain when I touch a human being, it's been a bit awkward between us. And by bit I mean unbearable awkward. I can barely meet his eyes without wanting to touch him again, without dying for him to hold me in his arms without having to carry with him the sorrows I'm so used to. I can't look him in the eyes without fearing he might see how desperately I need to feel that human contact after so much solitude. And because I can't control my emotions at will and I don't dare yet to take risks with James, I can't ask him to at least hold my hand again despite how much I need it, henceforth, I don't meet his eyes.

Later, after even watching a movie together in the same awkward silence, we realise it's late and he should sleep, because tomorrow he has classes and even if I don't need to sleep, he does so he can't stay awake all night just to keep me company, although it seems that's what he wants. He insists to stay with me in the living room, but I refuse.

"It's okay if you don't want to be alone and if it's hard. You probably feel the pull to your house," he continues and although I feel it, that need to go back home, I fight it. I'm conscious I can't go and it's not like I don't have control over my own soul.

"If I'm struggling too much I'll let you know, but as for now I'm perfectly okay," I reassure him but he doesn't seem convinced.

"I just feel oddly uncomfortable knowing I'm leaving you in the living room without even a blanket," he blurts out, cheeks flushed and anxious movements.

I chuckle, finding his attitude so charming and adorable, but keeping that to myself. "It doesn't make a difference. Even if you even lend me one of your hoodies I wouldn't be able to wear it. The moment you look away it'd fall to the ground."

"I just... I just don't think I can fall asleep knowing you'll be all night awake here, without anything to do."

"I'll find something to do. I've been doing this for fifteen years, remember? I haven't gone insane yet," I joke but he doesn't even smile. "What? Do you want me to sing you lullabies until you fall asleep?"

The jokes help me to ease the awkwardness between us, allowing me to actually meet his eyes.

"That wouldn't be that terribly," he shrugs and that light tone I had in my voice gets caught in my throat. "But if you're tone deaf, maybe you should stay here."

He gives me a smile that twists something inside me, so I have to look away for a second. I even have to cough to clear my throat before I reply.

"If that helps you, we can try that. Unless having a ghost in your room creeps you too much," I try to tease but he only smiles.

I know having a ghost around doesn't faze James, he's grown up surrounded by them, and he's really used to me. I even think he sometimes forgets I'm a ghost, considering he reacts the way he does, trying to offer comfort with a soft touch when he sees me so upset. I also think he doesn't like seeing me as a ghost, because he seems to struggle with the concept every time, and he avoids saying out loud that I'm dead. I don't dare to analyse that because if he's getting too attached to me that will only cause him pain, after all we're looking for the way for me to cross over. It's not just putting distance between us, it is actually leaving this realm to never see him again. If he is indeed growing fonder of me and even getting used to having me around, it'll only hurt him when I cross over.

Maybe that's why I make remarks of me being death so often. Things I never did before until he showed up, like joking about being a ghost, are now a thing as common as breathing for a living person. It's a way to remind him I am dead and I'll be crossing over, hopefully, soon so he shouldn't get attached to me. And I shouldn't get attached to him, either, because if I do then I won't want to cross over, to a realm I don't even know if exists. If I grow fonder of James

I'd have a reason to stay and something tells me that isn't a good idea.

"I'll go wash up then. You can go to my room in the meantime," he says, breaking through my train of thoughts, and I just nod.

I end up waiting for him in his room, walking around paying attention to all details. He has a king size bed in the middle with a dark cover and white stuffy pillows. Like in the living room, a whole wall is just windows that lead to another balcony with a better view. Next to the wardrobe he has more shelves with some comic books, but most are pictures, amazing pictures from every corner around the globe, and it's clear these are all professional takes. I wonder if these are his parents'. Maybe instead of family pictures this is all he has, the only way to have them close. He also has another desk with different brushes, pens, pencils, ink and stacks of paper. I think he works on his graphic novel there. He also has a great sound system that looks too fancy for my poor understanding.

Every corner of this place reminds me James is from a very different social status, and I think it makes me happy that he doesn't wear that. I don't think I would've even approached him if he was a posh jerk that thought too little of everyone else.

I'm too caught up taking a closer look to the pictures to notice James is in the room, I don't notice him until he's behind me.

"That's when they were in Vietnam. They send me some pictures from every place the visit, along with a lot of cash,"

James tells me, startling me and making me bump into the shelf, almost making the things inside and the shelf itself fall over us. "Oi, careful there!" James cries out, stopping the shelf from smashing us with his hands, but also caging me between his arms.

I find myself trapped, between the shelf and James' body. I try to turn around, only to find him still there, looking down to meet my eyes, so close I can actually feel his breath tickling my nose. His dreads fall like a curtain around us, leaving me with the only option to see his face.

We are so close but we still don't touch and I feel like all my skin is buzzing, especially when he looks at me with such intent eyes. Because I don't know what to do, I just grab one of his dreads, something I've been wanting to do for a while, and blurt out, "Why dreads?"

He blinks, his expression showing confusion before he steps back, taking the dread from my fingers.

"Well, I like them and I have an impossible curly hair. It was always painful so the only other option was to cut it really, really short. Buzz cut, you know? But I guess it was also my way to rebel, you know? And try to get my parents' attention. Even if I did it unconsciously back then, I think it's because of that. And I've just stuck with it. Plus, many people are judgmental and ignorant about them so it helps to keep those people away, using their own prejudices as a shield," he explains and I'm surprised at how deep the reason behind his hairdo is.

"I think I've grown really fond of them," I smile. "And I'm learning about them a little bit."

James smiles before taking another step backwards, turning to his left and walking up to his wardrobe from where he takes a clean hoodie he then throws at me. I barely catch it, looking at it with a puzzled expression.

"I know you don't need it but it'd make me feel better if I see you in something more comfortable than a denim jacket. At least until I fall asleep," he explains with an easy smile.

I keep staring at the hoodie in my hands. It's dark red and really big, but it's also really soft and I wish I could smell because I have a feeling it would smell like James. I shrug off my jacket and dive into the hoodie that almost reaches the hem of my dress and which sleeves are way too long on me.

"I look ridiculous," I say, flopping my arms like a bird trying to fly for the first time, but James' expression is nothing but mocking.

"No, you look really cute," he says instead. He then heads to his bed where he gets under the sheets. "You can sit here. The bed is huge, after all. And once you fall asleep you can go anywhere, read a book or watch another movie. I taught you how it works," he says and I nod because I'm afraid my voice will betray me.

I know it is ridiculous for a ghost to feel this nervous. It's not like something can happen if James and I lie on the same bed, but still, my guts twist and I want to hide inside this hoodie forever. Yet I still walk towards the bed and sit at the other end, as far away from him as I can, watching him getting comfortable.

"What would you do if you couldn't cross over?" James ask me and I have to think about it.

"I dunno. I guess I'd be the same, still pretending I'm not dead and repeating the same routine day after day. I guess after a while I would even forget what we learnt today and I'd go on believing I've been like this for less than a year." I look at him, shoving my hands in the front pocket of the hoodie, and pretending that it's James the one embracing me instead of this cotton fabric. "I'd probably even forget you."

Saying that stirs something inside of me that actually hurts. Differently from the memories of the bullying, different from the pain I carry with me. This is a pain I feel in my chest, making me feel heavy with grief and for a moment I feel like crying.

"But that's the case if I weren't around," James says and I shake my head, both to dismiss his comment and to shoo the pain I'm feeling.

"You can't stay here forever. You'd eventually have to leave and craft your future away from this city, and even if I have nothing else here, I wouldn't be able to go with you. You know that," I tell him and his expression darkens with the same grief I'm feeling in my chest. "If we can't succeed at what we're trying to do, the best option is to forget. It's less painful," I add.

"I don't think I'd be able to forget you, Paige," he confesses in a whisper, stirring something new in my chest that makes me smile sadly at him.

I wouldn't either, I say in my mind because I can't utter those words out loud.

"Then I guess we can't afford to fail. We'll figure what happened to you and make sure you can solve your unfinished business," he says with newfound determination, but there's still a linger of sadness in his eyes. "We'll look into the old newspaper's records until we find something about your... accident. And if there isn't anything, then we'll find your class generation and we'll ask. I don't think it matters if we shock them a bit with questions about what happened fifteen years ago."

"Maybe if I see their faces I'll be able to remember more," I suggest and James nods.

I don't notice how I get more comfortable on the bed until I'm lying on my belly and with my face turned to watch James.

"Yeah, that might work. It seems you haven't lost your memories, you just have them locked them up in your mind. Like touching the urn triggered something and you could remember that," agrees James. "And if your unfinished business is to make them repent for what they did to you, whether that led to your accident or not, then we'll find a way to accomplish that."

"Why do you say accident?" I ask, focusing on that instead of his plead. "Why do you always avoid saying death or that I'm a ghost?"

James stares at me for a few seconds, almost confused for my question, as if I should know the answer but I don't. I can't be sure about it and I don't want to speculate. But I don't really want to know. I'm wary of what he might say and I regret having asked that, but I can't take my words back.

"'Cos it's hard to see you as a ghost when you feel more alive than other people I've met, or even other ghosts. And 'cos I guess I don't want to believe it, even if I saw your ashes," he replies.

"Why?" I breath out, a sound barely above the noise of his breathing.

"Just because," he says, but his eyes are so intense and carry more words than I can read, making my chest feel tight and stuffed, making my ghostly heart race inside my ribcage. "Just like you pretended to be alive, let me now pretend you're still alive."

I want to refuse, argue that it's not wise, and that this is a mistake. Instead, I say, quoting one of my favourite films, "As you wish."

Chapter 25

It turns out that finding articles from fifteen years ago isn't that easy. There are many and not just one newspaper, so James and I spend several days looking through the registers but to no avail. Just like with the internet search we only find articles related to new polices after an accident with severe bullying. No names mentioned or anything. Just that. What happened to me is reduced to an 'accident'. That makes me boil with rage and frustration because not even after I died they cared about what happened to me. Not even an apology.

James tries to distract me but I think he's aware this frustration is taking away all the bubbling he knows me for, and it's turning me into a dark creature, filled with rage and thirst for revenge. Revenge against people that ruined my life but I can't remember. Written apologies on my desk are not what I need. I need to see them knowing what they did and how that killed my soul. Whether they pulled the knife in my flesh or not, they murdered my soul and no human can live much longer without it.

Either way they killed me, and I want them to never forget they are murderers.

"Hey Paige," James calls me when he notices that, once again, my mind has been drifting away with too dark thoughts to be allowed. "I asked around to know who's the person who's been the longest working here. Richard, the technician of the top floor of the E block, has been here sixteen years. He's also the one that takes pictures, and I've heard he remembers every student. What do you think if we go pay him a visit and ask him if he remembers what happened fifteen years ago? Maybe he remembers names and more."

He tries to smile to cheer me up, but I can't focus on that. I'm trying to remember Richard. Why is my mind so scatty? Why is that no one stays in my memory for too long? I wonder if that's a consequence for staying too long on this realm.

"Let's try that," I accept, pushing away those other questions. James says I just need to get my memories triggered; maybe going to see Richard will help.

I manage to see James' worried gaze on me, but I don't want to fake a smile when I'm so tormented and angry, frustrated because I can't remember what happened to me, and no one bothered to leave a clue or any register of what happened. Everyone just deleted me and disregarded me.

Fifteen years isn't that long, is it?

I stand up and head away from the rec and towards the E block, upstairs with James following me without uttering a word. Some other kids walk past us, no one noticing me but they do pay attention to James. Even if it's been a while since he joined us, he still gets attention because he keeps being a mystery for them. He is a friend to me, I know him better than anyone else here, but that makes no difference. He is as alone as if I weren't here.

We get to the top floor and James knocks at the door where we should find Richard. We heard a faint 'come in' that is the sign James takes to open the door and walk in. Now I'm the one following and staying behind whilst he greets the technician that smiles kindly at us. He's probably around forty-five with receding hairline and deep laughter lines. He has brown eyes that still look young and when I take a look into them I remember him. When he was near his thirty, full of youth and spirit, with the same warm smile and kind eyes. He was always around, taking pictures of the students and every event to remember.

I remember him.

"You're the transfer student, right?" Richard asks. "Nice to meet you, I'm Richard. How may I help you? Do you need something?" he offers a seat for James that he takes. His eyes briefly dart to me and I just shake my head. I can sit anywhere.

"Yeah, I'm James," he introduces himself. "And I was wondering if you could help me with something," he begins. Richard only nods to signal he's following and waiting for James to continue. "Well, it's about something that happened fifteen years ago." Richard's face shows recognition, like that number alone rings a bell. His body posture changes, becoming more alert and my own suspicion grows as I watch him. "There was a girl back then and she was severely bullied during her first year. Do you remember anything about that time?"

For the longest ten seconds of my existence Richard only stares back at James, who is growing anxious, considering how he slightly stirs on his seat. "Paige Samuels," he finally says and both James and I take an audible intake of air. "Such a broken girl." His once happy eyes turn melancholic, regretful. "We should've done more to help her, but everyone thought 'they are just kids. They'll grow up and stop.'"

"What happened, exactly? I've tried looking for articles or anything that mentions it but to no avail," James intervenes, his own anxiety dripping from his voice, his body leaning forward in anticipation.

"Why are you asking about her?" Richard asks back, making James retreat and use a more defensive posture.

"I can't really explain. Let's say it's personal. She's close to me," he replies but that seems to confuse Richard further. "Please."

Richard shakes his head and if he was debating himself whether to tell James the story or not, he comes to a con-clusion now. "I didn't know her much, she was always like a shadow, you know? I heard of her more later, after she died. It seems everyone underestimated the situation, and she never complained. After she died many people came forward, giving testimonies and sharing the horrors that girl had to go through, but when it was happening no one said a thing."

I brace myself. Hearing the events from a different point of view, from someone who had nothing to do with it and only heard of it, is wrecking. It shakes me from within, making me ache in a way no physical pain could compare. I hear from this technician's mouth how every adult ignored me, how no one could vouch for me and help me until I died.

Why did not anyone feel at least a bit sorry for me to even send an anonymous note to the principal or something? Wasn't I even pitiful for them? They definitely saw what was happening, but they turned the blind eye until I died. Why?

"The measures were taken too late. They apologised to the family, to the girl, gave her the best ceremony they could, the bullies were expelled and new policies were created to prevent that from ever happening again. But she was already dead and nothing could bring her back," Richard laments, telling a bit of what the articles covered.

My whole body shakes with frustration and fragmented memories. I see many people crying, apologising to my family. I see the principal handing a check with a lot of zeros to my mother and she rejecting it. I see grief, so much grief.

"How did she die?" James asks, his voice sounds constricted, as if his throat closed up and he can barely get the words out. I imagine my voice would sound like that, too.

"She killed herself," Richard answers and I feel cold wrapping me, like a frozen blanket, chilling me to the core. The words echoing in my head, over and over again.

I killed myself.

"The last thing the kids did to her was locking her up in a closet for a whole night. The next day, she stayed almost all morning there, she didn't even cry or shout for help at that point. She was found almost at noon, cold to the bone, shaking and she had even urinated herself. Instead of worrying, the kids that did that to her came to laugh at her. They humiliated her even further. I think that's why they did it to start with." I can't even blink as I listen to the rest of that memory I saw when touched my urn. "The family was informed and hell broke loose. The mother had been calling everywhere, trying to find her but you understand back then not everyone had a mobile phone like today. She tried to fill in a missing person file but they told her it had to be forty-eight hours after the person disappeared. When she learnt that her daughter had been locked in college she made sure to let everyone know how despicable everyone was. She filled in the transfer papers that very day.

"The girl didn't say a thing. She was too shocked and broken, I guess. The little I saw that day was enough to bring me nightmares even today. That poor girl... she was soulless, broken to the point of no repair but the most terrible thing was the hatred in her eyes. She blamed not only the kids that bullied her but everyone there. And I guess she was right, we were all responsible.

"The next morning there was another surprise, only that time she was the one bullying the rest. With her own blood she wrote 'I did it' on the board. The kids found her dead body on her desk. After that it—"

I can't take it anymore.

I stand up, shaking, throwing the table I was sitting to the floor, and more things with it, startling both James and Richard, but I don't care. I can't care.

The memories come rushing to me, reminiscences I crushed myself in my mind so they wouldn't torment me any further. The memories of that day and how I did it. The agony, the pain, the hatred and resentment. Rage, so much rage and detachment. I feel it all over again. It comes to me ruthless, tackling me from every direction, leaving me breathless and unable to see.

I tumble around, crushing against different things until I can reach the door and leave this room that has become a new form of hell.

I killed myself. I did it. Here in college. And I did it because they told me to so many times and the last thing I did was telling them they succeeded and I finished my own life. For them. I didn't kill myself to escape, I killed myself for them. To give back. To show them what they did to me. They broke me and I gave them what they sought from the beginning: my life. All for them.

I can't see and everything hurts. I feel cold consuming me and I think I'm losing my body again. The cold is burning and leaving me raw so I start screaming as the agony I felt that last day embrace me with a deadly grip. I shout because I can't cry, yet that's all I want to do.

I remember.

I remember all that happened that day. The moment I gave up in that closet, when the tears stopped coming and my mind came to a decision. I remember the moment my very soul left me. When I knew I would give them what they wanted and were asking me to do. How many times did they tell me to kill myself? I finally listened. I decided in that closet that I would give them the pleasure of seeing me dead. I had lost my soul already and knew that my body had to follow it.

I remember the coldness that I felt and how I knew exactly what to do to cause the most impact. I had to put on the perfect exhibition for my torturers.

I remember pondering all my options until I decided which one wouldn't fail. I knew I couldn't fail.

I remember sneaking out of my window and heading to college. I was so numb already that I couldn't even stop for my parents. I couldn't think beyond what I needed to do to the kids that drove me and pushed me over the edge.

I remember walking inside the E Block and heading to the Art History classroom. I remember the cold determination that took control over my body, and I remember that the pain I felt when I sliced open my own veins was nothing compared to the ache in my heart and the agony I had endured until then.

I remember taking one of my Stanley knives and soaking it in garlic before leaving home, just to make sure my own wounds wouldn't close and my blood wouldn't coagulate before I was really dead. I remember following the veins on my arms, from wrist until I could almost reach the shoulders, one after the other, opening them and feeling nothing but cold when the blood started pouring and splashing like sprinklers. I remember writing with that very blood on the board so they would all see it and be proud of what I did. It had to be my blood. They had to see my blood there, spelling the words I couldn't shout to their faces. My blood was my offering to them so they would be happy that I finally listened to them. It was all for them, they had to see it.

I remember putting on my denim jacket and seeing it getting soaked with blood, changing from a light blueish colour to burning scarlet.

I remember sitting and waiting.

I remember fading away, my own vision turning blurry from the corners and the cold consuming me. I remember the last tears I ever wept and how I kept mumbling, "I did it. Happy now? I did it..."

I remember wanting to see their faces. Wanting to see the moment they saw the my blood, hoping that image would never ever leave them. I remember the hatred in my heart hoping they would finally see what they caused and know this was their doing.

I was the one who opened my veins and let the blood escape me, but they pushed me to that. They didn't put the knife in my hand, but they told me so many times to do it until I obeyed.

I remember the last thing I saw before darkness took me away was the board with my handwriting in blood. The words that now echo in my head louder than ever.

"I did it," I whisper, my voice hoarse after so much screaming.

Hysterical laughter comes next because the cold is coming back, consuming me, taking control. The burning hatred and resentment possessing me. The same crazy drive to make them see, make them pay.

"I did it. For you all... I did it," I cry out. So loud I feel the whole building trembles. "I DID IT!" I shout one more time as faces, finally, come to my mind. I remember... I remember the people that did this to me.

Chapter 26

Their faces are so clear in my mind, and their names echo in my head. The same names I died with, repeating them over and over again, hoping what I did would get to them. Did they even see it? Did they care? Was it even worth it? I am a ghost now but they were less human than I am now, so I wouldn't be surprised if they didn't care about what happened and just laughed at my weakness.

I would expect that from those... monsters.

I died wanting them to pay for what they did. Wanting them to repent and be sorry. No wonder I'm stuck as a ghost now, that's clearly my unfinished business. If I died with that in mind and without completing that task or seeing the outcome, I'm still here to fulfil that. It's the only thing that makes sense in my head.

"Paige, Paige stop it! Paige!" someone screams, but the voice barely gets to me. I'm too consumed in my own rage and the faces that tormented me for so long.

One face... one girl.

She had been tormenting me for years. Back in secondary school and then when we met again in college. I thought... when I graduated from secondary school I thought I wouldn't meet any of them again. I regretted all my choices the moment I saw her again. She made friends immediately but I was alone, and she turned her friends into her new partners against me. She's the one that brought all this to me. Who never gave me a break.

"Paige, if you don't come back I'm gonna hug you!" the voice shouts again, trying to reach me, and my mind reacts to that threat.

No... I'm not scared of being touched, although I should be. Foreign hands only brought pain to me, I should be scared. But this voice doesn't affect me like that, on the contrary, I don't want to hurt the owner of that voice. And if he touches me... if he touches me, I'll be hurting him.

James!

I can't let James touch me.

I shake my head and try to get back to the present. I push to the back of my mind the faces that tormented me and I focus on the voice calling me.

"No," I breathe out. "Don't touch me."

"Oh thank goodness," he says. I can open my eyes now just to see him kneeling in front of me, his eyes charged with worry and sorrow. I look everywhere around but there's no one else. "You scared the living hell out of everyone. Richard fled like soul chased by the devil himself."

"I'm sorry..." I mumble, just thinking now how scary must've been for the poor technician. "I couldn't... think."

"I know. I'm just saying you shouldn't worry about someone seeing us now and even if someone did, I don't care what rumours they might come up with. There are enough already, one more won't make a difference," he says, and I notice the big effort he is doing to sound light and cheerful. Yet his eyes look nothing but happy, they look tormented and like he's enduring the biggest agony.

I want to comfort him and ignore everything I'm feeling... but then I realise he's feeling like that for me.

"I did it," I tell him. "I really did. I remember now and I... it was so gruesome, James. I really did that, just to get back at them. I didn't kill myself to escape the pain or anything, I didn't do it out of cowardice." I take a deep breath, holding his stare and doing my utmost best not to reach out to him and hold him, or on to him, I'm not sure. "I did it to bring pain to them. It was my revenge. I didn't think of anything else, consequences be damned, I just did it."

"Paige..." he murmurs my name. I can't read the meaning behind that, whether there's pity or understanding.

"And I don't even know if it worked," I laugh, losing it a bit once again. "I can't remember seeing them finding my body or anything. For all I know, someone might have found it first, someone who wasn't supposed to, and no one else because no one was allowed to see that."

I don't even know how to feel at that possibility. I don't know if I should scream, laugh or just cry-even if I can't.

"I remember their faces, but I don't know if those faces actually saw what I left for them. My revenge isn't completed, James. That's why I'm stuck here," I tell him, sharing with someone my theory. My voice drips desperation because I want him to understand and support me.

"Paige," he says again and I sense something in his voice this time, something that indicates we are not on the same page anymore. "I don't think that's really what you're here for," he adds, a mere whisper but that slaps me across the face harder than any hand could.

"I'M SURE OF IT!" I shout at him. "I died with that in my mind. It's ought to be my unfinished business. At least her... at least her," I break down, trembling like I did so many times when I was alive. When I was humiliated over and over again. Like I did every time I got home and I could only cry against my pillow, hoping Mum wouldn't hear me again. "You said you'd help me..."

"Who? Who is she?" he asks, and even if he is saying that, I can feel in his voice he doesn't want to do this.

"Dawson... Diana Dawson," I reply. James frowns, probably trying to think if that name sounds familiar to him. "She's the one... the one that bullied me for years and who made everyone here follow her. She... I just need her to be sorry and know what she did to me. Just her, James. Please," I beg, grabbing the fabric of his hoodie and pulling of him a bit, still careful of not touching his body anywhere.

"Dawson... like Roxi Dawson?" he asks and I have to think.

Roxi is always dying her hair, and Diana was a brunette, but they look similar. There's an evident resemblance that now makes sense. Now I understand why I hated Roxi the most out of everyone else. There's an attitude, the look, the way they treat others and think of themselves that show they are clearly related.

"Like her! Roxi must be related to Diana. A cousin or a sister or even a daughter!" I blurt out. "That's why I hate her so much, because she looks kind of like Diana and she reminded me of her and-James!" I keep rambling, my mind spinning with thoughts and all the pieces together.

"Okay... but calm down, Paige. You need to calm down. You're still shaking," James says instead. "Why don't we go home and think better about this? We need to figure out how to proceed and exactly how we'll get to find out whether she saw what you did or not. If she did, Paige, I'm sure that's more than enough. You don't need to torment her any further."

"Why do you make it sound like I'm the monster here?!" I spat, standing up and stepping away from him, feeling be-trayed and unstable. "I just asking for what I deserve. Don't I deserve an apology?"

"You do, Paige. You certainly do! And don't think I'm here looking after them or anything. I couldn't give two shits about what happens to all those people who hurt you, and the ones that turned their backs on you," he exclaims now, also standing up and sounding agitated. "I'm doing this for you! I'm looking after you 'cos I don't want you putting in jeopardy your own soul..."

His voice is barely a whisper at the end, but even if his voice is that low I hear it louder than when he was shouting. The power of those words is louder than whatever decibel he can reach.

"Let's go home, Paige," James calls again, and I'm so tired right now, so drained that I think my knees will give out. "Please."

I want to take his hand, let him hold me in one piece because I'm falling apart, but I don't dare to hold up my hand for him. I know the pain I'm feeling right now would destroy him and rip off his own soul. And I can't do that to him, to the only person-that is not related-that has helped me and showed me some sort of caring. I can't control my own heart right now and even if I need him so much, I can't do that to him.

"Let's go home," I agree in a whisper that he rewards with a smile.

I follow him downstairs and then to the bus and eventually his flat. I know he wants to talk to me on our way, distract me from the storm in my head, but I don't react to all his initiatives. I do my best not to let the memories consume me again, but it's hard. I can see that vividly that last day I repressed until today. The way I couldn't think of anything else but making them see their wrongdoings. I couldn't see past that. The worst thing isn't that I killed myself in such a coldhearted way, that I tortured my body worse than anyone did before. No, the worst thing is that I didn't think of my family at all. Not even once I considered stopping myself because that would hurt my parents.

I know that many times I wanted to kill myself just to escape the constant torture. More than once I stood in front of pills thinking of an overdose. Or in front of a rope, thinking of hanging myself, but I never managed to do it because I could always see my mother's face and that was enough to stop me.

I had no friends. No one cared enough for me to actually help me or give me a hand until I learnt that expecting people to care was pointless. I learnt that not everyone feared the bullies but they all feared ending in my place, so they saved only themselves. But even if no one would even look at me and offer me a smile, I still had my parents. And I endured it for as long as I could for them. I started hiding it for them, so they wouldn't see how their daughter kept being bullied. I hid it the best I could so they wouldn't worry and I faked all my smiles.

But that last day I was so consumed by rage that not even the face of my mother could stop me. Not even once I apologised to her.

And if all I did, if hurting and destroying my family like that, was for naught because Diane didn't even see my body, because she isn't even sorry and doesn't live with the weight of her actions, then I need to make it worth it.

When we get in the flat, James is babbling. I can't even understand what he is saying, so I stop him.

"Can we use your computer?" I ask, succeeding at shutting him up. "I need to find Diana and if she's related to Roxi, then she must be on the Internet. All people nowadays are there."

"Don't you want to rest?" he asks and I shake my head.

"I sliced my veins open, one after the other so they wouldn't close and I would surely die. I wrote with my blood so they would see and be disgusted. It had to be my blood so it would have a stronger impact. I doomed my family and my whole existence for this. I'm a ghost now, and I've been stuck for fifteen years because of this," I summarise for him, my voice as cold as you would expect from a murderous ghost. "So no, I don't want to rest. I can't rest until I finish this, James."

There's so much pity and worry in his eyes, but he finally agrees and goes to his computer. Over the past few days we've tried the Internet again so I'm a bit more used to it already, still, he is the one that types and I watch. And now I see him writing Roxi's name and then refining the results until he ends up on her Facebook profile. I've learnt that Facebook is basically all your information exposed for everyone to see and stalk you. On that profile James looks for her relatives and he stops when we see a name I've shared already. Diana Dawson... Roxi's sister.

James follows that link and we are on her profile, to see pictures from when she was a kid, then a teen when I knew her, then an adult after I died. When she got married and had her first kid. We see pictures of her perfect, normal life, and that fills me with even more rage.

How is that she has a perfect life when I am a ghost and broke my family? How is that even fair?

"She needs to be sorry, James. Don't tell me I'm wrong, this has to be my unfinished business. At least her... let me do something about her," I beg, still watching her picture in which she looks so bright and happy, with eyes that don't show any torment in her life. "Please."

I turn to look at him, all my desperation in my voice and I can see the struggle shadowing his expression. I can see the moment he gives up, as well.

"Fine," he agrees. "But I won't let you lose yourself again, Paige. Just be aware of that. I won't let you become the monster."

Chapter 27

"And what do plan on doing?" asks James later that same night.

As how it has become our routine, we lie on his bed, just talking until he falls asleep and I leave to mind my own business. I normally read a book or try to use the computer but that normally fails, so books and many of the graphic novels he has have become my companions when James is asleep. I don't go to his bedroom until he wakes up because watching him sleep is too creepy. I'm a ghost and I know I'm creepy in many ways, but watching him sleep is a whole other level of creepy and I will not cross that line.

"I will not cause her physical harm, if that's what you're worried about," I reply.

I'm still not sure how to feel about James' previous statement. I know what all I've said sounds like, and I'm touched that he cares so much about me as to try to protect me, but at the same time I'm hurt that he thinks I'm capable of such evil. I'm not like the ones that tortured me. I'm not a monster. All I want is a bit of justice, to be sure that they know what they did was horrible, and that somehow they'll try to make amends. Not to me, I'm dead. But maybe to my mother or any other kid at school. Diana has a baby now, I just hope that child will not grow into the kind of bully her mother was.

I just want my retribution. I don't want to kill them.

James looks a bit embarrassed after my snappy reply, he can't even meet my eyes. I sigh and look away, too, trying to collect my thoughts before continuing.

"I know, but—"

"But you still think me capable of it," I complete for him. "You think I'll drive Diana insane until she also kills herself so she can understand what she made me do. Isn't that your fear? Or that I'll coldheartedly kill her because as I'm not human anymore I don't have morals and I don't follow the social laws?"

I sound angrier and angrier as I continue with my rant, I can feel him stirring on the bed so I move away, leaving the mattress and walking towards the window.

"I'm a ghost, not a monster," I mumble next, feeling more hurt than I should.

"I'm not saying that, Paige! Don't say you're not human because ghost or not, you're more human than any other person I've met," he says and I don't have to look to know he's followed me and is standing behind me. "It's just that... the look in your eyes when you remembered, when you were talking about revenge..."

"I was shocked and terrified! How did you expect me to react? With smiles and say 'oh who cares, it's in the past'?" I shout, turning around to glare at him. "I remembered them and remembered how I killed myself. I'm sorry if I can't be happy about it."

"Stop twisting my words, Paige!" he shouts back, his blue eyes are hard and angry now. "You know that's not what I meant. I was just worried."

"Well excuse me if I don't know how to deal with trauma!" I raise my voice even louder, taking a threatening step towards him, but he doesn't retreat.

"Can't you stop? I'm not your enemy!" he shouts back, glaring daggers at me. Frustration wrinkles his face, there's a muscle ticking on his jaw and for a moment I get distracted. Just a second of weakness.

"Then stop acting like that! Stop treating me like I'm the biggest threat. She's a sociopath that drove me to suicide and she's out there. How many more victims are there because of her? Doesn't that worry you?" I retort, trying to make him see the real problem.

"I don't care about her or anyone else right now! I only care about you, Paige. Why don't you understand that?"

His voice, his words resonate around us, surprising me, startling me and making me take a few steps back, until my back hits the windows behind and I'm cornered. James stares at me so intently, breathing heavily. He takes another step towards me, making my heart race and my whole body shake in anticipation.

"I'm not attacking you, Paige. I'm with you," he says, more softly this time. My mind is going crazy, I can't quite process what it's happening now. I'm not afraid of him or anything, but this situation is too much and I do what any other girl would do.

I run.

I dodge his approach and leave the room. I hear him shout my name so I scream back that I need time. I can't face him right now. Arguing is a thing, but this last twist is very different from what we were doing. I could shout and let all my frustration and hurt out with a fight, but when his look changed and his words carried a different meaning, I didn't know what to do. I don't even know what to feel right now, I feel like my head is overheating and I'll collapse any minute.

It's been too much. Too much for any person, or for a ghost. I really do need time. Time to think, collect myself and put things in order. I existed for so long in oblivion, just carrying on without questioning, just pretending. Now the truth comes crushing down, drowning me in the facts of what really happened and how it happened.

It was like an avalanche, all my memories at once, all the horror I had buried so deep it couldn't crush me again. All my feelings raw and burning. I can't deal also with James' own feelings and the implications of these. I don't want to read too much into his words. I don't even want to think of the meaning of that statement.

I need a break.

□□

James and I don't even say a word to one another the next morning. He acts as awkwardly as I feel and every time our eyes meet he blushes. I thank all heavens that I can't blush because otherwise I'd be a permanent tomato with legs and arms walking around.

We head to college in the same awkward silence. Many times I want to say something but I can't make the words come out. I spent all night trying not to think of him and what he said. There are things more important that I need to deal with, like completing my unfinished business so I can finally cross over. Whatever he implied when he shouted that will have to wait.

Once in college and in the Ceramic studio, I see Roxi. I'm immediately reminded of her sister and my revulsion towards the girl grows exponentially. I can't even stand the view and even if they might look different at first sight, it's like I'm seeing Diana. I feel both fear and hatred, twisting my guts and making me want cause pain. But as I told James, I'm not the monster.

James goes to sit where he normally does and instead of staying by his side, I go to Roxi's, who's merrily talking with Adeline. I stand behind the now cherry blossom-haired girl, wanting so desperately to touch her, because I know that'll hurt her. She'll feel all my pain, this agonising sorrow that drove me to suicide. But I don't do that. I know James is watching me closely, I can feel his worried stare, expectant. Even if he says he doesn't think I'm the monster, he is afraid I might turn into one.

Does ghost become monsters? After all, they always star in horror films and books, they are never the main character. They are never good. They scare, they haunt. James has encountered many ghosts in his life, maybe he's seen them turning into monsters or just being that. Didn't he say he didn't like ghosts and he had bad experience with them? Maybe that is the reason why he is looking at me like that.

So instead of touching Roxi I just lean very close and whisper in her ear, "Call Diana. Tell her to come home."

Diana doesn't live in Street anymore, but as I can't leave this town I need her to come here, and the only way to accomplish that is for Roxi to beg her sister to pay the family a visit. Once she does I can meet her.

"Call her. Tell her you want to see your niece... tell her you want to see your sister. Tell her to come home," I insist.

I don't know if this will work because she can't really hear me, but I have to try. My presence can be felt, maybe my intentions can get to her. She seems a bit off when I'm talking to her, even leaving her sentence hanging, but I don't know if she can actually understand what I'm saying. For all I know, she could just hear a murmur or have a bad feeling, like someone's behind her, but that doesn't grant me she is actually listening.

"Text Diana. Do it now. Tell her to come this weekend. Make her come home, Roxi," I insist, barely touching her hair just to make her shiver, not enough to cause her pain. I just need her attention.

"Roxi?" Adeline asks, confused to see the other girl in such a state. But Roxi doesn't react. "What are you looking at?"

Adeline turns around and follows Roxi's stare. She finds James staring back first, his eyes fixed on me, not Roxi, but the black-haired girl can't see that.

"Oh my God, James Black is totally staring at you. You lucky bitch," Adeline says, her words breaking my own concentration. "Ignoring him was the key to draw his attention. You were right," she continues and now I'm frowning.

"He isn't staring at Roxi!" I complain. "Stop assuming things that are so farfetched!"

But Adeline doesn't listen, instead she keeps smirking and now that whatever hold I had on Roxi is broken, the cherry blossom-haired girl is trying to snap back to reality and understanding what's happening. I don't know if she does or if she's just pretending, but her arrogant facade is on.

"Of course. I told you he couldn't resist me," Roxi comments, making my inside twists with repulsion and something else, something dark and bitter that makes me want to push her so she falls off her chair.

Roxi looks at James and instead of smiling or even winking she just flips her hair and ignores him again, treating him as if he wasn't worthy of her time. I really want to smack her.

"By next week I'll have him eating from my hand," Roxi says, that disgusting arrogance dripping from her voice.

I get so angry that she's talking about James like that, treating and seeing him like that. I can't control myself, I pull her hair, making her jerk backwards, almost falling.

"He's not a dog, okay?" I snap, even if she can't hear me. "Do what you should instead of thinking you're the queen of the universe and call your sister. We have unfinished business."

"What happened? Are you okay?" Adeline asks, helping Roxi back to her normal position.

"S-someone pulled my hair," she says, looking back with a furrowed brow, but there's no one she can see there, just me, waving my fingers at her.

Adeline scans around, trying to find whoever did that to her friend, but no one is even paying attention to them. I decide to focus on the black-haired girl now, I even approach her and lean closer to her ear. "Ask Roxi about her sister. Tell her you want to meet her newborn niece."

Adeline seems confused, she blinks, trying to clear her mind, so I touch her hair just like I did with Roxi, making her shiver before I repeat the words.

"Anyhow, Roxi," Adeline says, sounding confused but speaking nonetheless. "How's your sister and her daughter? I saw... pictures on Facebook."

"Oh... she's fine... She hasn't visited us in a while. I should call her. It's unfair we have to go all the time there to see her, don't you think?" Roxi replies and I smirk, glad what I tried is working.

"Yeah, you should. I'd like to meet your niece. She looks pretty," Adeline comments.

Roxi smirks before adding, "That's because she looks just like me when I was a baby. She has a bright future ahead."

"You arrogant bitch," Adeline laughs. "Let me know when she comes to visit. I'll make sure to meet your successor."

"Will do. I'll text her right now," Roxi muses, taking her mobile and I clap.

Yes! It worked. Now all I need to do is wait for Diana to come back into town to finish everything between us. I'll make sure she remembers me and is aware of what she caused. She can't live without that weight in her conscience.

Chapter 28

I 've become a stalker.

No, I'm not proud of it, but what else can I do? I need to know a few things as I wait for Diana to come back to Street. First, I need to know where Roxi lives and when Diana will arrive. So I actually roam around her to hear her conversations, leaving James all alone, but that's actually a nice thing. It's actually a new type of torture to be around Roxi and Adeline a whole day. They are not shallow, they only have moments, but they are so mean. Not like Diana in the sense they attack the person directly, but in a more cowardly way. They talk behind everyone's back, making vicious comments, laughing at almost everyone. More than once I want to slap them for the things they say. I do mess with them a few times, though, when James is not around. Just scaring them, or just hiding their things. Nothing lethal, but enough to give them a headache.

I've tried a few more times saying things to Adeline and Roxi. What I've learnt about that experiment is that I can't exactly be heard or anything, but I can kind of transmit my intention. For some reason, Adeline is more perceptive than Roxi. Most of the time my coaxing doesn't work with the cherry blossom-haired girl, and more often than not it does work with Adeline. I assume it's a thing about mental strength.

I tried making Roxi poke her nose in public, many, many, many times, to no avail. There's no way I can make her do something, but I can bring up certain topics. Like put a seed in their heads and see what happens. Besides making her call Diana to come, nothing else has worked as I expected. I tried to make her think James hates her and to stay away from him. Apparently, all I could transmit was James so they spent about an hour talking about him. I hated that hour. Maybe it was two minutes, but it felt like an hour of torture.

Once I know all I needed, I go back to James. It was all the rest of Thursday and the whole Friday that I spent around Roxi and even if it's been barely twenty-four hours, I've missed James terribly. I can't believe how used I am to be around him. I've naturally forgotten that other people can't listen to me and that whatever I say is just a shout in the void.

I find James in the library. I stop a few steps away, just watching him. He's drawing again, with his headphones on, keeping the world shut out. That is how I met him, when he didn't let anyone in. Somehow he let me in his small bubble. He's let me see his smiles, his caring side. Something no one else has seen, not even his family because they've turned their backs on him, too.

I want to go up to him and hug him so tight from behind, to wrap my arms tightly around his waist, resting my chin on his shoulder, letting our cheeks touch. I want to comfort this lonely boy, but I can't do that. For as long as I keep carrying this sorrow with me I can't touch him.

I think another big reason why I want to finish this deal with Diana is so I can get rid of these dark feelings. To leave them behind so I can finally touch him, hug him, without letting him experience the pain I live with. It's okay if it's cold, but I don't want it to be painful.

Although I'm dying to hug him, I just walk up to him and sit on the table, next to him. The moment he sees me there his smile is automatic, the sparkle in his eyes comes back. He looks happy.

"Had fun with Roxi?" he asks me and I roll my eyes.

"The time of my life and no-life," I reply, making him chuckle. "She's bully just like Diana. The only difference is that she does it from behind. Not sure what's worse," I muse and James seems to ponder.

"I think Roxi's way hurts less, but it's equally low," he comments and I have to agree. "So, did you find out all you wanted?"

"Yup. Diana arrives tomorrow, but she can't come with her husband or child, saying it's too soon for the baby to travel," I reply, kicking my legs in a very childish way.

"And what are you gonna do then?"

"I'm not sure yet. I'll figure it out when I see her. I was thinking of going at night, sneak in the house and find her. I won't just scare her, I don't want that. Or maybe I'll make sure she knows it's me, that I'm hunting her. Maybe the fear will make her apologise, don't you think?"

James nods. "You're good at scaring people," he comments and I give him a bright, happy smile, and a peace sign.

"The best ghost around. I should get a medal or something."

James laughs and shakes his head, but we leave the topic there. He just goes back to drawing and I watch him calmly. That's how the rest of the day goes by, in our normal routine and the same for Saturday. Although as the sun goes down that day, I get more anxious. We've checked on Facebook and know Diana is already in town. Which means I'll be done with this soon. I'll complete my unfinished business and be able cross over, finally, after fifteen years of just wandering, repeating the same routine over and over again.

It'll be done. I'll be done with this life.

I can barely hold my own anxiety when James and I head to Roxi's house. I can feel James' own nerves and fears, I know it by the way his eyes watch me so carefully and that little crease between his brows, telling me about all his worries. But I can't really focus on that when I'm so close to finish this. I'm both eager and terrified because I can't be sure of what comes next, but I know I'll finally put this chapter behind.

An apology. That's all I want. An honest and wholeheartedly apology. I need to know she regrets what she did. If I can get that, then I'm sure I can move on.

"We're here," I announce. James stops, watching the big house that seems so carefully taken care of. I wouldn't believe such poisonous people live in there if it weren't because I followed Roxi here.

"I'll be waiting for you here once you're done. Be careful, Paige. And whatever happens, whatever you feel, remember you're better than them, okay?" James advises me and I nod. I need to keep that in mind.

I will not lose myself. I won't let his fears come true. I need to hold on to that. If not for me, for James. I can't let my mind forget there are people out there who actually care about me. If I do that, like when I killed myself, then I'll really become a monster.

James eyes are so intense on me, so apprehensive and wary. He takes a step closer and my breath gets caught in my throat, but I don't move, even when he leans closer. I freeze when his hands grab my face and that same shock helps to keep all my other feelings at bay, controlled some-how. He then leans forward, his lips finding my forehead for the briefest moment before I'm released from his hold. I'm left there, blinking quickly, with a racing heart and slightly shaking hands.

"Good luck and come back to me, okay?" he says but I can't reply, I just nod.

James takes a few more steps back, giving me the space I need to collect myself and remember why I'm here. I nod to myself and take deep breaths before turning around and focusing on entering the house. I'll have to do something I hate, something that hurts, but it's the best way to do it.

I let go of the grip of my own energy and matter, until I lose my body and can walk through the door. It hurts, but I can control it because I'm doing this consciously and it's just through inanimate matter. When I walk through people it's normally unexpected and I can't really prepare myself, so I am never ready for the pain. It surprises and consumes me.

Once inside I hear the telly so I go there to find two old people watching a film together. I assume they are Diana's parents and I want to throw cushions at them. How can people actually raise kids like Diana, who actually torture the weak as a form of amusement? How can they fail that much as parents? But I don't throw cushions at them, I just walk up to them and blow air to their napes, scaring the living days out of them.

This whole family is toxic. I hate them all.

I run upstairs, looking for Diana. I don't find Roxi although I do walk into her room. I assume she's out, partying with her friends. So I keep looking for my nemesis and after a few more doors I find her in front of a laptop, typing with the ease of an expert. I stand behind her just to see her writing what looks like an article. On her Facebook it said she works for a magazine, maybe she's writing for it.

"Diana," I call, my hand brushing her hair. That makes her stop, a shiver running down her spin.

The rage in, all that hatred that has consumed me for so long roars to life, consuming me and I have to actually fight to remember to stop it from taking control over me. A part of me wants to hurt her so bad. I could do that. I could grab her and throw her against a wall. Do to her the same things she did to me, give her the same bruises she left on my own skin. But I won't do that.

"James," I whisper to myself, calling the boy that isn't with me now. "I won't hurt her like she deserves because of you."

Instead, I keep brushing her hair, alerting her of my presence somehow. She isn't alone anymore.

"Diana... do you remember me?" I talk in her hear, making her shiver more violently.

She turns in her chair, eyes wide and scared. I take a few steps back when I see that face fifteen years older now, as old as I should be if I hadn't died when I was just seventeen. Those same eyes that tormented me for years. The same eyes that hunted my nightmares and that I feared so much, but at the same time hated with a burning passion. I see her eyes and I want to make her cry and beg for forgiveness. I want to destroy her completely.

I start shaking, my mind going numb, my vision getting blurry and it's getting harder to remember why I shouldn't kill her right now. She killed my soul, it's the least I could do.

An eye for an eye, a tooth for a tooth.

But there's still a little voice in my head telling me no, to stop, to control this. I'm not Diana, I will not lower myself to her level. So I close my eyes, I don't want to see her because if I do then I won't be able to listen to that little voice anymore. So, with my eyes still closed, I approach her, carefully walking towards her chair. It's just three steps until I feel her. Her energy colliding with mine. I open my eyes then, just to see her shivering.

"You killed me, Diana," I say. "You pushed me. Over and over again, you told me to kill myself. And I did, your words got to me, you see? Look at me now. LOOK AT ME!" I shout, grabbing her shoulders and pinning her against the chair. She screams, all colour drained from her face. "Look at what I did for you!"

Tears start falling from her eyes and I know why. She's feeling my pain because my head is plagued with the memories of my last day. All that hurt and hatred, all that numbness that made me slice open my veins. She's feeling all that now. She's feeling my emotions.

"Did you even see my body? The message I left for you... Because I did it, Diana. For you and all your friends, I did it," I continue, my own hands sneaking up, cupping her face. She's breathing hard, her whole body shaking violently.

"P-Paige," she breathes out, barely a whisper.

"That's right. It's me... I'm here, making you sure you don't forget me. You've carried on with your life and I lost mine. Is that fair? And you didn't take only my life, you also took my family. Have you thought about that!? Do you even feel sorry about what you did!?" I keep shouting, holding her face even tighter, my own hands shaking with my own pain and sorrow.

I think of my mother, of her hollow shell that has been existing for fifteen years. I think of a father I can barely remember by now. A father that left my broken mother to suffer on her own. All because this girl couldn't leave me alone.

"You made me kill myself, Diana. Your hand guided mine as I pierced my flesh. It was you," I tell her, practically pressing our foreheads together. "Do you even feel guilty?"

"I'm sorry..." she says. "I'm sorry, Paige. It's you, isn't it? You finally came for me. I'm sorry," she cries and even if she's saying those words I'm not okay. It doesn't fix anything. "I'm so sorry. Please... don't kill me."

I let her go, I release her as if her skin were burning me. She falls off her chair, ending like a sobbing mess on the floor. I watch her, feeling, for the first time, pity for her. For this murderer who drove me insane. As she keeps crying, I only feel cold. She apologised, she's sorry, she cries and she is scared. She felt all my pain, I made her know... but I'm still here. I'm still dead. My family is still broken.

I go to her desk, grab a piece of paper and a pen and write my address. Below that, with big letters I wrote 'apologise,' and throw it at her. She grabs it in her shaky hands and reads it.

"I-I-I will. I'm sorry, Paige. I really am. Don't take me with you. I was stupid, and immature. I never thought you... I'm sorry."

"I hope you don't fail as a parent like yours did. I hope your daughter doesn't make your same mistakes. I hope you realise how horrible you are and will always be."

And with that, I turn around and leave, feeling as heavy as when I walked in. Feeling my emotions choking me because her apology didn't change anything.

I made her feel, I made her cry, I scared her... but I only feel worse.

Where did I go wrong, then?

Chapter 29

I slowly walk towards the spot I left James at, feeling heavier with every step I take. I can only see Diana's terrified face, the tears streaming down her face. She was just scared, I don't even know if she really regretted what she did. She said sorry because she was afraid I would kill her. Maybe she lives with that fear, I can't know, but the thought doesn't comfort me. Even if her soul is eternally tortured, that doesn't soothe my pain. That doesn't change anything and noticing that now makes me feel worse.

I was so certain this was it. Making her pay, making her know I was still here and didn't forget what she did... but that didn't change anything. If that was my unfinished business, this wasn't the way to fulfil it.

I have no idea what to do now. Where to go. I was wrong and I'm even more lost now. Seeing Diana in such pain, feeling my own agony didn't give me any sort of peace. How... how can some people enjoy torturing others? How could she enjoy seeing me cry? How could she find amusement in pushing me, hitting me, humiliating me? Where is the pleasure in bullying someone else?

I see James standing there, watching the house as if he expected it to burst in flames any moment. Or maybe he is just waiting to see where I come from, because the moment his eyes find me his smile widens, his eyes sparkle and he breaks in a jogging to catch with me. But as he draws closer he notices my expression, he reads all my emotions and his own face mirrors mine.

"What happened?"

"I did it," I say. "I found her and I was so angry. I wanted to harm her do badly, but I didn't. I did touch her so she could feel my pain. She knew it was me. She said she knew I'd come for her one day. She cried and said sorry... but nothing changed." My voice breaks, more than frustration I feel disappointed and confused because I'm once again back to where I began. But I lost all direction now.

"Oh Paige," he laments, his own voice as broken as I feel now.

I want to cry. I want to sob and whine and just let it all out. But it's stuck inside of me, stuck forever, just like I am.

"I gave her my Mum's address and told her to go apologise to her. She can at least do that now that she's in town."

"That's a good idea," James points out and I just heave an exhausted sigh.

"I think I should give up on this whole unfinished business and just worry about Mum until the end. Can we go to my house and check on her? I've been so busy with this that I don't even feel drawn to there anymore," I say and he nods immediately.

"Yes, let's do that. In all honesty, you sound more regretful about her than anything else," he comments as I walk past him heading towards my old house.

"That's because it's my fault how she ended up. I feel so sorry to her. And if I'm stuck here to repent for what I did to her, then that would be fair and I should stop trying to escape my punishment," I muse and I hear James' steps cease.

"Don't say that, Paige. Don't become a martyr."

"Whatever," I mutter next, defeated. I can't even think of being positive or pushing away all my own sorrows, I don't have the energy. I can only see Diana crying, and as the seconds go by I feel more remorseful for falling so low as to torture her. I went to her house with the intent to cause pain, thinking that would give me peace.

How could I be so stupid?

For the rest of the way we don't say anything else. I try to focus on James' steps by my side, the constant rhythm of his boots against the concrete. It seems like three lifespans go by before we reach even my neighbourhood. And once we are there I stop thinking of all those conflictive thoughts or anything else. I can only see the commotion around.

Firetrucks and an ambulance, neighbours watching, in their pyjamas, wrapped in blankets and gathering around, whispering to one another. I feel dread consuming me, I'm not even able to take another step. I notice the smoke coming out and it takes me a while to understand that there was a fire.

Everything gets blurry around me because I cant see any-thing else. I'm just looking ahead, to where my house should be, and the firemen coming out. I don't care about all the people whispering and watching as if this were some circus exhibition.

"You think it was intentional?" I hear, somehow the words carried with the wind to my ears.

"No. The firemen said it was an accident. It seems she left the the iron on," I hear again. Whispers carried by the night wind, chilling me.

I start shaking, fear and horror taking control over me. All my selfish worries vanish because I can only think of my mum. Where is she now? Did they take her to the hospital already? To what hospital? What will happen next?

I don't realise how I start running until I'm in front of a burnt house. Smoke is coming out from every corner, but the flames have disappeared already, completely extinguished. Then it means it happened a while ago. My house caught in fire and I wasn't even aware of it. I was too busy seeking revenge to be around to stop this. Mum always left the iron on but it was me the one that unplugged it, making sure an accident like this wouldn't happen. But I wasn't around this time... now the house is lost.

"M-mum," I breathe out, my voice so shaky even if it's such a small word. "Mum... where are you?"

In that exact moment I see another group of firemen, these carrying a stretcher with them and it looks like they've got something on it, but it's covered. Mum is walking beside them and the relief I feel is so strong my knees give out.

"Mum. Oh dear God, Mum," I cry out, my hands trembling as I touch my mouth, covering it.

But then my Mum's head snaps towards me, as if she heard me. Her eyes widen and I freeze again because it seems she is seeing me here on the cold hard ground.

"Oh shit," I hear someone from behind. James, I realise. He's standing behind me.

"Paige?" Mum says before I can even think she's just watching James. "Is that you, Paige?" she asks again and I can't even blink.

Mum can see me... she can see me now. She's calling my name, her eyes are meeting mine. Why can she see me now?

She stays behind whilst the firemen keep walking, and then she takes a step towards me, and then another, never ceasing to call my name. In the background there's a cacophony that sounds muffled, a small sign that the world keeps going on around, but I can't focus on anything else but my mum walking towards me.

"It is you, my baby. Paige... why are you here? Paige!" she cries out, running towards me, kneeling in front of me and grabbing me in her arms next, pulling me towards her.

It's electricity, just energy and nothing else. It's not like when James touches me and she doesn't seem to be in any sort of pain. She's not crying or shaking, she's just hugging me tighter as she keeps repeating my name. But I can't react, I can't even hug her back because my mind is working so hard to understand what's happening. I think I already know why this can be possible now, but I'm still trying to deny it. I don't want to believe this.

But my mum is finally hugging me, she can see me, and once again I'm in her arms.

"Mum," I whine, finally hugging her back.

"My girl, my baby girl," she does the same and I can't stop shaking. "Where have you been all this time? Why did you leave me?"

"I'm sorry, Mum. I'm so sorry," I beg, hugging her as tight as I can. "I'm sorry for what I did, Mum. I should've... I should've thought of you. I should've stopped."

"It doesn't matter now, you're here," she says, pulling back to just look at me. Her hands cup my face, fingers brushing my hair and her eyes looking at me with so much love. There's no resentment, even after what I did to her, she never blamed me. "We are together now. It'll be all fine. We'll find a new house and we'll be okay," she promises me. The lump in my throat is choking me.

She doesn't know. She hasn't seen the police and forensic team, the firemen carrying what now I realise was her body. She thinks she's still alive but she isn't... she's a ghost just like me.

"We can't," I breath out, confusing her. "Mum you... in the fire... I'm a ghost, mum. I'm not alive," I let out, not exactly making sense but trying to make her understand. "And now you..."

"What?"

"I'm sorry, Mum. I'm so sorry! I should've been here, making sure this didn't happen. I had to protect you. I'm so sorry!" I cry out again, but my mums shakes her head.

"No. How can you be dead? I'm seeing you, I'm touching you," she protests, shaking her head more firmly.

Why can't I cry right now? Why?

"I've been dead for fifteen years. You know that. You had my ashes with you. I'm sorry, Mum. I should've saved you from this fire."

Mum freezes, then looks around, taking into notice everything that's happening around. She sees how no one is paying us attention, despite what is happening between us. No one is actually dragging her to an ambulance or anything, despite she was in a fire. I think just now she realises she doesn't even feel dizzy or anything. She's not even dirty. She's perfect. And a person who was in a fire can't look like that.

"Mum," I breath out, feeling terrible for not saving her. I had to save her. That was my mistake, to be focused on seeking a pointless revenge instead of looking after her. Why do I keep making her suffer like this? Why can't I do anything good for my mum? "I'm sorry."

"No," she says. "You don't have anything to be sorry about. It's not your fault," she says. I want to refute, to tell her it is my fault. To beg for forgiveness. "Nothing is your fault. It is mine. I should've taken you away from that place the first time you came home with that broken look in your eyes. I should've taken you away from this town when kids didn't stop bothering you. A mother is supposed to protect! I didn't protect you. It was my fault, Paige. I should've heard the truth behind every time you lied saying you were fine. Please, forgive me, my girl. I should've protected you from all those other kids. I'm so sorry," she is the one begging now, stroking my hair, cupping my cheeks and smiling so sadly. "I'm so sorry."

I shake my head now. "It wasn't your fault, Mum. Don't... You did all what you could. You always loved me."

"I'll always love you, my girl," she corrects me and the desire to cry is breaking me.

"I love you, Mum."

Her smile is sad and broken, but it's a smile, and for the first time in so many years, she looks alive. She looks like the women I remember, the one that hugged me and told me things would get better in the future. She's the one I tried to protect by hiding the magnitude of what was happening. This is my Mum.

Someone else approaches us, but then I notice it's not someone. It's just... a blur. It has the shape of a person, but nothing can be distinguished. There's no face or hands, just a blurry image of what a person should be. That thing approaches us and stops behind Mum. It doesn't say anything, but Mum tenses, as if she knew.

Then it's hand is on her shoulder. Mum faces relaxes, her whole body language changes.

"I have to go," she says and I panic. She rises to her feet and I do the same, the thing behind her never breaking the contact. "I'm done here."

"But I can't... not yet," I whisper and she nods.

She knows now. Her expression has changed, it shows a serenity that avoided her for so long. She looks as if everything is sorted out and her smile is a reassuring one.

"But you're not alone." She looks at James who is still behind us, giving us space. "Take care of her. She isn't done here, yet."

"I will," he says. I can feel him closer to me now, right behind me.

"Paige," Mum speaks to me again. "Don't worry. Everything will be sorted out when it has to be. Your time on this realm isn't over yet," she explains.

"Why am I here? Mum, answer me that before leaving, please."

"You died before you had to. You have to fulfil your time here before crossing over. You need to learn your lessons first, only then we will meet again," she tells me with her reassuring smile, her motherly one. "For taking your own life you soul has been punished to stay on this realm, alone, until you learn your lesson. Here but not quite," she continues. "Only when your soul learns the lessons you were supposed in this life, you will be forgiven and admitted where you belong."

"We'll meet again?"

"Of course we'll do, my girl. And it'll be forever then," she replies, cupping my face once again. "And even then, it'll depend on you. It's always your choice."

"I'll meet you again," I blurt out. "I'll learn my lessons and I'll cross over. We'll be together again."

"Yes, we will," she smiles at me once again. "Until then, My girl. Thank you for staying by my side all these years. I knew you were there."

"That harmed you more," I mutter but she shakes hear head.

"Thank you, Paige, for never really leaving me. I'll see you again," she bids her goodbye, smiling one last time and kissing my cheek. "I love you, my girl."

"I love you, Mum," I reply. I hear a little meow bellow and find Luna, rubbing herself against Mum's legs.

"Time to go, little Luna," she says, grabbing her in her arms. "Say by to Paige."

My eyes widen in horror, realising what this means. Luna meows to me and with a shaking hand, I pet her head one last time. She purrs and I start shaking.

"Bye, Luna. Thank you for being with me all this time," I say.

The thing behind Mum takes a step back this time. Mum turns around with Luna in her arms and starts walking away. I stay where I am, watching her retreating figure that gets blurrier with every step she takes away till she's as blurry as the being by her side. Eventually, they disappear. I can't even say a word, it's all stuck in my throat. My mind can't even process what's happened.

"Mum," is all I can say, a broken and pitiful cry that reflects the shattered pieces of my heart and soul. "Mum..."

Chapter 30

I 'm not sure how I get back to James' flat. Whether he dragged me or I followed him, I don't know. I just know we are here when James says so. That is the moment my knees give out and I end up on the floor. I can't cry, I don't even shake, I just stay there, numb.

Is this how my mum felt during fifteen years? Did she live like this?

"Mum," I whisper once again, my heart breaking at the thought she's gone, I couldn't save her. It's all my fault, now she's dead because I lost focus of what matters most.

If I... If I had been home instead of seeking for Diana this wouldn't have happened. And what did I get from scaring her? I didn't really fulfil my unfinished business, I can't even go with Mum to wherever this different realm is. She's gone, forever. And I'm still here.

I know she said it wasn't my fault. I remember how she thanked me for being by her side. But that doesn't take all the guilt away, all the sorrow because I've lost my mother. And I know the irony of being like this when a part of me should be happy that my mum could see me, that we are the same now. But no, it's not the same. I'm a soul that's being held for killing herself before her due time, whereas my mum is a soul that left to rest already because she did nothing wrong. I can't even see her anymore. I've lost her the same as any living person loses a loved one. The same way she lost me fifteen years ago... at my own hands.

I cover my face with my hands, looking almost as someone who is crying, but no tears can come out. Yet I'm sobbing, my shoulders shake and I can't breathe, I whine and let all my feelings our of every sob, even if these are dry ones.

"Mum, I'm so sorry... Mum... together, we should be together."

What can I do? How do I follow her when it's not my time? She gave me answers no one else could, but these only add up to the sorrow burning my soul out.

"Agh, fuck this," I hear James' curse, breaking through my own mourning and giving me the enough time to look up and see the moment his hands reach out for me, his arms wrapping around my frame and pulling me towards him.

I freeze, the knowledge of what this is causing him the most important thing on my mind right now, like an alarm going off, telling me to take care of this first.

"No, don't do this. No!" I protest, trying to escape but his grip is made of iron.

"No, let me do this... let me do this much for you. Let me help you somehow," he says, his voice tense because it's clear he's clenching his jaw. "Don't feel it on your own, Paige. I'm here with you. Share your pain and don't force me to just watch you. I can't do that. Let me at least shed the tears you can't."

I stop struggling, not knowing what to do. I want to spare him this because hurting him is the worst I could do, but I need him so much. Someone to hold me because I'm in pieces and I'm afraid I will just fade away if I don't have his arms around me.

"You're hurting," I protest.

"I can endure it... for you," he replies stubbornly, burying his face in my hair, his mouth next to my ear, his words being whispered right there. "Leaving you alone right now would hurt me more."

I give up. I can't fight him anymore, so I wrap my own arms around his neck, clinging to him for dear life and letting him hold me in one piece. I keep sobbing in his arms but the tears fall from his eyes. The same pain I'm feeling is the one he's experiencing, we are sharing my own agony and even if it's painful, it isn't lonely.

I squeeze the fabric of his hoodie in my fists, hiding my own face in his neck. His hands rub my back and his breathing moves my hair. It's ragged and hard, it speaks of pain and sorrow, but at the same time it's the most comforting thing someone could do. I don't know what I would've done if James hadn't been next to me. I don't think I would be able to keep a hold of my own mind without him next to me.

I don't know for how long we stay like this and I can't tell it gets better because everything in me hurts and I can't even call my mother's name without breaking all over again, but I stop shaking and even James' breathing becomes more regular. Either I've calmed down or he's gotten better at enduring and controlling the pain. Just like I have. At the end of the day, a person can always learn to live with the pain and heartbreak. It hurts, it's hard, but not impossible. That's how we survive, we adapt.

"Feeling better?" he asks at some point but he never looses up his hold on me. We are still on the floor and I'm on his lap, curling next to him. Although my body can't hurt, his probably does.

"No," I reply honestly. "I don't think I can ever feel better about this. It was my fault, James," I blurt out, still hiding my face in his neck. "I was so busy seeking revenge that I even forgot about my mum. I left her all alone and couldn't stop this stupid accident to happen. If I had been there she wouldn't be dead now. It's all my fault!"

"No, no, Paige. It's not your fault. Didn't you hear? It was her time, that's why she could cross over. If it hadn't been that accident, it would've been another. You couldn't follow her and save her from everything. It was her time, and I'm sure the reason why you two could meet one last time was because she needed to apologise to you, face to face. She lived with that guilt that she could't save you. You can't do the same."

"How can I not?" I snap, pulling back to glare at him. "How can I not feel guilty about this?"

"Because one can't control death and accidents happen. It was her time and yours will come, but it isn't now," he insists, cupping my face in his hands and looking at me with such sweet eyes, so caring and loving. "It's not your fault and I'll repeat that until you believe it. If it's up to me, I won't let you live like that."

"I'm not living," I tell him, and my voice is so sour. He even cringes.

"You are, unconventionally, but you're still here. In my book, you're living."

There's a lump in my throat and I don't know how to answer to that, I just stare back at him, into those blue eyes that look at me like no one else did before. My own hands reach to cup his cheeks, barely touching his skin. He shivers and closes his eyes in an attempt to control the pain I bring with me. Yes, he's enduring it, but that doesn't mean it's not really painful. My heart breaks even more because I want to touch him without hurting him. I want to control my emotions and make him feel nothing but my gratitude, and every other happy emotion he makes me feel. I want to let him know it's not all agony or pain in me, there's more. But I don't know how to do that. All my feelings are so raw and I can't refine them.

"You're like an angel sent to me," I mutter. Cheesy as that sounds, it's true. There's no better way to express what he is to me, how much he's helped me.

"But I don't have wings," he says with a small smile.

"Wingless angel. No one said you're perfect." I try to smile, too. "Even angels can come faulty."

He chuckles softly, and then presses his forehead against mine. His hands sneak to the back of my head, his fingers buried in my hair, stroking softly, sending shivers down my spine.

"I should've stuck with the angel theory," I mumble next, causing his chuckles to cease.

"Pardon?"

"When you came here there were a bunch of theories, remember? My favourite was the werewolf one, but now that I think back, I should've bet my fortune on the angel theory, even if it was fallen angel," I explain and he laughs again.

"You bet your fortune?"

"No, it's just a way to speaking, don't be silly," I reply, even rolling my eyes and making him laugh even more.

"I really like your sense of humour. I love that it's so out of the blue," he confesses and his voice is so soft and careful, carrying more meaning than the one I dare to read. "I love that despite everything you can still joke and laugh. That no matter how hard your life was, you can still smile, even if it means you have to block the dark memories." I gulp, thinking how to reply to that, a thank seems too poor and I need to find something better. "I love that despite what they did to you, you didn't lose yourself. I love than even in death you care more about your mother and couldn't leave her on her own. I love how you smile, laugh. I love the way you look when you talk about your mother and how much you love her. I love that you even try to take all the blame."

He stops talking to take a deep breath, he even closes his eyes for a few seconds before he pulls back a bit so he can look me in the eyes more comfortably this time.

"I know you're a ghost yet it's so easy to forget you're not like me. It hurts me helping you to find your unfinished business because I don't want you to leave me. I don't care about anyone leaving and turning their back on me, but it scares me if it's you. If I can't see you ever again." He stops once again, just staring into my eyes. I can't do anything else but stare back. I can't even take a breath, which makes me very thankful that I don't need to. "And I know you won't ever be older than seventeen, I know you can't grow older with me, but I wish you could. I wish you could stay always by my side even if it means we'll never leave this flat. I selfishly want to keep you next to me and I'm sorry I'm telling you all this, but it's the truth."

His breathing gets heavier and he looks tense, almost scared, but at the same time certain. His eyes are sure and determined.

"Paige, crazy as it is, this is how I really feel." He takes another deep breath and continues. "I love you. Crazy, impossible and painful as it is, I love you."

My eyes widen and my breath gets caught in my throat. My own hands fall from his face, ending on his chest just because we're so close, but aside from that I can't move. I can see the fear in his eyes but there's also relief, like he's finally free from a heavy weight on his shoulders.

Love... the word echoes in my mind, pushing aside everything else just to play on repeat.

I love you.

James loves me, impossible, crazy and painful as it is, he loves me, and as I start to process the words, understanding what he just did, happiness starts bubbling inside. I can't really think of the consequences right now or how impossible it is. I can't think of anything else but the fact he loves me. And even if a part of me suspected this, it is different to hear the words, to be certain about it.

It's not only that someone loves me, it's that James loves me. If it were other hundred guys feeling like that, none of them would make me as happy as James does. If the rest of the world hates me I don't care because James loves me. Just me.

He starts smiling, the signs of pain leaving his features because he can feel my own happiness. Just how he felt the horrors he now feels this bubbling happiness, he can feel my own love bursting out of every part of my soul, burning in there like a fire. He feels it and it doesn't hurt him, it makes him happy, as well. So I hold on to that feeling, I won't let it go for as long as I can.

He presses his forehead against mine, his nose brushing mine as I squeeze in my fists the fabric of his hoodie, my right hand feeling the strong heartbeats as he leans closer and closer. I close my eyes because he's just too near I can't see anything but his blurry face.

It's soft at first, his lips barely touching mine, but they are there, testing. It tingles, everything tingles in me and the feelings that swirl in me are all happy, exhilarating ones. The same feelings he is experiencing now and that must be enough for him to decide it's safe. This works.

He kisses me, his lips really crushing against mine and although I have no idea what to do, I enjoy this. The warmth I can finally feel and all this happiness soothing the pain, the loneliness that's living within me for so long. I follow what he's doing it, imitating his own movements until we can match and make it work, until the kiss becomes a real one.

His arms wrap around me once again, pulling me even closer, almost crushing me against him as he depends the kiss and I give in, forgetting everything else but this moment. These feelings. This boy. This love.

Chapter 31

I pull back when I feel James shivering. Even if it feels warm and like being alive when I'm in his arms, it's not the same for him. Maybe it isn't painful right now, but it's cold. He doesn't let me retract much, though, still prisoner in his arms. He looks at me with soft caring eyes and a lazy smile. He looks happy and for a second that makes me forget that his face looks paler than usual and his lips have a bluish tone. He is really cold, it's almost as if I have stolen his warmth.

"You're cold," I state the obvious.

"Well, kissing a ghost has its drawbacks. It can't be all rainbows and unicorns," he teases, pecking my lips as if a way to reinforce his statement. "That was quite the experience."

"I'm sorry," I apologise, even trying to pull back but he doesn't let me.

"I didn't mean it in a bad way, Paige. Don't apologise. It was just... different." He chuckles and I see his cheeks blushing, bringing a bit of colour to his face. "I thought about this a lot, I must confess. Like, I realised my feelings a while back and I wasn't sure what could happen. I didn't even know if I could kiss you. I'm glad I can." He cups my face in his right hand, looking at me with such warm eyes. "It's so easy to forget you are... a ghost, 'cos you feel so real in my arms. I know that if anyone could see us would think I'm crazy or schizophrenic, but it feels so real and tangible. Just a bit cold. Next time I'll kiss you by the fire, and away from everyone else so I'm not sent to the asylum.."

I'm once again thankful I can't blush because I'm certainly feeling embarrassed right now. He says 'next time' so naturally and I'm not sure how to react to that. The weight of these events hasn't even fully sinked in yet, and I'm scared of how overwhelming that might be. Love or any sort of relationship is something I never contemplated before, not even when I was alive and now that I'm dead I have no idea how that might work out. Can it even work out?

"Hey, look at me," James says, breaking through my train of thoughts, probably feeling the change in my emotions. "Calm down, don't freak out. We'll take this slowly. There's nothing to be afraid of."

"Nothing? How can you say that?' I snap, tensing and surprising him. "I'm a ghost and you're human. I don't exist for anyone else but you. How can you not be scared of that? What's even the point of something that is impossible? And I have to cross over, I can't stay here forever, watching you grow older until you also die and leave me behind."

"Paige, please, calm down. We'll think about that later. Just stay with me on this moment and we'll figure out the future later on. I'll still help you fulfil your unfinished business, and to cross over even if that means breaking my own heart. But I don't want to lose this moment for that."

Even if I can't feel his emotions like he feels mine, I can read the sincerity and desperation in his voice. So I calm down for him, pushing aside all my worries and fears. I try to ignore the dark emotions that still lurk in my head, emotions that will only hurt him. Instead, I focus on being in his arms and what I feel for him. What he makes me feel. I let him comfort me. I need to have a better control of my own emotions if I hope to stay by his side a little while more.

But he soon shivers more constantly and I know I have to break the embrace. Even if he tries to stop me, he's too cold to offer more resistance so I win. I go to his room and look for blankets to wrap around him. I also prepare hot chocolate and turn up the heating system for him. I sit next to him but without touching him, just waiting until he warms up again.

Without his arms around me and his breathing in my neck my walls crumble down and everything comes back at me with the strength of a tsunami, the waves of angst and sorrow swallowing me from within. It's not only the hatred, loneliness and pain I died with, it's also the disappointment for seeking a wrong path and leaving my Mum to die alone. It's the heartbreaking agony of losing my mum, knowing I won't see her until I solve my business here, until I learn whatever experience and lesson my soul was supposed to. I wonder what would happen if I don't do anything at all, if I wait... will I stay for as long as I was supposed to live? If I was supposed to live until I was, for instance, eighty-five, then that means I'd have to stay for another fifty-three years. Another fifty-three years just like this. Here but not quite.

I don't think I can endure that.

I don't even know if the whole concept of heaven and hell exist, but I'm inclined to believe hell is the world we live in and being trapped here as a ghost is the worst kind pf punishment.

I'm so happy Mum didn't have to go through that. So happy she crossed over immediately even if it means I might never see her again. I would never want her to exist like this, even if we were together. Being stuck is a torture, not being able to move on like everyone else around, not being able to be part of the world you once belonged to.

"I'm so glad you moved here, James," I say, being completely honest. I wouldn't have anyone to talk if it weren't for him, I wouldn't even remember what happened and I would've ended all by my self when my mum's time arrived. I wouldn't have had anyone to hold me and tell me it wasn't my fault.

"I'm glad I moved here and I met you. I'm glad you nagged me and never left me alone at first," he laughs.

"I was really annoying, wasn't I?" I ask, looking at him. We are still in the living room of his flat, with our backs resting on the sofa but still sitting on the floor instead of on the very sofa.

"A bit," he chuckles. "But I grew fond of your babbling. It was so quiet when you weren't around. I missed you immediately. I thought I had gone crazy for missing a ghost."

"I'm like mould: I grow on you without noticing."

James laughs and grimaces at the same time. "That's disgusting but accurate. You're really one of a kind."

"If it weren't because you've met many other ghosts I'd say it's because I'm dead, but you ruined that pun." He still laughs though, so I guess it doesn't matter. "I know you don't like much talking about the past, but can you tell me a bit more about your experiences with other ghosts? I don't know if it'l help but I'd like to know more about you, as well. I feel like we've only focused on my unfinished business."

"Is there something in particular you'd like to know?" he asks me and I give it a though.

"What did they exactly did to you to hate ghosts?" I ask, because that's been on my mind since the beginning. "You said they hurt you."

James rounds his shoulder, sinking deeper in the cocoon of blankets I made for him. His expression turns serious and I guess it is because he's reminiscing the past, looking for those memories he surely doesn't like thinking about. I feel bad for asking him this, for causing him this kind of pain, but I also think its good if he tells someone else about this, someone who doesn't think him crazy for seeing ghosts.

"They are always lonely so the moment they figure out someone can hear them, they become obsessive. Some weren't that difficult, especially when I was a kid. They probably knew I couldn't do much for them and they just wanted to talk. I met kid ghosts and they just wanted to play or find their parents. Once I met a kid ghost who wouldn't stop crying because he couldn't find his parents. He followed me home, crying the whole time. I couldn't sleep or concentrate. I was fourteen by then," he explains and I know I should worry more about James, show my sympathy for him, but I can't.

Why was a kid stuck as a ghost? I doubt he killed himself so maybe he was killed, without his parents. Maybe he died crying, terrified, and my heart breaks when I imagine that. I wonder if that kid found his parents or if he is still crying somewhere.

"Because I couldn't concentrate or sleep or eat, I had to move. I literally ran away."

I know I shouldn't feel disappointed in James for what he did, for abandoning that child, but I can't help it. I don't know if I could've ever done that, I would've probably stayed with that kid, trying to stop him from crying and helped him find his parents again. But maybe that's my sympathy because I'm just like that child.

"Every time I moved it was because a ghost. They don't tend to be violent, but some are. Vicious even." I get chills going down my spine when he says that. "I was probably nine or eight when I saw something I should've ignored. I was playing outside and noticed a man following a person. I'm not sure what made me notice him, or even throw a rock at him. Maybe it was the way he looked or something. The rock went through him, but that alerted him of my presence." He stops for a moment to take a breath before continuing. "I remember his smirk, the eyes and the fear I felt. I ran but he followed me. I screamed and kept running, and I guess people just thought I was crying because I hurt myself or something, 'cos no one helped me or they didn't have time to help me. The ghost grabbed me and threw me to the street when a car was coming. Thank goodness the driver reacted fast and hit the break, otherwise I wouldn't be telling this story now."

"Oh my God!" I gasp, covering my mouth with my hands in shock and horror.

"I got a few broken bones, bruises and an internal bleeding, but I survived. I was in the hospital for a few days and believe me, that's the worst place for someone who can see ghosts. I avoid them the best I can since then."

"That's horrible, James. I'm so sorry," I say although it wasn't my fault, but it was by one of my kind.

"That was probably the worst experience, that ghost really wanted to kill me. The other things that have happened are ghost that got angry because I didn't want to help them or ignored them. They would mess with me, hide or destroy my things. They often pushed me or tripped me. Once I fell off the stairs because a ghost tripped me. Needless to say that ghost never showed up in front of me again after what she did. She probably didn't mean it, but still, I got bruised ribs and a sprained ankle."

"Oh dear, no wonder you hated me at first."

"The best way to avoid all those kind of things was avoiding everyone. If I did react to anyone then I was safe from reacting to a ghost's presence," he explains and I can't blame him for that. I can't blame him for running away from ghosts or for hating me at first. I can only feel sorry for the boy that had to go through all that alone.

"When I was a baby I would get sick very often, and I was always cold. I guess it was because of ghosts, as well. I was told that when I was three I ended in the hospital because I was near hypothermia. No one understood why. I think probably a ghost didn't let go of me. Maybe a mother, you know? Missing her child so she grabbed me."

I want to touch him, to offer him some comfort like he did with me, but I'll only make him colder, if I don't hurt him with my emotions as well.

"I'm so sorry," I repeat because there's nothing else I can do or say for him. He smiles at me, a bit sad because it's been charged with painful memories. I can only imagine how many more of those stories there must be in his mind, of every time a ghost hurt him. I can't blame him for wanting to shut everyone out and just wanting to be left alone.

"Would it make me an idiot if I say I'm glad all that happened?" I frown, very confused by his words. "For starters all that led me here, to you. Besides, I can kind of understand what it feels to be bully like you were. The difference is that I was bullied by ghosts and you by living people."

"Let's not figure out who had it worst, please," I beg and he nods, leaning on to me until he rests his head on my shoulder. I freeze, and then slowly focus on only his presence. I let this love overflow so I won't hurt him.

"We have each other now. It's okay," he murmurs and I have to agree. It isn't all bad, somehow we found each other. We were both very lonely for different circumstances, but now it's different. He has someone to lean on, even if it's cold, and I have him.

"We're okay," I confirm, a small smile playing on my lips as I rest my head on his.

Chapter 32

"Do you think your unfinished business could be me?" James asks out loud when he is having breakfast on Sunday morning, after such eventful Saturday night.

After James fell asleep last night, I spent all night thinking and mourning. Without him, I could only think of all the new things I'd learnt, and above everything else, the loss of my mother. I've thought so much about it that I can finally realise that the reason why it hurts so much is because I'm selfish, because I want to have her here. But after all I've done to her, after breaking her the way I did, I have no right to miss her or want here with me, where she is miserable. She left with a smile on her face, like she didn't look in fifteen years, so she was better then. Wherever she left to, she must be better off than she was here. The least I could do is to be happy for her.

I've controlled my mind for fifteen years, making myself forget I was bullied until I committed suicide. I have also almost forgotten my father and every other face that I knew when I was alive. I can surely make myself feel happy when I think of Mum because she is okay, she's just waiting for me. It might take a while, but all minds can be set to work in certain way, even ghosts' minds.

I also tried thinking of what could be the lesson I have to learn for me to cross over and reunite with my mum, but every time I tried thinking of that, James' face came to my mind, reminding me that crossing over means leaving him behind.

A relationship between a ghost and a human is impossible, even if I manage to learn how to control my emotions in order not to hurt him, and I don't mean it because he is the only one that can see me because that's irrelevant. A relationship isn't to display to others, it's between two people, and those who have that mindset are wrong and are missing the real point of a relationship. The problem isn't that I remain unseen for everyone except James, it's that I'm not a person anymore.

"That sounded so narcissist, I'm very sorry," James adds next, realising what his words sound like. An embarrassed chuckle escapes his lips.

"It's okay, I'm no one to judge you. And to answer your question... hmm... I don't think so," I reply, not sounding like my usual self.

"I'll try not to feel offended with that, but I don't think you really understand what I meant," he jokes a bit, his nervous smile still on his lips.

"I think I do," I say, and as my mind is still trying to cope with every change, I can't really feel sympathy for him now, or to mind how he seems hurt with my words. "You don't mean you, but finding love, or being loved by someone aside from my family. That is probably the most logical thing that could keep me here because it's something I never experienced."

James' eyes widen a bit, surprise clear in his features. "But many people die without experiencing so many things, and those don't keep them here. It's not a experience, it's a lesson what I have left."

I try to give him a smile, one that doesn't feel that honest, but it's the best I can manage right now.

"Besides, if it were that, then I would've crossed over already. But here I am, still stuck. It has to be something else," I add and I hear him sigh. "I tried figuring it out last night, but I didn't come up with anything. The only option I have is forgiving my bullies, but how can I do that?" My voice carries the weight of that statement, how reluctant I am. "Saying 'it's okay, I forgive you,' and really meaning it are two very different things. I honestly don't think I can ever really forgive them. I can accept their apology but that doesn't mean I can forgive them."

"Maybe you should, that resentment weights in on you," James comments, and I heave a frustrated sigh.

"Easier said than done!" I snap. "Can you forgive those ghosts that did all that to you? That psycho that almost got you killed?"

James is taken aback by my sudden outburst and how I just throw at him what he shared before. I immediately feel guilty after I say those words, looking away and trying to put myself together. I can't keep snarling because I'm frustrated, angry and heartbroken.

"I think I could," replies James, surprising me. "If I think about it and consider how things have changed, I can forgive them. If I hadn't run into them, I wouldn't have moved away.

I wouldn't have come here and met you, Paige. So yes, if I put things in perspective, I can forgive them."

I meet his eyes and his are so intense, determined to get the point across and make me change my mind. But I don't have it in me, even if it means I got a chance to meet him, I can't do the same. If I put things in perspective, I can't forgive them for what they did to me.

"It's not the same," I breathe out, feeling a lump in my throat. "How can you even compare it, James? You're still alive, you still have a chance. They broke me to the point I killed myself in the most horrendous way, bringing my mother with me, killing her in life. I killed myself and broke my family and I've been stuck for fifteen years. Did you forget all that?" He doesn't reply, but his eyes look pitiful now. "How do I forgive the people that pushed me to this point? They drove me to the edge and then pushed me off the cliff, laughing as they did."

"I know it's not the same... but can you even try?" he insists and the fact he is doing it makes me so annoyed I can't even look him in the eyes.

I stand up and walk away, towards the window, wrapping my arms around myself, trying to calm down. Why do people do that? They advise you as it everything was that easy, as if it just took a few words to fix everything. If it were easy, if one could just do as told, then no one would be in a mess. If I could forgive them by just wanting to, then I wouldn't be stuck.

If that is even my lesson! I don't bloody know by now.

It's not that I don't want to forgive them, if that's what will get me out of this, then I'll do it. The problem is that I'm not physically capable of such thing. My guts twist at the idea and I just want to scream and break things. I can't let go of this resentment, I lived with it for years and then carried it for even more. I can't just let go of it.

But what happens if that is really the lesson I'm supposed to learn? It makes sense, considering I've only remembered that for fifteen years, that being all I held on to. Then letting it go, learning to forgive and move on, could be what I need to in order to cross over.

If that is really what I'm supposed to learn, then I'm doomed. I can't do it.

"You don't need to do it overnight," James speaks from behind. I didn't notice he followed me

I heave another deep sigh. "I don't think I can, James. I... it's like this resentment has become all I am and I don't even know what I'll be without it."

"Then you need to find something else to hold on to until you can let go of that, right?" he proposes, standing next to me and grabbing one of the hands I kept at my side. "I'll help you in every way I can."

I look at our hands together and call out for all my feelings for him. These are stronger than the bad and dark ones, or maybe as they are new and unfamiliar they seem stronger, whatever the reason is, they work at pushing what could hurt James to the back. I feel a bit lighter, more comfortable when I let these feelings take control. I know it's working when James squeezes my heart a bit tighter before tangling our fingers together. That is when I can look up and meet his eyes.

"I'm sorry," I say. "For snapping before. It's just... overwhelming." I sigh because I can't come up with a better description of all what I'm feeling. But he probably gets an idea and he doesn't blame me for being all bitchy first thing in the morning.

"It's okay, I understand. I'm sorry I can't give you a solution." I shake my head before he pulls me a bit closer to him, passing our entwined fingers above my head until I'm wrapped and pressed against his chest. His other arm wraps around my waist and his chin rests on my shoulder. "I'd like to solve everything for you, and I wish I could have all the answers you seek. I know it's hard and it seems impossible right now, but don't panic because it's like that. We are getting there, just slowly."

I smile sadly at his words, leaning a bit more onto him.

It impresses me how much he can love me and care about me. This boy that has been alone for so long, with no one to love, or to love him back. His parents have always neglected him, and he grew with people that were paid to take care of him. For all these years he's needed someone to pour all that kindness to. AS the song goes by, he needed someone to love. Ironic how he ended up doing that for a ghost, the very reason why he had to turn his back on to everyone.

"James," I call, feeling sorry for something else. "I am grateful that I got to meet you. I know that if I hadn't killed myself, if I had been stronger, we would've never met each other, and if I think about that it actually breaks my heart." I turn my head a bit to see his face, even kissing his cheek. "I mean, being a ghost even keeps me from being a cougar."

I manage to make him laugh with that. If I were alive I'd be thirty-two, but as I'm dead, I don't really have an age. That's for living creatures. I'm frozen at seventeen, not a day older. Just like James, but contrary to me he does get older, every day.

"I'm very grateful you came to Street. Grateful you enrolled for the same diploma, and even more grateful that you can actually see me." I touch his cheek with my palm, and even if it's cold, he closes his eyes and seem to enjoy it. "Thank you for that, James. For not leaving me alone, for caring and for learning to love me."

James doesn't reply with words, he just looks for my lips and I help him until we meet in a kiss. I slowly turn in his arms until our chest are against each other and in a better position so we can kiss comfortably. It's not like last night, it's not as overwhelming or weird, and I guess we are slowly getting used to this; but it's precious nonetheless.

When we break the kiss I pull up his hoodie and smile before taking a step back, breaking the contact because he must be cold.

"You can't dress lightly from now on. Always with five layers of clothes," I instruct, trying to sound severe, but he only smiles.

"Dating a ghost will come in handy in summer, when the heat wave strikes."

I laugh at his joke, smiling honestly this time. "Who needs AC when you can get your personal ghost hugging you when it's just unbearable hot?"

He takes a step closer and traps my face in his large hands, next thing I know he's kissing my lips again. Just a short peck before stepping back. "Until summer comes, I'll just wear loads of clothes. And drink loads of hot chocolate."

"Surely that will help."

"If not, then I'll also carry a blanket with me." I chuckle, feeling a lot better. "Anyhow... I'm not sure about this but... about today..." he starts mumbling, the mood immediately changing. "Do you, perhaps, want to go and see what happened with your mum? I mean, her body. If it's too much we don't have to go, but if you want to know where she'll be put to rest, then we can go and ask some questions."

I think about it, scared of seeing her body, lifeless. Even if she was like a corpse before, she was still breathing. I don't know if I could do that. But then, I guess I should know if she'll be buried or cremated.

"Also, maybe we should go to your house and try to find your ashes. We can bring them here," he continues and I nod absentmindedly.

"I..." I start, but I don't know how to finish that sentence. "I'm not sure I can see my mum's body, but I'd like to know what happened to her. I mean, she doesn't have anyone else here. Maybe they called my father or something."

"Then let's go. We'll see what we can find out," he smiles encouragingly. "What about your ashes?"

"I don't think they survived but we can look for them."

"How can you tell?" he asks.

I shrug. "I don't feel drawn to there anymore. It's like whatever tied me to that place is gone, now I only feel drawn to college."

"Well, if that's the case we'll make sure to find out today. Shall we go? There are many places to go."

I smile at him, grateful that he is giving me something to do instead of just thinking. "Let's go," I agree, ready to make myself busy for the day.

Chapter 33

It isn't that easy, as it might seems; it doesn't take just asking to get answers. It turns out there are many protocols that need to be respected. Officers, or even any person in the hospital, won't share information to just anyone. There's a thing called confidentiality, and unless you are a direct relative, then you can't obtain personal information about a patient.

When James asks for Daphne Samuels, he is asked back what his relationship with the woman is. He can't lie and say he's the son, or some relative, because he will have to hand his ID and his lie would be discovered.

James is a really nice person, very asocial so the few social skills he has are fairly rusty. Hence, his lies, or any kind of deception, get easily caught.

We first went to the firemen and at that time he said he was Mum's son. They didn't even hesitate, they just looked him from head to toe and said, "Son, that woman was alone. There's no relative that can be contacted. Her only daughter died long ago. Now tell us what are you planning unless you want us to call the police."

Needless to say, we ran before he could answer.

It's obvious that after so many hours they made all the inquires necessary. Probably, even he neighbours explained how lonely my mum had been for the past fifteen years. And there's no point in James telling that I've been here all along because no one else can see me.

At the hospital James says he's a friend of the family, but that's not good enough for them to provide information.

"I'm sorry, kid, but we are not allowed to give that kind of information to non-relatives," the woman behind the desk replies, giving James a pitiful look.

"Can you at least tell me when her funeral will be held or something?"

"I shouldn't tell you this, but..." the woman takes pity of him. "We've contacted the ex-husband. Mrs Samuels's body will be cremated and the ashes taken to Cardiff, where he is living now. Her funeral won't take place here."

I can't say a thing and neither can James, so we just stare blankly at her.

"Now leave before you get me in trouble." James nods and his hand almost automatically reaches for mine. "My con-dolences," she adds before we take a step away and even if she is saying that to James, thinking he looks that devastated because my mum's death, in fact he's just feeling my own grief.

"Thank you," I say in a hoarse voice and then James repeats my words out loud for the woman to listen. She just nods with a tight smile.

Next thing I know, James is dragging me away from the hospital and doesn't stop until he finds a spot where we can be left alone, where no one will notice him talking to the thin air, and where he can hug me without anyone reporting him, thinking he escaped the mental ward.

I don't fight him when he wants to hug me anymore, even if that hurts him; instead, I just let him comfort me and make the pain go away so I won't hurt him any further. I'm numb right now, knowing that my mum's ashes will be taken away from Street, away from me. I know she isn't here anymore, but what was left will be in a place I can't go. I was hoping she'd be buried here or something similar so I could at least have a place to visit her, like normal people do. It's just a way to soothe the pain in our hearts, an illusion... but I won't even have that now.

"I'm very sorry, Paige," James says in my hair, hugging me ever so tightly. "I wish I could've managed to find out more."

"It's okay, you did your best," I say, pulling a bit back in order to meet his eyes and try giving him a little smile. "At least I know Dad will take care of her body."

He smiles at me lovingly before cupping my face with one hand. I lean in his hand, finding the contact so soothing and warm. Then I feel his lips on my forehead in a slow and calm kiss.

"Let's have lunch and then at night we can go to your house to see if we find your ashes," he proposes. I nod, pulling back completely because it's been long enough and he's getting too cold.

I follow him to a restaurant he picks, and to avoid making people stare, he wears his headphones and pretends to be talking on the phone, that way we can have a normal conversation even when we are outside. He asks for loads of food and I just sit across, watching him because I can't really share a meal with him. James asks me what I remember about my father but there isn't much. I don't even know if he has a new family. Maybe I have half siblings now, but I'll never find out. I don't even remember his name or what he did for a living, and if James asks me to describe him, I wouldn't be able to. The only image I have of him is from the pictures at home, but now even those are gone.

"Is it stupid that I feel sad because all my things are gone?" I ask out loud later in the afternoon. We've moved from the restaurant to that church where he took me before, just because it's pretty and quiet, and he doesn't need to wear the headphones.

"I don't think it's stupid, but it isn't really rational," he replies honestly.

I sigh, rounding my shoulders a bit. I bring my legs up, hugging them and resting my chin on top of them. "Mum made sure to keep everything as I left it, and now all that is gone. The clothes I couldn't wear, the toys I had when I was a kid, all my posters and notebooks, and everything I had." I look at him, hoping he can understand why I'm also sad for losing things I didn't even use anymore. "But what I miss the most are all those pictures I took when I was alive. There are gone forever."

I think he understands, or he tries to understand, because his eyes show sympathy, his lips curling in a sad smile.

"If it's true that we put a bit of ourselves in all the things we make, then it's normal to feel sad for losing them, considering that with that you are also losing a bit of ourselves," he tries to explain and I nod, following the logic in his words.

"I guess that by keeping my room my mum could pretend one day I'd come back from college, and I could pretend I still had a place in this world. Now all that is gone," I muse as I feel James arm wrapping around my shoulders, brining me closer to him. I rest my head on his shoulder, my eyes fixed on the space ahead.

We don't say anything else for a while, we just stay there until it starts getting dark and James too cold for holding me. I accompany him to get dinner, opportunity he uses to warm himself up, and once all that is done we head to my old house, which now is just debris and ashes.

On our way to my home—my old home—, we walk in silence. I have too many thoughts in my head as to keep a conversation and I guess James does not know how to break the ice. I'm not sure how I'll feel when I walk in. Last night I didn't focus much on my house, Mum consumed all my thoughts. I know I'm a ghost and I shouldn't have any attachment to material things, but how can anyone not feel attached to the place one lived for so long.

I feel really nervous when I'm in front of the house, which it burnt. It still has its normal shape, It doesn't look that terrible from outside. I'm not sure how Mum died, but I hope it wasn't burnt. I hope it had been intoxication for the fumes. I think that's more merciful.

There's no pot left, it broke, but I don't think I need a key to open the door. And I'm proved right when I just push the door and this opens for us. I can't walk in first, so it has to be James guiding me inside, taking my hand so I don't stay behind.

It still looks like my house, but everything inside has been destroyed. Whether it fell and broke or it has been burnt and now it's half ashes, half object. The frame pictures are broken, the furniture half burnt, the ceiling with holes and debris on the floor. And on top of all that, everything is wet. I walk around slowly, trying to see if something survived. If it wasn't victim of the fire, it was of the water used to extinguish the flames. It's hard to see it like this, when it looked the same for so long. It's all destroyed, what once was my home is forever gone.

"I'm homeless," I mutter. "A homeless ghost. I can't stop getting weird."

Even if it's actually quite sad what I'm saying, James chuckles. I look over my shoulder and see him pressing his lips tightly to hold his laughter.

"Why are you laughing?"

"Sorry," he apologises. "It's just... they way you say it. Regardless, I don't think you're homeless," he says next, making me frown.

"Then what? The house is ruined and now that Mum is gone I don't even know what's going to happen to this."

James shakes his head before taking a step closer and wrapping his arms around my waist to pull me against his chest. "I mean, you have a home. A new home." I think all this tragedy made my brain overheat because I can't really understand what he is implying. And James knows I'm not following, which makes him chuckle again. "My place is your place now, too. You can't be homeless if you have a place to stay."

I just blink up at him, too flabbergasted with his words. I know I've been staying there for a while but I never considered it my home. I also know he's referred to it as such a few times but I never took it too seriously. Knowing he is sharing his home with me stirs something inside, it makes my heart race. Or well, it makes me feel like my heart it's racing. It's hard to describe without using human analogies.

I never lived in his place, I can't really live there, but this is still really meaningful. So I lean against this chest, taking deep breaths and closing my eyes, listening to his heartbeat.

"Thank you," I say. "For not letting me be a homeless ghost."

Chuckling, he replies, "Thank you, for not leaving me alone."

"You mean for following around at the beginning?" I smile widely and he does the same. "Like a stalker?"

"Yeah." He kisses my forehead. "From that moment onwards."

I pull back although I keep my smile. I'm very thankful he's come with me, it makes things more bearable. Although I don't think I would've come if he hadn't suggested it this morning. And because he suggested finding my ashes, I head to Mum's room. It's in a very similar condition as the rest of the house. It breaks my heart to see it like this, the place Mum slept at every night, where I carried her to sometimes.

I look at the shelves where I saw my ashes the last time, that urn that kept my remains. It's all broken, everything Mum kept there is on the floor. The wood of the shelves gave out after being burnt and couldn't hold the weight of small things anymore. On the floor, broken and with ashes spread around, a bit wet, lies my urn. I know it, I can recognise it, and I feel it. That's me. On the floor. Scattered like that.

It hurts seeing that, in a level no words can describe.

I stay there, standing, watching a broken urn and my ashes without being able to even utter a word.

"There's still something inside," James mentions, walking towards it and picking the urn in his hands. "I guess we can't save all your ashes and it doesn't sound that bad leaving a bit of them at this place, but we can take the rest. I'll get a new urn or something for you."

I don't know what to say or how to feel, not even when he grabs the bottom of the urn that holds the bit left of my ashes. He rises to his feet again and turns to see me, a little smile on his face.

"It's not all gone," he adds.

"I don't even know how to feel," I mutter. "I know that's me, or what I once was, and I just..." I close my eyes, trying to collect my thoughts and put myself together. "I will not touch it. I'm scared of what I might remember if I do."

"It's okay, you don't have to," agrees James. "I'll take care of them... and is it okay if I keep them even when you cross over?" he asks next, a thing I didn't even consider before.

"If I cross over," I correct him but he shakes his head, dismissing my statement. "I guess... If that's what you want, I'm okay with it."

"It's just a way to keep you with me when you're not around," he confesses looking down, at the urn and ashes in his hand. "So I won't feel like you're completely alone. That's probably why you're mum kept the ashes in her room."

I don't say a word, I just stare at him until he meets my eyes again.

"Shall we go to our home now? We found what we came for," he changes topics.

"Let's go home," I agree, trying to smile, but there's still something bothering me, and I think it's the fact I don't like the idea of leaving James.

Whatever it is, I'll have to deal with that later.

Chapter 34

Without a clear goal ahead, James and I just sink in a normal routine. We go to college together, listen to the teachers, and I watch him work, too. As I have him I don't feel that need to ramble because I'm bored out of my mind, I just have to wait until we are alone to talk to him, and that is not hard when it's not me talking to myself the whole time. Having some feedback helps to tone it down a notch.

When we are alone I help him as much as I can with his college work, things I didn't do in so long because what was the purpose? I am dead, it doesn't count. But I get to do something productive with James, and that is really cool.

There's something magical about doing art with James, helping him with his sculptures, or even the dull task of organising his photographies, even more, tracking the progress of his work. It feels really good to be part of something, to add a bit of me on to something other people can see, even if they have no idea I was involved. Besides, it's my way to pay him back.

James has been so focused on helping me with my unfinished business, revenge, and all those things we've achieved already, that he was left behind with his college work. The least I can do is helping him to catch up with everything he missed for being busy with me. And I enjoy helping him, so it's a win-win situation.

It feels like a normal life, just the two of us, something I haven't had in so long. These days with James have made me feel more alive than ever, even when I was really alive. I don't have people tormenting me, and even if I don't have my family, I do have him, constantly reminding me he loves me. It's not always with words, sometimes it's with a tender touch when he brushes a lock of my hair away from my face, or the way he smiles lovingly, or how he insists to wrap me in blankets when we watch movies together, even if I don't get cold. Sometimes it's the way he holds my hand over the table when he's eating, just to make me part of what he's doing. And sometimes, it's just the way he says my name.

It's really nice. But also extremely heartbreaking because this is just temporary, until I learn my lesson and can cross over, to reunite with my mother. It makes me reluctant, so reluctant to actually do that. Every day I fall a bit more in love with James, discovering just how kind and caring he is with me, even if he is cold and even rude to other people, to me he shows a side no one else has seen.

Maybe it's wrong of me, but I kind of like that he doesn't let anyone else in, just me. I actually enjoy how he pushes other people away, because he has me. Like he did to Adeline the other day.

The girl grabbed his arm when he was leaving after Photography, making him wait until everyone left before smiling at him.

"Hi," she purred, surprising me. Until today, just thinking about it gives me the chills. "I thought we could talk for a bit. You're always the first to leave. I barely see you, lately."

"Hm," James only muttered, quickly turning to look at me, almost asking me to help him. I laughed, thinking of scaring Adeline, actually considering to give the girl a back hug.

"Roxy says that it's a matter of time you ask her out, but she's wrong, right?" Adeline asked next, clearly surprising James who stared at her wide-eyed.

"What?" James muttered. I had to press my lips tightly together not to laugh.

"I knew it," Adeline smiled, content with the kind of response she got from James. "I knew you wouldn't like a girl like her."

"Oh?" I still find extremely funny that James only gives her monosyllable answers, and Adeline is doing all the talk.

"I think you're just shy so I thought of helping you out a bit," she added, stepping closer, pissing me off in that occasion. I took a threatening step towards her, even if she couldn't see me doing so. "Why don't you and I go out? I'll let you take me on a date."

James couldn't even answer, he just looked dumbfounded, blinking his confusion away, even shaking his head ever so slightly.

"Uh?" His response, however, made me laugh.

"You know, let's go out. I think we'd match well together. You're cute in that mysterious kinda way," she tried explaining, winking and making me gag. Was she taking her lines from cliché chick flicks? "What do you say?"

"I uhm..." James began. Adeline smiled confidently, and for half second I felt sorry for her. Just half second. "I have a girlfriend."

"What?" Then it was Adeline using monosyllables. "No, you don't."

"Yes, he does," I intervened.

"Yes, her name is Paige," he explained and I couldn't help my huge grin when he said that.

"What is she taking? Do I know her? Why haven't I ever seen you with her?" she demanded, as if he owed her a sort of explanation.

"You don't know her, but I'm always with her. We live together," he shrugged.

"But... that's impossible. And your parents?" Adeline asked, her shocked expression was priceless. I walked up to James, wrapping my arms around his waist and giving him a back hug. I felt proud at that time, happy that he was actually telling someone about me... about us. I let him feel that.

I have to say I'm getting better at controlling my emotions. It's not about shutting out the ones I always carry with me, it's about letting the good emotions overflow, and in that way balance the pain so it's only cold for James.

"They don't care. I don't live with them, they are too busy travelling the world," he explained, shrugging but also leaning closer to me. Adeline didn't notice that, of course. "So it's only Paige and I."

"I— but you— I—" she mumbled, causing me to chuckle and James to smile, at me, not her, needless to say.

He didn't say anything else, he just walked out, leaving a very confused and shocked Adeline behind. I couldn't stop smiling for that whole day.

The rumour has spread, of course, now our whole group knows James is dating a girl named Paige, and that is why he doesn't bother to look at anyone. The rumour has twisted a bit, saying how we had been engaged since childhood and that's why we live together, or that he is forced to marry a girl he doesn't want. Some other are nicer, saying we've always been together and the like, but his parents opposed to our relationship so we ran away together and are living our romance in secret.

These kids, they have a lot of imagination.

But that is also how they comfort themselves, like Roxy and Adeline, saying that because James is a nice guy who can't be unfaithful he never gave her the time a day, which isn't entirely wrong but it isn't correct either.

"Did you hear what the kids were saying today?" I ask James after dinner, when we are working on the progress of his Photography project. I help him sort out and paste the photographies.

"What were they saying now?" he asks absentmindedly, too focused on his work to actually look at me.

"They said we are actually married because you knocked me up, and that's why you left your precious home, to stop people from talk about us or notice my pregnancy. We had a boy and his name is Clyde," I explain and James stop working for a second, just to burst out laughing the next at the absurdity of the rumours.

"Seriously, don't they get tired of talking about us? More things need to happen for them to change topics," James muses, going back to his work, but the smile still lingers on his lips.

I find this last version of the rumour a bit bittersweet, though, but I don't mention that to him. The truth is, those rumours are the closest we'll ever be to actually have that kind of future. It's not a matter of choice for us, it's just impossible. Whether we want it or not, we'll never be able to marry, or have kids. Those rumours the kids at college spread are all we'll ever have, because then I'll leave James here when I cross over. He'll form a family... with someone else.

I'd tell that to James, but I think it would only make him sad, and that is the last thing I want.

"I wish they could see you at least once and realise this isn't a Romeo and Juliet sort of story," James muses next.

"People are too obsessed with a story they don't even understand," I comment. "Besides, two barely-teenagers can't compete with a human and a ghost," I joke, even winking and making him laugh again. "If there was a contest for freaky couples we would win the first prize," I sing-song, standing up and spinning in a sort of pirouette.

"You're so cute," James mumbles next, smiling fondly.

"I'll never be grateful enough that I can't blush." He laughs again as if I had told a joke when I'm speaking the utmost true.

"I'll paint you, and when I do, I'll make sure your cheeks are very rosy, as if I just said something that made you blush," he almost challenges me, kind of forgetting his work.

"You think I can stay still enough for you to paint me?" I remind him. By now he is very aware I can't stay still, I'm always moving and talking.

"We'd have to try. I could even present that at some point and when they ask me who the model is, I can proudly say she's my girlfriend."

"Oh, you just want to brag you're not single," I laugh at my own words and how my voice sounds, so cheeky and playful.

"Of course I want to do that," he confirms, completely ignoring his work and walking up to me, stopping only when there's one step between us.

I stand straighter, rocking on the ball of my heels and raising my chin to meet his eyes, the grin still on my lips. His blue eyes sparkle with amusement and love, I can see it so clearly. James' hands tangle behind his back and he also rocks his weight, following my lead, and it almost looks like we're dancing. I even mimic his posture, causing my grin to widen.

"I want everyone to know how pretty you are, and how lucky I am for having you. I also want to to rub in their faces that I'm the lucky one who can see you."

"That certainly helps with jealousy, doesn't it?" I ask teasingly, he just shrugs, trying to keep his smile at bay. "You don't have to worry another guy will hit on me."

"It's one of the perks," he admits, leaning closer, and in a heartbeat, pecking my lips before I can even realise he's done that. "It comes with many others."

"Is that so?" I ask.

You know how it is by the end of a romance film? When everything is solved and the couple are just in this blissful happiness? Being cheesy and enjoying every second? That is how this feels and how it probably looks. It's not like everything is solved, but isn't life like that? You can't fix everything because as soon as you deal with something, a new issue comes out, so it's never-ending. But as of right now, it feels like it's time for the credits to roll down.

"Paint me like one your French models!" I exclaim, overly dramatic, even striking a pose, stealing his beanie to help me, but then I realise that quote has another meaning. "On a second thought," I add in a higher voice, exactly remembering the scene of that film. "Never mind. You don't have to do that. Forget I said it. Forget it, forget it!" I cry out, feeling so embarrassed and self conscious.

James seems utterly confused, though, and he's watching me with a frown. When I pull his beanie lower, covering my face that should be blushing if I were human, he connects the dots. His response is an explosive laughing fit.

"Oh my God," I groan, turning around and running away, locking myself in his room.

"Oh, come on, Paige! That was funny!" James says from the other side. Of course he followed me, but I locked the door. I'm too embarrassed to meet his eyes.

"I'm never coming out of this room!" I shout. I can't believe I suggested him to paint me naked. That's so humiliating.

I can only hear him laughing at the other side, having the time of his life at my expense. Not even as a ghost I can't stop being an awkward teenager.

Chapter 35

It gets easier and more comfortable to be with James. It stops being awkward in the sense it is already normal we are together. When we are at his place, just the two of us, it's so easy to forget we are a ghost girl and a human boy, because nothing reminds us of that. Maybe when he starts to get too cold but then he just wraps himself in more layers and he even puts some on me. It turns out it works for as long as he's watching me. The moment he leaves the room or I do that, the clothes I'm wearing fall to the ground and I'm back with only my usual outfit. If I focus a bit more I can keep them, but I get too tired. So we leave wearing three hoodies each for when we cuddle together.

James had a collection of hoodies, by the way.

I notice the severity of the situation when he's taking a shower and I'm helping him by leaving the clothes he'll change in on top of his bed. It's just to do something in the meantime. I had taken a peek inside his wardrobe before but never paid attention to it.

It turns out James has a few pair of trousers and shorts, quite a few tees and like three times that amount in hoodies. Different colours, designs and styles. He has one particular hoodie two time times! I think that's his favourite one. Some have bands he enjoys, some have illustrations or cartoons, but most of them are plain. It's impressive. I wouldn't be lying if I say he has like fifty hoodies.

So it's not an issue for him to wear three of those at the same time and hand me other three for me. It's funny, I always laugh because we look like astronauts. I like messing around too, pretending to be one and such. But the outcome is always the same.

"Come here," James says, opening his arms for me and I just jump on to his lap, cuddling up to him like a little puppy. Or an adult St. Bernard that hasn't realised it stopped being a puppy and is suffocating its owner. I think in size we are about the same.

James gives me so many happy feelings and even if he seems serious and taciturn outside and to everyone else, he is very cheerful and loves laughing. He enjoys my humour and outbursts of nonsensical sentences. When we are to-gether he's always smiling and I don't even need to feel his emotions to know it's like that. And maybe he can give some of that happiness to me, too, because I don't feel that heavy. When I'm in his arms it seems like everything is okay, there are no worries. When I'm with him it isn't hard to let go of all that is choking me. When I'm with him, I can actually believe I can let go and forgive the bullies that drove me to the edge, but that's only when I'm in his arms. The moment I'm alone, like when he's sleeping and I have nothing to do, all those dark feelings come rushing back, making me sink in despair and agony.

One Saturday morning James wakes up with that expression that says he's got an idea. He smiles widely and excitedly, and I mirror his expression.

"What are you planning? Are we gonna go play and scare people on the streets?" I guess, getting excited. I clap my hands when I think of something better. "No! We're going pretend to be superheroes and help fight crime. If that's the case, I can't wear my underwear on top of my dress and I strongly oppose to you wearing your on top of your trousers. Like hell to the no!"

James loses his smile and I think he's just precessing all the incoherence I've said. Three seconds later he bursts out laughing, probably picturing what I suggested. It is quite a sight, if you ask me.

"No, we are not doing that. We're gonna get Clyde," he explains and now I'm the confused one.

"Clyde as in our son Clyde?" I ask, remembering one of the rumours the kids have spread in college. "Are we getting one of those like animated dolls they use for health classes in movies?"

James chuckles again before walking up to me and grabbing my face in his hands, squishing my cheeks. "Nope. We'll get a lovely, cuddly kitty that we'll name Clyde. He'll make you company when I'm sleeping and I can actually say Clyde exists. I bet you'll enjoy the kids' reactions."

I imagine that and my grin is humongous.

"And he'll stay with me when you have to cross over," he adds next in a whisper, a bit more serious.

We haven't talked much about that, I guess he's just giving me time, trying to distract me from my grudges so I can let it all go and learn my lesson. And if we talk little about that, we talk even less about me leaving him behind. I guess adopting a kitty is a good idea, he won't be left all alone. But even if it's like that, it squeezes my soul the mere thought of not being with him.

I am aware a ghost isn't the best company ever, and it is still so lonesome, but it's better than nothing and without me James has no one. I don't think his parents will change and realise that having a child isn't just providing money, it's caring, it's being there. I can't go to them and teach them a lesson either. I can't leave Street, how am I supposed to go wherever they are? And in all honesty, I doubt James would like that either.

"Like Luna made Mum company," I murmur but then I think of what I've said. "Oh dear, it feels like I'll die all over again, this time leaving you behind."

"Hey, hey!" he hurries to my say, his expression changing to show his concern and anxiety because my chest feels tighter. He is touching me, he is feeling what is rushing like waves on me. "No, don't think like that, okay? It'll be like... like ah... like a breakup. Everyone goes through those."

"And everyone goes through losing someone loved, that doesn't make it easier," I refute and James sighs. I can see the struggle on his face, the way he is coping with the emotions I'm giving him. I try to step back but he doesn't let me.

"It's fine, it's something you have to do. I always knew it. But what will eventually happen won't stop us now, right?"

I take deep breaths, trying to calm down. I close my eyes and think only of his hand cupping my face, the warm and familiar touch. That helps, enough to put myself together. I take a step forward, wrapping my arms around his waist and hiding my face in his chest. He accepts the embrace without a complaint, rocking us ever so slightly.

"I'm sorry," I apologise in advance, but he just hushes me, patting my head.

"It's okay. Shall we go for Clyde now?" he changes topics, so I take a deep breath before stepping back and agreeing.

We leave the house together and head to a shelter James looked for prior. We don't chat much, I just sit by his side on the bus, resting my head on his shoulder as we watch outside the window. Once we arrive James takes care to inform why we are there and after filling in some forms, we are guided where they keep all the animals they rescue from the streets. It's fun seeing how they all react to me, even if James isn't next to me. I play with some dogs but they tend to be a bit more hesitant to approach me, whereas cats come calmly to me, rubbing themselves against my fingers through the cages.

At some point, I see a lovely little kitten. It's a fluff, there's no other way to describe it. It's grey and so extremely fluffy, with big blue eyes and such a small face that looks even smaller among so much fur. It's sleeping on its back, exposing its belly and then twisting a bit more. A think it's dreaming and it's the most adorably thing I've ever seen. I'm drawn to it immediately, and when I get there I can see the thick blue collar, indicating it's a boy.

"Clyde," I whisper, chuckling a bit. I make sounds for the cat to wake up and when he does and sees me, comes almost running, meowing so adorably to ask for attention. "James, come quickly. This is it, this is Clyde," I call out loud. James hears me immediately and leaves the cat he was playing with to see the one I've found.

"Oh boy, that is adorable," he mutters, opening the cage to take the cat in his hands. He fits perfectly, he's that tiny. And he rubs and kneads, getting comfortable. I pet him, rubbing his little head and then his chin. The kitty exposes his tummy again, asking for more love and I can't contain my squeal. "He's so cute."

"Can we have him? Please?" I beg, giving him my best pleading eyes, even if it's not necessary. James is as enamoured of Clyde as I am.

"Of course," he replies and I giggle overly excited.

"Did you hear that, Clyde? You're coming home with us!" I tell the kitten, even kissing his little nose and he meows in agreement. Is it just me or is the kitten smiling?

James informs we have decided to adopt the kitten. They tell us he is the only survivor they found after an old cat gave birth to five on them. The other four died of pneumonia and he was the only one that barely survived. He was very sick at first, but they fought really hard to save him. He's barely two months old.

During our ride back, we can't stop playing with Clyde. We also make sure to buy everything we need for him: his bed, food, his box, cat sand, a collar and all sort of toys. The kitten sleeps most of the ride back home and once we are there, we take him to explore every corner. He meows cutely and always comes to where we are standing, rubbing his nose against my legs and then James', like marking that we are his.

"We have the cutest baby," I tell James, hooking my arm with his; he chuckles.

"I agree. Should I go for my camera to start taking pictures?" he muses.

"Oh, I'll go for it!" I offer myself. "I wanna take pictures."

James agrees so I leave them alone to go to his desk, where I last saw his camera. In my rush I knock one of his notebooks, dropping and spilling all its contents. I have to put the camera aside and pick everything up, but I stop when I find a few polaroids. James doesn't have that kind of camera, he has photographic printers so it is kind of pointless, then these aren't ones that he took. When I grab the pictures I recognise myself in them. These are old pictures, ones that were in my room. There's also a picture of the two of us, one that we took that first time I took him to my house.

"Oh," I mumble, realising now, after quite a long time, he brought those pictures with him. Pictures that if he hadn't taken would've burnt with the house. These are actually the last things that survived from when I was alive.

I stare at the pictures, especially the one that has the two of us, the one that managed to capture me next to him. A sad smile comes to my lips, I don't even know how to describe how I feel right now, it's so conflictive. It's like there's a lump in my throat and my stomach is tied in knots. It's almost as if I wanted to cry, but I'm not sad... yet I am.

I don't really want to leave James behind, and I don't want this to be the only picture of us. A part of me wonders if it'd be too bad if I never move on, if I stay with James forever. Would that be a bad thing? Would it be that terrible?

But I died, I'm a ghost now, I don't belong here. If I stay forever, there must be a price for that, right? Nothing is free in this world, even the things we think free come with a price at the end, a price we don't even realise but that it is there. I assume that staying for longer than I should can't be cheap.

How different would things have been if James and I had gone to college together, whether when I went the first time or now. I don't think I would've made the same decision, or maybe I would have and James wouldn't have cared, he would have never talked to me and I would have never chased him until he reached his limit. We would have never got close. If I really think about it, the only reason why James and I became as we are today is because I'm a ghost, and not any ghost but once that has been stuck for fifteen years, one that didn't even remember how she died. One that needed his help, but one that didn't force him to do that. If the situation had been different, then we would have never got together.

"I guess it was only meant to be like this," I muse, barely a whisper.

I put the pictures inside the notebook, just like they were, and grab the camera again, going back to where I left James and Clyde, just to find them playing together, James wearing the most beautiful smile ever, his eyes sparkling with love. I immediately take a picture of them, only then alerting them of my presence. James holds up his hand, inviting me to join them and I do that, sitting on the floor right next to him. He holds Clyde in the middle of our faces and takes a picture of the three of us.

When I see the preview I feel so many things I can't even pinpoint each one of them. It's gratitude, and love, and a bit of heartbreak, among many other. So I lean closer to James, hugging him tight when he lets go of Clyde so he goes to explore some more. I don't say anything, I just let him feel everything that's keeping the words inside.

He doesn't say anything, either. He lets me hug him and wraps an arm around me, keeping me close. It's just after a while, before he gets too cold, that I look up to him, touching his cheek ever so lightly and say, "I love you, James Black."

Chapter 36

His smile is radiant and oh so happy. James forgets about Clyde and focuses all his attention on me, cupping my face in his hand. I lean closer in the warmth of his touch. As he can feel my emotions I'm pretty sure he was aware of my feelings even before I acknowledged them, but it still makes him happy that I say it out loud. I don't know exactly what is that makes it important, to utter those three words. They don't really change anything, not technically speaking, but at the same time they change a lot.

"And I love you, too," he replies, kissing my forehead.

"What if..." I start, feeling hesitant but going for it anyway. "What if I stay with you? If I don't cross over?"

That's something that's been in my mind for a while, the chance to stay with him. I know my mother is waiting for me, hopefully, but I'm happy here with James. I feel loved and accepted, I don't have to deal with bullies and I do feel like I am alive, despite the irony that I am a ghost. I feel terrible for saying this, but I'm happier now than when I had my parents, when I was alive. I know they loved me, but maybe I was faulty or too immature, maybe too weak, or maybe the bullying and constant harassment was too much for one person alone.

Even if my parents always showed me how much I meant to them, they couldn't measure up to the bullies. Right now, James is the only one that loves me, and he only has to fight the loneliness that comes with being a ghost. It's not that hard, he just needs to stay with me to push all that away and fix everything that's wrong. Just a smile of his and I feel good, warm emotions coming to me, wrapping me like his arms do. James only needs to touch me to push the hatred and resentment to the back of my heart. It is possible to let go of the grudge I hold, but only when I have him to focus on, when there's love to give and receive. If I don't have him, then that thirst for revenge and justice is all I have, hence all I hold on to.

If I can't move on, if I have to be in this world, then I want to be with James. But I can't be certain that he'll want to stay with me forever. I only have him, he's my only option, but for him it's very different. He has a world of opportunities and options, he can choose. I only have two paths I can possibly follow, one leads to him, the other to my mother. Right now, I'm thinking of choosing him, even if that breaks my heart. But if I chose my mother then it means leaving James behind and that hurts more, so much more.

That is why making choices is so hard. Because it hurts, because no matter what, you're losing something. At the end it's not about what you win at the end, it's about what you give up on. You chose letting go of that one that hurts less, and stay with the one that hurts the most to let go. And at the end, if you can live without that one, then you did well at letting it go.

Right now I think that I can live without my mother. After all, that's a natural thing, to leave the nest and make your own. But I don't think I can live without James, even if I'm not really living.

I don't think I can exist without James. Leaving him behind, breaking his heart and leaving him all alone hurts more than not ever seeing my mother again.

"What?" He asks, confused that I'm bringing that up now.

"That. Me, staying here with you. Would that be that bad?"

James doesn't react at first, I think he's too surprised and is still thinking about it, trying to process my words and find the best way to answer without making a mistake. It's a delicate subject, so he's only being careful. Or that I hope.

"Are you giving up crossing over?" James inquires next, his brow slightly furrowed in concentration. "Is that what you're suggesting?"

"No," I shake my head. "Yes." I frown, confused. "Maybe? I mean... would it be that bad if I don't try to find my lesson and I just... continue like this?" James doesn't say anything, he just stares at me. I don't think I'm making enough sense for him to follow me. "I mean..." I take a deep breath, trying to sort my thoughts out and put them out there for him. "Every time I think of just... leaving you, it breaks me. You know when you feel like you're drowning and you're desperate for air? Your lungs burn and you can't even see? Well, kind of like that. But instead of water or lack of oxygen, it's just all that... hatred in me. Without you, it consumes me. Maybe it's me being selfish, but I want to stay with you. I want to feel happy, even if it's when I'm just a ghost. I couldn't have something like this when I was alive, this peace and love... and now I don't want to give it up."

I look down, feeling embarrassed for exposing my fears and those aspects that make me so weak and dependent. I'm actually confessing I need him to be happy because I can't do that on my own. How pathetic is that? That's probably why I couldn't deal with the bullies, why they took away the life in me... because I'm weak like that. Because I can't stand on my own.

I don't think that's a crime, though, not everyone has to be strong and independent. It would be good if it were like that, if every one was strong enough... but I am not like that. I need James and I don't want to give him up, even if that makes me pathetic and selfish. I just want to be happy. How do I know that I'll feel like I do when I'm with James when I cross over? Is it wrong wanting to stay where I'm all right and content? Is that really a crime? People always speak of leaving the comfort zone, but why do I have to leave a place where I'm satisfied in?

"It kills me thinking about that, too," James says, moving his hand to grab my chin and make me look at him again. "I don't want to lose you, ever. But... is that wise?"

"I don't know," I honestly reply. "That's why I'm asking, what if. Would you... would you like that? Can we start with that first?"

James smiles fondly at me, easing away a bit of my insecurities and fears. "I would, very much. I honestly don't need anyone else buy you. I don't even want to think about the days when you won't be with me. But I don't want to...

jeopardise your li— your existence in any way. Can you really stay here with me?"

"I've been here as a ghost for fifteen years already, and aside from forgetting, nothing more has happened. If you stay with me, I won't forget your face or you, like I didn't forget Mum," I think out loud, James nods along, probably agreeing my my theory. "If my lesson is really forgiving, then I might not be able to do it. And if that happens, then I could... I could stay with you."

"Although I like the idea of you staying with me, I don't think it's wise. You shouldn't give up on learning your lesson," he tries saying and his expression, the way his eyes stare into mine, tell me this doesn't please him. It hurts him saying this, just like it hurts me thinking one day we'll have to part ways.

A fear I have, one that really scares me, is that if I ever cross over I'll forget him. I'll forget everything because why would I need to remember? What if I cease existing as I am, what if I'm not Paige Samuels anymore but just a soul and I can't even recall James' face? What happens then? Then it would only be what we have now. As a ghost I forgot many things, many faces. What do I become when I cross over? What will I forget then? What will I keep with me?

That scares me enormously.

"I don't want to leave you," I whine, feeling my voice breaking with fear and apprehension. "I know..." I add before he can open his mouth. "I know it's almost impossible for me to stay with you. What can you do here? You need to go to uni and get a job. Will you grow older and lose all your chances at life because of me? Someone who can't even grow older with you? You'll become an adult and I'll be stuck as a teenager forever. But I want to, I want to stay with you forever. Why is it so hard?"

James doesn't say anything, he just grabs me in his arms and pulls me for a tight hug. I wish I could cry, but all that comes from me are the sounds. My face is dry, my eyes only burn with the memory of what it feels to cry.

"I want that, too. I want it so much. I want you by my side every day, even if we can't grow older together. Even if it means missing many things. I'd choose you over anything, except your own life."

"But we don't even know if it'd be dangerous for me!" I refute. That's the thing with us, we don't know many things, it's always just guessing what could happen and what we should do. "Maybe nothing will happen to me. Maybe I'll just stay the same forever and ever."

"And if something happens?" James counterattacks, and I shake my head.

"If nothing happens... if it just meant forgetting a few things, what would you say then?" I ask him, because I need to know that. "Hypothetically speaking."

"Then I would hold you forever. Even if it means I have to work from here and never leave Street. Even if I can't go to uni or anything. I would choose you, over everything else. And somehow, I'd manage. I'd take online courses and maybe get a job from home. Who knows? It could work. I don't need to be successful. I never really expected anything from life, Paige. I had no ambitions, I was just... going with the flow. Besides, if I leave this place and you, more ghosts would follow me like before. I'm sure that it's because of you that it's been so quiet for me, but the moment you'r not around, it'll be hell again. I'll have to shut everyone out once again." My heart twists at the loneliness of that situation. I hate that, I hate so much that he doesn't have anyone else. We are both so alone without the other. "The only real ambition I have right now is you; keeping you with me. And you talking like this is making me so greedy. If you keep saying these things I won't be able to let you go, Paige."

"Don't let me go, then," I plead in a small voice. "Let's stay like this."

I have to shut my eyes so tightly, because as soon as I say that I can't stand how selfish I am. It's beyond the limit, because I'm costing him so much with my own greed. A degree, a good job, a family. He never had one, his parents left him always alone, but he could change that. He could be a good father... but he'll never be that if he stays with me.

These are things so normal for people, they came with growing up, and I'm taking them all from James.

"What about your Mum?" he asks, his voice sounding as conflicted as I feel.

I really want to stay with him, but it isn't an easy choice. There's so much at stake, for both him and I. We both lose something when choose one another, and because we love each other, what the other loses also hurts us. It's a double loss, that's how it feels.

One can endure one's pain and accept the consequences of one's choices, live with the losses... because that's what one's decided. But when we are the cause of someone else's loss...

of someone we love, then it becomes harder. It's carrying with your pain and someone else's, because you're responsible.

It's so much harder.

"Can you really give up on your mum?" he insists, and I close my eyes tightly.

It hurts so much to think about her and never seeing her again, because I think that if I stay with James I'll never cross over. Even when he dies and moves on, I'll never move on. If I give up on learning my lesson when I'm with him, then I'm giving up on that forever because I won't find someone else to help me in the future. And just how it happened before I met James, I'll forget. I'll be stuck, repeating forever, without James. For as long as James lives, I'm giving up my entirety.

"I—" my voice fails me, because it just hurts so deeply. It's unfair, so unfair that I have to give up on one to have the other. If it's my Mum, then I leave James. And if it's James, then I give up on my mother. Either way, I'm shattering my soul. "It hurts more giving up on you."

"It's not easy, is it?" he asks, a smile that has no hint of amusement or happiness. It's sad, defeated.

"When has making decisions been an easy thing? That is why we avoid them so much and would want someone else to make them and take responsibility for them, because it hurts. Because it's scary."

James chuckles, pulling me closer again, letting me rest my face in the crook of his neck.

"It also hurts more letting you go, but I don't want you to ever resent me for giving up on your mother," James confesses. I can feel him breathing, I can hear the beating of his heart. It's fast, scared, anxious.

"And I don't want you to resent me for stopping you from having a normal life." I smile sadly, realising how similar our fears and concerns are "Do you think you'd ever resent me for that?" I ask, pulling back again, just to look him in the eyes.

He shakes his head as he cups my cheek with his left hand. "I think it's impossible, because I'm choosing you, and I'm aware of what I'm giving up to keep you with me. What about you? Would you resent me when you keep missing your Mum, knowing she's waiting for you?"

I wish I could answer as fast as he did, but I have to think about it. It breaks me, I feel like I'm being torn apart, but at the end... it takes just a look into his eyes to know the answer.

"I wouldn't... because I'm choosing you, and I'm aware of what I'm giving up to stay by your side." He smiles, stroking my skin with his thumb.

"Then... does that mean we've made a choice? Are you sure?" he asks one more time, and I can feel the slight tremble of his hand.

"Yes, I'm sure. I'm staying with you," I affirm, as confidently as I can, smiling bright and hoping this is the right decision, hoping we can be happy together like this. Hoping the price for this choice is something we can pay at the end.

Chapter 37

The decision has been made and maybe we are sacrificing too much, but this is what we've chosen, what we think we can live with. Maybe it's foolish, maybe we're being just teenagers and we aren't really seeing ahead and planning for a realistic and comfortable future, but right now this is what we feel, what we want.

Many things might change tomorrow. Maybe I have a limited time, whatever amount of years I was supposed to live, and once I fulfil that time I'll cross over whether I want it or not. Maybe James will meet another girl and fall in love with her and will want to have a family with her. Maybe I'll stay with him until he dies and then follow him to wherever we have to go next, because we are supposed to be together. There's so much uncertainty that it does not make much of a difference what we choose at the end, because we don't really know the consequences of those decisions. What matters right now is that we have each other and for once, we are not lonely.

James takes a bit of my pain away every day, and I make him company, to the point a smile is the most natural aspect of his features. I bring happiness and company to his life, he brings love and acceptance to mine. Is it then wrong to stay together if we help each other like this?

Of course, there are many difficulties that come with staying together, especially for him. I'm basically an anchor to Street, a small town with little possibilities. His parents won't provide for him forever, he needs to make his own life and forge his future, but I narrow his options. For as long as I'm bound to college, and he stays with me, he'll be glued to this town.

"Paige!" James screams one morning, running into the room where I have been, organising his wardrobe. I have learnt that organising his hoodie collection in different ways every once in a while is actually really good to kill time and relieve stress.

"What's wrong?" I immediately ask, dropping the red hoodie in my hands and turning to look at him with wide eyes.

"I've got an idea," he says, wide smile on his lips and eyes full of excitement and anticipation. "I was thinking and then I saw it and it hit me!"

"What?" I ask, because I'm not following him. He's like skipping words in all his excitement.

But he doesn't answer, he only grabs my wrist and drags me outside the room and towards the living room. I just follow him, confused and a bit worried, but I don't say anything. We don't stop until we face the shelves where he keeps many films and books, where he's also put the new urn with the remains of my ashes. Since we brought them home it's become easier for me to stay and I naturally feel drawn here when classes end.

"Your ashes!" he points out, as if I hadn't noticed them already. I turn to stare at him, letting him see my concern because it almost seems he lost his mind.

"Are you feeling well?" I question out loud, instinctively, I raise my hand to touch his forehead, as if it to check for a fever, although that's pointless. He's always just warm to me.

"Yes! But Paige, don't you realise? Your ashes are a bound point to you, and contrary to having been buried, you can move your ashes. Like form your home to here. You've felt the difference, right?" I nod. I think I know where he is going with this, but still then I don't interrupt him. "I thought that maybe you can leave town if we take your ashes with you, or maybe you can get a bit farther than just the town limits. What do you think?"

I stay quiet, giving a thought to that idea. It seems like a logic option, and he is right, I have felt the difference of staying here when the ashes were still at home, and then when we brought them with us. It might not work, but I think it's worth giving it a shot.

If... if it worked, then James could leave this place and look for better opportunities out there. And I could go with him, see other places, as well. Maybe I could go to uni with him and learn new things. Maybe we wouldn't need to stay in Street until the end because there's an option.

Excitement begins to bubble inside of me as a wide smile shows up on my face. I'm probably James' reflection right now, looking as thrilled as he is at the new possibility. It almost looks too good to be true.

"We have to try," I blurt out, almost bouncing on my heels. "See how far we can get."

"Indeed we have!" he agrees, grabbing my two hands and squeezing them hard. I chew on my bottom lip, trying so hard not to burst out giggling right now. "Let's take a trip, Paige."

"When can we go?" I immediately ask. If I could have it like I want, then we would be on our way to somewhere, I don't care where. "Now?"

James laughs, that glorious and full of joy kind of laughter that makes one happy with just hearing it.

"I'd like to say yes, but I have college work. Let's go this weekend, what do you think?"

The pout I make can't be stopped, but I do understand we can't go now. I'm just so excited I wish it were different, but even if I'm being childish, James doesn't mind. On the contrary, he just raises our hands until his lips find the back of mine in a gentle, romantic kiss.

Friday is just two days away, I surely can wait that much for our trip. And in the meantime, I do get everything ready. We make plans, deciding to go to London as it's been so long since I went there, probably when I was seven or so. We also decide to take the train because I like it and it seems like a nice option to enjoy the scenery.

In preparations, college work and so much anticipation, Friday comes and we take a bus to Cary that will take us to the train station. James has carried my ashes with him the whole day, in a different, very secure urn. It's creepy, I have to admit it, but we are in a very serious experiment.

I have noticed so far, that when the ashes were in college I felt the strongest I've ever done. It was like I was almost corporeal again, like I wasn't just energy trying really hard to stay there. It was such a weird and powerful thing, and it gave me hopes this would happen.

Maybe we should take my desk with us, I have kept it here for fifteen years, stubbornly bringing it back every time they tried to get rid of it. I technically died there, so maybe if we move that we can also expand the ratio of how far I can get.

In the bus I can barely control myself, I'm bouncing the whole time, talking non-stop. James just smiles and shakes his head, wearing a glove where he is holding my hand even if it isn't cold anymore. Whether he's making a fool of himself, he doesn't mind. He even wears the earbuds with microphone because I insist, otherwise he wouldn't care if people see him talking to the thin air. I just don't want to bring unnecessary attention to him, especially if we're going somewhere away from Street where I have kept all the ghosts away from him.

I get nervous when we approach the next town, paying attention to every part of me to notice the changes. The last time I tried leaving street it was draining me, to the point I fainted. Kind of. So now I'm expecting the same feeling, but it doesn't come. Yes, I do feel like invisible strings pulling me back to college, but it's bearable. It doesn't hurt, it doesn't drain me out. It's just... bothersome.

I actually make it out of Street and to Cary to the train station, and when we get off the bus I can barely contain myself. I actually hug James, making him lose his balance and almost making him fall.

"I made it! I'm outside Street. For the first time in fifteen years!" He hugs me tightly, not minding all the people staring at him like he lost his mind. "It worked."

"I'm so glad it did," he whispers in my ear, hugging me tightly before letting me go. "Shall we continue?"

"Please!" I chirp, holding his hand that the then puts in the front pocket of his hoodie and we go to get on the train.

He bought two tickets, even if that meant waisting money, but that way I could comfortably sit by his side without having to scare or do anything to anyone. Although I do that unconsciously, when he hands me his mobile phone to play and the person near sees a gadget operating on its own.

It turns out, touch screen technology it's really hard. Most of these gadgets work with warmth or like texture and such, so as a ghost, it is almost impossible to make it. But James hands me his mobile for me to practice, even if it means I end up completely exhausted because I've put everything I've got to unlock the screen and launch and app. Depressive, I know. But it's okay, a ghost doesn't need a mobile phone.

After around two hours, we make it to London and I'm like a child in Christmas morning, too excited to be contained. I don't even know where to go first, the fact of being there is already too incredible. I can't believe it's worked out, that we really made it this far. It means I'm not an anchor for James anymore, we've found a loop hole and can work around that.

James is the one that tells me we need to go to the hotel were he'll be staying for the weekend, and where he goes I go with him. He leaves his small bag there and uses that chance to ask for delivery for lunch.

"Now that we know this works," he says when the food has arrived and we're watching telly while he eats. "We could try other farther places in the future. Get to travel like that," he suggest. "We could go to Scotland, or Ireland. Maybe to France next, and other countries."

"Oh my! That would be great! Yes, let's do that!" I exclaim, clapping in excitement. "You need to see what uni you're going to, and what program, and I'll go with you and it'll be so great! We can actually do that. I still can't believe it!" I burst out giggling again.

"I guess it was the right choice after all, we can have more than what we expected," he muses and I nod frantically. "Shall we go sightseeing now?"

That's what we do, leaving the room and only taking the urn with us to see how I react to that. I can totally endure the pull, and having my ashes with us works like a buffer of some sort, reducing the strength of what pulls me back home, and at the same time stabilising me. I do notice I have to concentrate more to stay in one place and not to walk through objects. Also, as London is so very crowded, I have to be very careful not to run through anyone. That would be a tragedy. But all in all, we have a great afternoon, going to those landmarks that make it to every London postcard.

The next day is a bit harder, though. We leave the ashes in the hotel, just to see how that works. At the end, coming on this trip was just to test the limits. And this part of the experiment isn't working out so well. I have a hard time managing to stay in one piece and keep coherent thoughts. I can't control emotions and it seems I'm colder than usual because James can't bear my touch. And as the hours pass, I have trouble even walking. It's like it takes everything in me to make myself stay with him when everything pulls me back home and not being next to my ashes is too hard.

By lunchtime, I can't really carry on. I can't even sit without going through the chair. I can't touch anything because I'm not strong enough, and James doesn't dare to touch me for fear he'll go through me and hurt me enormously.

"Let's go back to the hotel," James says, his expression looking dark and anxious. He's the opposite of what he looked like yesterday. "You're not okay."

"Not yet... it's still early. I can do this," I insist, but even against my own words, I can't do it for much longer. I grow too weak and not even being next to my ashes help. The pull towards college is too strong for me now, I can feel myself slipping and I think that if I close my eyes, I won't open them again.

James is so worried next to me, looking even guilty for even thinking of doing this. And I start feeling depressed, too. I was so happy yesterday, but today all the hopes and dreams crushed. Yes, we can make it out of Street, but not for too long and I grow weak. The bond with my ashes is there, but it isn't as strong as the one I have with the place I died in. And if I put distance between college and I, then I can't really separate from my ashes, which makes it quite uncomfortable. I'm basically glued to the urn if I'm not in Street.

"I'm sorry," I say, when we are back in the hotel. I'm basically hugging the urn, trying to stabilise myself like that, but it isn't enough. I still feel so weak and like I'm fading. Like when I was trying to get away from Street that time and I passed out.

"I'm sorry for suggesting this," he says back. "It wasn't a good idea."

"Don't say that," I protest. "We learnt that I can actually leave Street, and we managed to have this little trip. Let's pretend I just got food poisoning," I try to reassure him somehow, lightly smirking. "Because I just ate too much despite you told me not to, but I'm a child inside."

James chuckles, barely touching my hair to stroke it.

"We'll go back tomorrow morning, okay? You'll be okay," he promises and I nod, knowing it'll be like that and trying to push the sadness and disappointment for this failure to the back of my mind.

I guess we'll have to figure out another way to make things work, this isn't enough. But there must be a way, I have to believe in that at least. It's not like I have anything else but that future with James, so I'm holding on to it with both hands, and I'll keep doing it, until the end.

Chapter 38

James and I try new ways to leave town without exhausting me so much, but the results are basically the same. I need to be next to my ashes if I distance myself too much from college, and if when being away I dare to step more then five metres from my ashes, then I'm left completely drained out.

Another thing we've tried is James putting a bit of my ashes in a smaller container and carrying them with him. It's easier than with the whole urn, but still, it doesn't allow me to stay more than a week away from Street. I think that if we leave Street then we'll have to come back quite often, which means we can't go too far if we have to travel every weekend.

But aside from figuring out what to do, we've been together. There's no purpose, nothing we're after aside from finding the best way to be with the other. Yet, it's been the best time of my life. It's mundane and ever so simple, just the two of us. Cold hand in warm hand. Blue eyes staring into brown ones. James and Paige, Paige and James... even if no one else an see us. Even if what we have exists only for the two of us, and Clyde.

I can't have a life on my own, but I'm still enjoying so much my time with James. Living through him doesn't seem like such a bad thing when it is working so well. I get to work on pieces and help him lessen the burden from all the college work. I know I can't grow old and I'll never have the things every human being is granted in one way or another, but I'll experience them through James and that feels okay. I'll be there somehow when he gets his diploma, when he goes to uni and then gets a job. I'll be there when he gets sick and when he feels the strongest. I'll be there when he has a rough day and when everything is working for him. I'll be there.

Our future is clearly complicated, but it's something we're working on.

"What if..." James ponders one night when we've finished watching a family comedy. "If we ever want to have a family, we look for a kid that's like me?"

My brow furrows in confusion, not sure what he exactly means. "Can you rephrase that?"

James blushes and seems to struggle with the words, as if it were too embarrassing for him. "I mean in the future. It seems that it weights on you that I'm giving up on having a family of my own, but I was thinking maybe it isn't a complete lost cause. We can adopt a kid, and look everywhere until we find one that can see ghosts like I do. Someone that can see you, too. I can't be the only person in the world with the ability to see ghosts." Words are stuck in my throat, prisoner of the surprise his idea has brought upon me. "It's just an option, I'm not saying we should try that, but if we ever want that, then, well, we could try it."

"Oh," I mumble as I try to process exactly what he's said and what that means.

A future, even a family. We've been planning our lives together for a while already, seeing how to work around that, but every once in a while he comes up with a new thing to give more normalcy to our uncanny situation. James and Clyde are all I have right now, but that could be different in the future. We could find someone like him, a kid that we could give a good life to. I didn't think I wanted such a thing, I honestly gave up on the idea the moment I realised I had succeeded and ended my life; since I knew I had become a ghost and was stuck in the same day for eternity.

Perhaps it won't be possible, maybe I will never be ready or able to be a mother to anyone because I'll be seventeen forever, but there's also a possibility that I might be able to do that, and it's so soothing knowing there's a chance. It's reassuring knowing there isn't just one way.

"It's an option we should keep in mind for the future," I add next, a slow and almost lazy smile coming to my lips. "It's good knowing not all is lost in that sense." I chew on my lower lip, trying to contain my excitement because there's another way.

"Really?" James sounds so relieved, and only then I realise he was nervous about bringing this subject up. It must be nerve wracking, especially when he's still so young.

I nod, smiling fondly at him just to let him know it is really okay and that his idea makes me happy, the possibility makes me feel so hopeful.

"Working on a future with you is such a beautiful thing. The closer we get to that, the happier I become," I confess, leaning a bit closer to him. "The fewer things I take from you, the better."

James doesn't reply, he just wraps his arm around my shoulders, bringing me closer, kissing the top of my head. At that same time Clyde climbs on to James' lap, curling there and starting to purr. My smile grows wider at the sight, knowing that even if we never adopt a kid or that even if we don't even leave Street, we've made our family here and we are having a life together. Unconventional. Impractical. Difficult. Unseen. But it's a life together, nonetheless.

Summer holidays come and like that, James' first year of college is done. He still has to do a lot of college work to prepare his portfolio for his uni application, but we'll get on that little by little, and I'll help him on every task.

The weather is great, maybe too hot for everyone, but he has a ghost girlfriend who's cold as corpse and keeps him cool even when everyone else is agonising. I'm better than any AC, and it is great we can have much more skinship without risking a case of hypothermia.

We go out a lot, and we take Clyde with us to have picnics or just to spend a few days outside. I work every day on improving my cooking skills just to do something for him, just so I can take care of him, too. I think that once he finishes college, or even uni, I shouldn't follow him everywhere. And I can stay at home, helping somehow, finding something I can do. I never expected or wanted to become a housewife, to be honest I never even had time to have those thoughts before, but now it sounds nice. Maybe it's because it is something I can do, whilst everything else seems impossible.

It seems funny how now I think of a future. It is ironic how I had to become a ghost to be able to dream, because when I was alive these thoughts never made it into my mind. I was in constant agony and fear, so much pain I couldn't see beyond the blackness that threatened to consume me every day. But that is gone now, along with my life, yet only now I work for a future.

Only after I lost it all I found myself, I found my happiness and a reason to fight. It's heartbreaking I couldn't find it when I was alive. Just one reason to keep fighting, one more thing to hold on to and fight against my torturers would have made a difference.

I thought it was too late for me, I had resigned and fallen into a constant pattern where I didn't even think, I just kept doing the same day after day. But it wasn't all lost, when James came into my life he brought so many thing with him. He ignited the life that had left me and made me dream again. He made want to do things and try hard to accomplish them, even if they seemed impossible.

It wasn't that late, then.

And because I have him now and all these possibilities, all these dreams and plans, the darkness within me starts fading away. No. That's not exactly what happens. Darkness doesn't exist, that is just the term for the absence of light, and what happened to me is that the bullies had taken all the light in me, leaving me only with darkness. I couldn't ignite a spark on my own, but James did that, and slowly that flame grew up, consuming the darkness and lighting up every corner of my soul.

There isn't absence of light in me anymore.

Until him it was only despair, a thirst for revenge and so much sorrow for the unfairness of what had been my life. But now there's more. There's hope, there's love, there's dreams. And if someone asks me what road I'd like to take, I'd chose the latter, the one that leads me to light and warmth. The one that leads me to James.

So I let go of it, without even noticing it. Of the grudge that consumed me and kept me going, even if I didn't even know whom I was holding that grudge against. I let go of that darkness and cold that was all I was made of before. I don't realise how this happens, it's so gradual and natural. I guess it happens because I wasn't paying attention, and most things in life go away when we turn our backs on them. Good and bad things. The moment you walk away, what's at the other side will unstoppable get away from you. The first step is turning around, the second is taking the hardest first step, and the third is keep going until you can't see what you walked away from.

It happens that if you have someone to hold your hand and help you take all those steps, then it's more bearable. James helped me, but I let go of it. I walked away from what was holding me back and decided to focus on something different. I did it... and succeeded at it.

I realise that one hot Monday afternoon when we've come to the countryside, renting a cottage to enjoy the weather on our own. I'm outside, by the pool, facing the sun with a smile on my face feeling warm without having James around because he's gone into town to buy groceries. I guess it's the fact I feel warm what makes me notice the change in me, and when I think about it I notice as well that I can be in James' arms for longer without freezing him, or that he doesn't seem to struggle when we touch. I also notice that whenever we touch I don't have to work hard to push the darkness back, because there's so much light already.

Now that I have a life, a future to fight for and dreams to feel excited about, I can leave behind the past that tormented me. I am happy today, like I wasn't before.

"It's in the past," I thing out loud, closing my eyes and keeping the smile. "What they did to me, it's in the past. It's behind me."

Life itself will teach them a lesson, it's not in my hands. And even if that doesn't happen, that's okay, too. I don't care anymore. I have so much more, important things to focus on. What happened in the past belongs to a life that isn't mine anymore. I don't think I can forgive them for what they did to me, but I can let go of the pain and resentment. Maybe that's forgiving. And I might even forget about it in the future, who knows? It doesn't hurt me anymore. They can't hurt me anymore.

There's a shift around me, something changes. The energy, the mood, I can't pinpoint it, but there's a change that makes me tense up and freeze. It's not cold, but it's not warm either. It's just... like static. Like white noise.

I open my eyes and at the other side of the pool there's a man staring back at me. I think it's a man, it has human shape but it's also blurry. But the more I think of the creature as a man, the more the creature looks like a man. His features change, blur together and make it harder for me to distinguish anything. But I don't feel scared when I see him, maybe even if I should.

"You are ready," he says, and I think he's smiling at me. "You can come with me now. You have learnt your lesson."

I blink five times before I realise what he is talking about and what he is.

I saw him before, or something like him, when my mum died. Something like him came for her and took her away... and now he's here, for me.

This is the moment I panic, when I get scared to the point of standing up and taking a few steps back, away from him. There's a pool between us, but I want a ocean. He's a threat to everything that makes me happy now, to all my hopes and dreams. He comes to take me away from James and our plans, to take me somewhere I don't know. To uncertainty.

I'm scared.

"Let's go, Paige," he invites me, his voice warm and welcoming, but it sends shivers down my spine.

"Where?" I breathe out, barely a squeak, like a little mouse.

"Where you belong. Come with me," he insists, extending his hand but I take another step back.

No. James isn't even here. I can't just go when I have decided to stay, when I have so much to look ahead. I won't go.

"No," I whisper. "No," I repeat louder this time, closing my eyes and covering my ears with my hands. I crouch down as if like that I could be saved from this creature. "No. I won't go.

No!" I shout, shaking my head, refusing to give up on what I've been building up with James. "NO!" I scream at the top of my lungs, pushing everything and everyone away.

"Paige!" Someone else cries out, louder than me, and it's a voice I recognise. I open my eyes and turn around, finding James there, his worried eyes on me. He's the only one with me, the creature is gone. "What happened?"

"James," I breathe out, standing up and running to him. I've chosen him, I did it long ago. I won't be leaving him.

"Paige, are you okay?" he asks, receiving me in his arms, hugging me tight.

"Now I am," I reply in a deep sigh, smiling and pushing back any other thought.

This is rights. This is okay. I'll be fine... won't I?

Chapter 39

Without asking anything, James only comforts me. I feel shaky and ethereal, as if all I am has been ripped off of me, and now I'm a shadow lingering on this dimension, holding on to whatever I can get my hands on. I think I'm taking energy from James because after a while he can't even hold us both, his breathing becomes hard and uneven before his knees give out.

"Are you okay?" I ask him when we have collapsed to the ground. I pull away just in case it's my fault he's like this. I've hurt him, I've almost frozen him, but I have never drained him like this.

"Just... let me catch my breath," he asks, struggling to do so.

I watch in concern how he takes deep breaths just to pull himself together, but not even that helps so I head to the kitchen in my weak state, stumbling and tripping, but I make it there and I grab a cup that I fill with lukewarm water, and put some sugar in it before going back to James. I notice then he's lost all colour and looks as pale as a ghost, pun intended.

Hands tremble when he grabs the cup I've brought for him; weakly, he takes a sip and cringes at how sweet it is. I don't even know if it works, I think it does, I might've heard about it when I was alive or dead, who knows?

"Are you feeling any better?" I ask, completely ignoring how feeble I feel, I'm more worried about James.

"Yeah, I'm not sure what happened. I suddenly felt like I had run three marathons," he comments, his voice low and whispery.

"I think it was my fault." The guilt rushes to me like waves in a tsunami, I don't even receive an alarm, beforehand, I'm just drowned in it before I realise what's happening. "I... I think I stole your vitality."

"But you've never done that before," James refutes, already trying to ease my worry and guilt.

"I think I was in desperate need now, like never before. I was... feeling weaker than I've ever felt."

"Is it because we're here? Should we go back home?" James asks in panic but I shake my head. I'm pretty sure the real reason why I'm feeling like this is because of what happened after James arrived.

Shaking my head, I add, "I just... I shouldn't be here?" It ends like a question because I'm not even sure about what I'm saying. This is unknown to me, I've never crossed over before and no one has prepared me for it.

"What do you mean?" He asks, his hand trying to grab mine but I avoid him. If I'm right and I'm the one who stole his vitality, then I can't touch him until I feel more like myself.

"Something happened before you came," I start, feeling a lump in my throat already at the mere memory of it. In my head I see the creature again, what came for me, and I shiver.

Was that supposed to be the Grim Reaper? "I... I realised I had finally let go of my grudge and that I was happy with you, and I guess... I guess you were right. My lesson was letting go and living my own life. If I had done that when I was alive, if I hadn't listened to the bullies or given them the power to break me, if I had forgiven them for being so wrong and lived my life instead, holding on to my family, it would've been different. If I had even told my parents the hell I was living in and asked them to look for a better life, away from here... everything would've been different. But I held on to their words instead, I listened to them and believed them right. I focused on what they thought of me instead of looking for my own future and happiness somewhere else. I started hating and resenting them when I should've ignored them or turned my back on them."

"It's hard to know what to do when you are under constant attack," James reminds me and I nod.

"It's just darkness and self-hatred when you're living that. It's impossible to see logic, even if someone is telling you what to do. I was weak back then because I couldn't under-stand what I had to do. Fifteen years later I learn my lesson."

"That's good, I mean at least now you..." James' voice fades away as he starts realising what he's said and the implications of it. I can't meet his eyes, my heart racing at the memory of the fear I felt when the Grim Reaper came for me.

"I can cross over now," I reply for him and even if he tries to control himself, I can see in his eyes his own fear and reluctance, the panic he feels when I tell him this. He tenses and drops the cup, instinctively reaching out for me.

"When? How can you be sure? Is it really all you need?" He sounds stronger now, but I know it's not due to his sudden recovery of strength or because the sweet water worked, this is just panic giving him an adrenaline rush.

"Well..." I don't even know how to explain what happened, or where to begin. "I was just here, thinking of what I told you and just how happy I am right now with you... And then something showed up." James frowns, confused with what I'm telling him. "He was just there, at the other side of the pool. It looked like a person, but he wasn't. I couldn't really distinguish features or even call gender. It was just there... blurry, but as I thought it could be a man, it looked more like a man."

"Are you telling me it was taking the characteristics you gave it?" James suggests, trying to help me make sense out of what I'm telling.

"I guess." I shrug. Just talking about it is making me weak again, my vision becoming blurry like the Grim Reaper, hard to focus on. "I think he was a Grim Reaper."

"How do you know that? Maybe it was another ghost or some other kind of spirit?" James suggested but we both know it can't be like that, ghosts look just like any living person, that's why he can't tell one from the other, the only difference is that ghosts can't be seen by ordinary people.

"He told me to go with him, I had learnt my lesson," I finally reply and James' face is drained from all colour again. The panic that had made blood rush to his cheeks is working against him again, probably even his heart has skipped a beat.

I can't see the dread and disbelief in his eyes, the denial and surprise.

"But... but you're here. You're still here with me," he mutters, sounding as puzzled as he looks.

"I... I got scared," I confess. "I don't know what happens when I go, I don't know if I'll remember you. I don't know and that scares me."

"Where is he now?" James asks next, looking around, seeking for that Grim Reaper I was talking about.

"He was gone when you arrived, after I... after I..." For some reason I'm scared of telling James what I did, even if it was accidental and I wasn't really thinking. I am not sure it was a good thing. "After I refused to go with him. I just... I couldn't go if you weren't around and without saying goodbye, and not knowing what really waits for me there."

"Your... your mum waits for you," James reminds me with a small voice. It seems he's having trouble breathing again, but he's doing his best to look whole.

"Really? How? Like her or something else? What happens there? Do we live in a paradise or what? I killed myself, why would I be allowed where my mum is?" I snap. "I don't know what happens next, James. But I know what happens if I stay here with you."

"No one knows what happens," he comments ever so sadly, but I shake my head.

"It's not the same! When people die they don't get a choice, they just take the next step. I decided my death and then stayed over here, and now it is my choice to go somewhere I have no clue about. It could be hell for what I know!" I'm shaking but it's not due to how weak I am, it's just fear that has taken control of me. "You think if people had a choice they would always cross over? Or even die? You think it's easier taking that step when you don't know if there'll be a ground to step on once you cross the door? It could be a cliff, too!"

James takes my wrists in his hands, trying to calm me down but when he touches me he retracts immediately, hissing as if I've burnt him, which, of course, must be my fault.

"I have a future with you, I have plans. I don't want to give them up, when I finally have something to look forward. So I said no, I didn't go with him."

"Paige... we talked about this," he reminds me and even if he wants to sound confident and reassuring, he only sounds hurt and scared. "We were supposed to find your lesson and help you cross over, but changed planes because you thought you couldn't do it."

"No! We changed plans because we wanted to be together! Or was that just me?"

I don't know why I'm yelling at him, why I feel like he's betrayed me somehow. I crawl back, away from him, still shaking in both fear and frustration.

"Of course not! I want to be with you, too, but if you found your unfinished business and fulfilled it, if you had a chance to cross over, then you should've taken it."

"You want me to leave? Is that? Without even saying good-bye? Is that why you're saying that, James? You wanted to come back and not find me anywhere, not knowing what happened to me or where I went?" It hurts, my throat closes up and I want to cry, I feel like I could burst out into tears, but I can't and it's as unnerving as it's always been.

"Of course not!" he repeats. "Paige, stops putting words in my mouth! I'm just saying this was important, you didn't have to just plain reject it. What happens to you now? You lost your chance! You think it'll come again?"

"And what if it doesn't? Is that bad? I had accepted that already."

James rubs his hands over his face, clearly as frustrated as I feel. I'm sure he would've stood up and come over if he wasn't as weak as he is.

"I couldn't leave without saying goodbye, James. Even if that was what I had to do, I just couldn't. I can't. I won't!"

"Aren't you scared of what might happen to you for rejecting your opportunity?" James asks, his voice shaky and I think tears are welling up in his eyes. "I'm terrified of what might happen to you."

"How can you ask me to leave you?!" I cry out, clenching my heart in desperation and heartbreak. "How?" I break down.

"I'm not asking you that, I'm just... I'm just..." James looks down, the ball of his hands pressed to his eyes and I can see his body trembling. "I'm just saying that you... you should've thought of you and do what you had to." He looks up, feebly, timidly.

"I couldn't," I insists. "I said no before I could even realise what I was doing."

"Paige," he calls my name, a plea. The emotions that one word carry are so conflictive, I can hear the longing and the fear, I can feel the despair and the determination.

"I know," I breathe out. "I know I should've gone but how can you ask me to do that? If you were in my shoes what would you have done? Would you have just left without a word?"

James looks away because the answer is clear: he would've done the same thing. Even if it was wrong, even if it was probably dangerous and it meant I lost my chance forever... I just couldn't go. I'm sure that if people had a chance to say goodbye before leaving, they would all take it. If people could say no to death and get a chance to stay, they would all take it. I didn't know it was going to work, I didn't think the Grim Reaper would just go when I said no, but it happened.

"I had... I had embraced the chance of never cross over already. It makes no difference now." I try smiling, hoping to reassure him with my words, but it seems my actions can't touch him. "I'll be fine."

"How can you be sure?" James asks. "How can you be sure something else won't come for you and drag you without a warning? We don't know anything! We have no clue what might be the consequences of this."

"We've never known!" I shout, insisting on something, holding desperately on to something. "But I know I have you and that I won't leave you unless something drags me away."

"Paige." This time is a scold.

Shaking my head, I ask him, "Why are you so ready to let go of me?"

"It's not that, you know it. I'm just... scared for you."

"Just hold my hand, then!" I insist, crawling back to him, slowly, hesitantly. "Until the end, don't let me go. I don't want to say goodbye."

James doesn't reply, he can't even utter a word, he doesn't even grab the hand I'm holding up for him, and that... that hurts more than anything I can think of. I understand what he means so I drop my hand, turn around and leave him there, as alone as he wants to be.

Chapter 40

I was scared, nervous and unsure. Couldn't James show me a little bit more of support instead of scolding me like that? Okay, so maybe I did something wrong, but it wasn't consciously done, I was driven by the panic of the moment. I was still shaky and confused, but he didn't give me time to recover before rubbing in my face the thing I did wrong.

And still! I thought we had this settled. Why is it so terrible if I stay forever? It's not like I can die again, I'm already dead. What else do I have to lose?

Is it so wrong that I want him to hold on to me even tighter?

As I hug my legs with my back pressed to the door of the main room, that is all I can think of. How I just want him to want me around as much as I want to stay with him. But he always has an excuse, some fear, and I'm honestly starting to believe he doesn't want me to stay with him. Maybe he's scared, maybe such a serious commitment is a terrifying thing, especially for a guy. Perhaps I'm asking too much of him, what normal seventeen-year-old guy would want to commit himself to a ghost girl until the very end?

All sort of insecurities don't cease to attack me, from every direction, ruthless until I don't know what to think or to feel.

I thought I had everything sorted out, my decision made and everything else clear, but now my head is in a haze and I don't know where to turn, which direction in order to escape this.

"Paige? Are you there?" a voice asks from the other side, accompanied by a soft knock. "Paige, let's talk."

"I don't think there's anything else to say," I reply, although my face is still between my knees, hence why my answer sounds muffled.

"Of course there is!" he shouts, startling me. "You always decide what I say or think, you never let me explain things to you! You put words in my mouth and you need to stop doing that! Right now you're thinking I don't want you with me and you couldn't be more wrong about it!"

I lift my head a bit, blinking in surprise because James has never talked to me like that. Only once he shouted at me with such rage in his voice, only once he sounded as fed up with me as he does now. Right after I discovered he could see me, and he realised I was a ghost. When he hurt me so deep with insults and cruel words, telling me to get lost because he didn't want me around.

The memory, something that happened so long ago, hurts. All that I felt back then comes to me mercilessly. James is angry with me right now, and I don't even know what to do.

"I don't want you away from me," he says next, his voice sounding weak, shaky, almost broken. "I can't even describe how much the mere thought hurts, but I'm just so scared of what might happen to you." There's a soft thump against the door, I think he's just banged his head against the wood, or something like that. I stand up, feeling still so feeble and out of my element, but I manage to face the wall and press my hand against it. I don't know if he has his at the other side or anything, but doing this soothes my heart somehow. "Ghosts aren't supposed to be here. Ghosts exist because their time on Earth was cut short, because they weren't supposed to die so soon. That means... that means you're not supposed to be here if you learnt your lesson already. And I'm scared that something might happen to you now that you're not just staying because you haven't finished your business but because you're overstaying."

"What could happen to me?" I say, my voice low and fragile, like his. "I'm already dead."

"You think that's the worst that could happen?!" snaps James. "Do you know what happened to you when you disappeared for a week? Where did you go back then?" I can't answer that and he knows it, that week is completely gone from my memory, not even a slight recollection of where I went or what I became during that time. "What if something like that happens again, permanently?"

I gulp, my eyes widening at the possibility. There's a difference between unknown and nothing, and I can't tell exactly what's more terrifying right now. Both options chill me to the bone and fill me with dread, so much that I feel like crying and calling for my mum, as if I were three years old.

"I'm scared something worse could happen to you, Paige. If I... If I could secure you somehow, if I could find a way to make sure you'll be all right, I'd give anything. I'm just... I'm assuming that crossing over is what you should do, the natural course, even if that... even if that takes you way from me."

His voice is so strangled, so broken and painful that it feels like my own heart is being ripped off my chest. A trembling squeak escapes me before I slam the door open, making James almost fall because he was indeed leaning against the wood. The moment he looks up after regaining his balance, and our eyes meet, I can see the bloodshot eyes, the tears streaming down his cheeks and all that angst consuming him from within. I know this time he is not crying for me, those tears are only his, a reflection of his pain. Yet... yet I'm still part of why he's crying.

Hesitantly, trembling, my hand reaches out for him, not really daring to touch him for fear I might make things worse, although comforting him, taking his pain away, is all I have in my head right now. But James doesn't care if I might hurt him or take all his energy with me, he only cares about getting to me. He grabs my hand and pulls me until I'm trapped in his arms, so tightly that if I were a human I wouldn't be able to breathe.

I close my eyes and think of only taking all that pain, fear and uncertainty from him. I want to take all what's bad and keep it with me because I know how to handle it. It's basically the only thing I'm good at.

I don't know if this works or James just refuses to let me go, but we stay like that for a while. Eventually, our legs give out and we end up on the floor, but not even then he loosens the grip on me.

"What are we going to do?" I ask feebly, my face in the crook of his neck.

"I don't know. Pray that nothing bad happens? Hope that the worst case scenario is that you can't ever cross over?" he suggests, but I know it pains him to barely suggest that. He doesn't want me to lose that, and I guess that if we traded places and he were the ghost, then I would think the same.

"I guess time will tell."

The problem is that time does tell us indeed, and time also happens to be part of the problem that threatens us now. Time is what we don't seem to have now. Oh the irony, at some point I thought I had all the time of the world, I thought I had forever.

When you're young you think, and are told, you have your whole life ahead. But life is so unpredictable... an so is death.

No matter where I am, even if I'm with my hand buried in my ashes or resting on my desk, I'm still fading away. My energy, whatever I was made of, starts escaping me. It's like everything takes twice or even thrice to accomplish, I can't focus and do more than one task at the same time. If I want to touch something I can only do that. Talking or anything else stays at the back of my mind because trying to not go through things is taking all of me.

I think I'm becoming a creepy ghost, the type that is weak and kind of translucent. I feel like I'm disappearing and that is more horrifying than I can put in words. James is freaking out, every passing minute he gets more worried. He can see how I'm slipping away, too fast for his hand to grab me and hold me. And I can't deny it's happening because I don't even have the energy to lie.

James' eyes scream words he does not need to tell, I can read them clearly in his blue gaze: 'I knew it was wrong.' And yes, he is right. I did wrong when I refused to go, and the consequences started that very moment, I just thought it was the shock, but since the moment the Reaper left, I started to get weaker.

We had to come back and even go to college, thinking that could help, but it didn't. I was still getting weaker, and James more frantic.

On the first day I have trouble doing most normal things like walking or just keeping a conversation. On the second day I can't focus for more than ten minutes on a single thing. By the third day I can't touch James. By the fourth I can't even stand up. By the fifth, I can't leave my desk, which is the biggest drawback because James can't stay there with me. By the sixth day James can't take it anymore.

"There must be a way!" he shouts, only desperation dripping from his voice. "You can't just... fade way like this. It's happening too quick. We need to stop this."

I can't really reply, it takes too much energy. I'm just lying on my desk, eyes closed, listening to his voice that seems to be too far away although he's in front of me.

"Paige, please... something, there must be something. I can't... I can't watch you like this." His voice breaks and I don't need to see him to know he's tearing up again. He's been doing that quite often, in sheer terror of what's happening to me, overcome by frustration for not being able to do anything to stop it

"I... did wrong," I mumble, barely intelligible. "I should've... gone... with... it." I try to smile, or I think I do.

The irony of my existence, doing everything too late. Learning to let it go, but too late. Learning to follow the natural course, but too late.

"I... regret...it."

"Paige," he whimpers, there's such a painful edge to his voice.

I use everything I have left to open my eyes and meet his. I don't think I'll be able to do this again and if I'm fading away, if this is the last bit I have with James, then I want to look him in the eyes.

"I wish... I wish I had gone with him. I would... I would at least... wait for you there. Wherever that is."

"Paige," he says with a broken voice, there's so much pain in the way he calls my name. It's such a big difference from when he said it so cheerfully before, so lovingly. Now it's filled with sadness and fear.

"I'm sorry," I mutter, wishing I could touch him one last time, but I can't even lift my hand, let alone touch him.

The energy around us shifts, buzzing and sizzling. James also feels it, he visually tenses up and stays alert, like looking for whatever is now with us. It takes me three seconds to understand that this has happened already, I felt this before. I'm not even surprised when I look past James and I see that creature, blurry and kind of creepy, like it were just made of light being reflected but not quite clear. It is intimidating but calling, and this time it doesn't scare me.

"Have you changed your mind?" the Grim Reaper asks, smiling at me. I think of my mum, of how much easier it would if this creature were her. "Your mother is waiting for you, Paige," he adds, as if he could read my thoughts.

I gasp, and so does James, turning around and watching with eyes wide open the blurry creature in front of us.

"You can come with me if you want. If you don't, you only have one day left," the Grim Reaper says. "It'll be okay, I can help you."

"Help her," James blurts out desperately before I can say a thing. "Please, help her."

The Grim Reaper takes a step closer, the energy becoming stronger, making me feel stronger, too. It's like the creature is giving me back the vitality I lost. And the Reaper doesn't stop until it's next to me, its hand on my shoulder, fixing it all.

One touch, that's all it takes.

It's soothing, it's relaxing and so peaceful. It's warm and light, cheerful and welcoming. I feel like I have never felt before, all the pain, all the angst I carried with me for so long is gone and I'm myself again, I feel alive again. My mind is clear and I have no fear, I know I'll be okay. I don't know exactly where I'm going, but I'm certain it's the place I have to go, where my mother is waiting for me and where I'll wait for James.

I look at him, the boy crying in fear for me, looking at us with such terrified eyes. I can sit up straight, I can smile and I can talk.

"I have to go," I say, looking only at him. "I really have to. I can't stay longer."

"I know," he whimpers, brushing the tears with the back of his hand, trying to pull himself together. "I know."

"I'll be okay and so will you," I say next. James has been kneeling in front of my desk the whole time, so I just have to lean forward to cup his face in my hand. He closes his eyes and I know this time it's not cold, or painful. This time is warm and loving, like every time he touched me. It's finally equal for the two of us. "I'll be waiting for you, we'll meet again."

"I'm going to miss you so much," he confesses. There's no fight, he knows he has to let me go now because I can't stay. He's prepared himself for this as I was fading away, he made a choice back then, now he's just seeing that decision happening. "Every day."

"You'll be in my mind every day, too. Don't rush, okay? Your time will come and we'll meet each other again. Be careful, live fully. There's so much for you," I tell him because I know it.

It's not like I can see the future or that I have all knowledge now, it's more like a certainty in my heart. I know he'll be fine, he'll do great and that we'll meet again. And I know it because his soul and mine are connected, because we come in a set, because no matter what, we were supposed to meet.

And we'll do that, over and over again. We've done it before, even if we can't remember.

James nods, accepting my requests, promising to do as told. "I love you, Paige. I'm so... thankful that I transferred here, that I met you."

"I love you, too," I reply, because now, as I'm about to leave, I feel this love stronger than ever, so powerful and overwhelming. So lasting. "And I thank you for everything. You guided and helped me to find myself again."

"I won't forget you," he promises, slow and painful tears falling down. I brush them with my thumb as I smile at him, reassuringly, lovingly.

"I love you, James Black. You gave me life even after I gave up on it. Come back to me when it's time," I tell him at what he nods before standing up.

"I will," he promises.

I stand up, too. Leaving my desk and breaking the connection I had with it. I died there and now I'm definitely leaving. I shouldn't have done that, it wasn't my call, but I paid the price and eventually learnt my lesson. The natural course of actions was restored, I can cross over now.

One step closer, then another and I'm in James' arms, tightly wrapped, and it's the warmest hug we've ever had. I can feel him sighing in delight. I try to give him all the reassurance I can, all the love I have for him.

"I love you," he whispers in my ear yet once again, so I nod before pulling a bit back, enough to meet his eyes.

"Goodbye, James. I'll see you again," I bid him with a smile, brushing his tears away one last time.

He doesn't say anything, he just leans down and kisses me for the last time, and I close my eyes, kissing him back, knowing it will never be like this again. The next time we meet he'll be like me. So for now I melt in his warmth and love, I drown in his essence, and I know it's the same for him.

When we pull back and break the kiss, he's smiling sadly at me.

"Goodbye, Paige," he whispers as I start stepping back. He holds my hand, reluctant to let it go so our arms stretch till their limit, until only our fingertips brushing. Till I'm back with the Grim Reaper who has waited for me to say my goodbye. I turn to look at it, the smile still on its blurry lips.

"I'm ready," I tell the creature and it nods. One last look at James, whose tears can't stop falling, whose lips are tightly pressed together, but who is still holding it all in. "I love you," I say one last time before the hand of the Grim Reaper is back on my shoulder, filling me with peace and certainty.

We turn around, the energy around us buzzing with a new life, a new existence that awaits for me. I take a first step towards it, leaving James behind. But that's okay, it's only temporal, we'll see each other again. Soul mates are always supposed to find each other, and that's what James and I are.

James gave me back the life that was crushed. Time will fill the absence I leave in his life, but when we meet again it'll be different, because for every other soul with us, we will exist. James, I and our love will be seen.

Epilogue

I remember blue eyes like the deepest ocean. Long hair worn in dreadlocks. I remember a kind and loving smile. Big and steady hands that could create a new universe. I remember arms that held me so tight, even when it was cold and painful. I remember bubbling laughter, happiness, love.

I once was an ordinary girl, and although I can't really remember that particular life, I know I had it. I was named Paige Samuels, and I had it hard. I was tormented, I was chased and pushed off the cliff. I made a decision that wasn't mine to take, I took in my hands what I shouldn't have touched.

I killed myself.

And I was punished for that. I had to stay for so long, stuck in an endless circle until those blue eyes came, until those big and steady hands took mine and pulled me away, showing me what life was supposed to be about. Until that kind and loving smile was only for me. Until those arms held me when I was slipping down, when I was breaking and aching. Until that bubbling laughter, happiness and love was what I was made of instead of the pain I took with me the moment I took my life.

I remember a bittersweet goodbye and a promise to meet again.

I remember a boy that gave me back my life after I turned my back on it.

After all these years, after all that's happened for him, I still remember him and they way he looked at me. From the first to the last. He is the most vivid thing in my memory from that life, the one I decide to hold on to. I still remember how much I loved him... as much as I still love him.

And because I remember him so clearly and vividly, I recognise the blue eyes when they are in front of me. That loving smile that still warms my heart. That big and steady hand reaching out for me, bringing back the bubbling happiness that he once gave me.

I laugh, I jump, I run to him. "James!" I cry out, now trapped in his arms, because it's finally time.

We are together again.

9 781934 232590